"You're going to be a pain about being my bodyguard, aren't you, Thorne?" Amanda demanded.

"Only if you fight me every step of the way. I *have* to be with you wherever you go."

"But there's no rule that says I *have* to like it and act like some simpering child obeying your every command."

"*You*, obey *me?* By choice?" He shook his head at that hope. "I'll settle for low-level compliance." Then he turned and, in a flash, gripped her arms and moved her into the darkened shadows of the porch.

"What are you doing?"

Suddenly he kissed her. Amanda felt all the strength go out of her legs. He didn't deepen the kiss, but Amanda couldn't have denied the race of sensation that rushed through her even if she'd wanted to.

Finally he lifted his head. "Someone is watching us."

Dear Reader,

Once again, we're proud to bring you a lineup of irresistible books, something we seem to specialize in here at Intimate Moments. Start off your month with award-winning author Kathleen Eagle's newest American Hero title, *Defender*. In Gideon Defender you'll find a hero you'll never forget. This is one of those books that is bound to end up on "keeper" shelves all across the country.

Linda Turner completes her miniseries "The Wild West" with sister Kat's story, a sensuous treat for readers everywhere. Award-winner Dee Holmes once again demonstrates her skill at weaving together suspense and romance in *Watched*, while Amanda Stevens puts a clever twist on the ever-popular amnesia plotline in *Fade to Black*. We have another Spellbound title for you this month, a time-travel romance from Merline Lovelace called *Somewhere in Time*. Finally, welcome new writer Lydia Burke, who debuts with *The Devil and Jessie Webster*.

Coming soon—more great reading from some of the best authors in the business, including Linda Howard, whose long-awaited *Loving Evangeline* will be coming your way in December.

As always—enjoy!

Leslie J. Wainger
Senior Editor and Editorial Coordinator

Please address questions and book requests to:
Silhouette Reader Service
U.S.: 3010 Walden Ave., P.O. Box 1325, Buffalo, NY 14269
Canadian: P.O. Box 609, Fort Erie, Ont. L2A 5X3

WATCHED

Dee Holmes

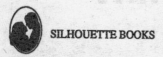

SILHOUETTE BOOKS

ISBN 0-373-07591-X

WATCHED

Books by Dee Holmes

Silhouette Intimate Moments   Silhouette Special Edition

Black Horse Island #327   *The Return of Slade Garner* #660
Maybe This Time #395
The Farrell Marriage #419
Without Price #465
Take Back the Night #495
Cuts Both Ways #541
Watched #591

DEE HOLMES

would love to tell her readers about exciting trips to
Europe or that she has mastered a dozen languages.
But the truth is that traveling isn't her thing, and she
flunked French twice. Perhaps because of a military
background where she got uprooted so much, she married a permanent civilian.

Winner of the 1990 Romance Writers of America
RITA Award for her first novel, *Black Horse Island,*
Dee is an obsessive reader. She started writing casually, only to discover that "writing is hard! Writing a
publishable book is even harder." Involved in her local
RWA chapter, she says that she loves to write about
"relationships between two people who are about to
fall in love but don't know how exciting it is going to
be for them."

To my mother,
In loving memory

Prologue

At eleven minutes before midnight, the dark vehicle without lights swung onto Town Beach Road behind Amanda Delaski's car. She'd just passed through the last intersection.

Amanda didn't notice the car until its high-beam headlights exploded in her rearview mirror.

Squinting against the blinding white, she adjusted her mirror to get rid of the glare. She expected the car to go around her since she wasn't going all that fast and there was no one else on the road.

But the vehicle didn't pass her nor did it turn off its high beams. It crept closer, dangerously closer to her rear bumper.

Amanda sped up a little, but the vehicle did, too.

She slowed. So did the other driver.

A tinge of fear spread through her and she tried to shake it off. The darkness and the glaring headlights made her feel as if some monster was bearing down on her.

What's going on? she wondered. Teenagers having some twisted fun? She doubted it was a drunk, for the driver exhibited steady skill and obviously knew how to ride a bumper without touching it.

Amanda thought of movies she'd seen where one car would force another off the road, but dismissed them. Whoever was behind her didn't seem interested in doing anything more than taunting and scaring her.

She eased as close to the sandy shoulder as she dared, hoping to urge the vehicle to pull out and pass her.

It didn't. In fact, it shadowed her driving with a predator's precision.

Her fear formed a life of its own and clawed deep into her stomach. No turnoffs on the road and frighteningly sloped shoulders made her all too aware that she had to either stop on the road or continue five miles to the end.

Earlier that afternoon, she'd enjoyed the June solace and coolness of the sparsely traveled road and had even used the miles to mentally plan out her day in preparation for the arrival of the troubled teenage girls she'd be working with for the next month.

Now the miles that had been tranquil and enjoyable were terrifying.

Suddenly the lights were gone.

Amanda blinked. The driver couldn't have turned off—there was no place to do that. Could they have simply stopped? Her heart pounded and her hands were sticky on the wheel. She slowed a little as the road curved and was just about to take a breath of relief when the lights came back on again.

Now they were some distance behind, but coming at her fast.

"My God, they're going to ram right into me," she said aloud, her voice shaky and astonished. She had nowhere to go. To leave the road would bury her tires in the sandy shoulder and that would leave her really vulnerable. Her best bet was to outrun them.

She touched the gas pedal, pressing it down as the speedometer climbed. Still the car kept coming.

Forty-five.

Fifty-five.

Amanda clutched the wheel to negotiate the next curve, mentally giving thanks that she was so familiar with the road.

At sixty-five, the dark vehicle was once again melded to her bumper. Her hands gripped the wheel so hard the tension climbed up her arms and down her sides. Her legs were rigid and her body braced.

The lights went out again.

This time she felt no relief that they were gone. She knew they were there in the dark, grinning, no doubt, like a huge cat with a cornered mouse. Whoever it was obviously wanted to play games.

What made her turn her head, she didn't know. Instinct, perhaps, for she'd heard no noise. But when she did, every terror, every fear, she'd ever imagined rushed through her.

It was here.

So close that, if her window had been open, she couldn't have slipped her hand between the two vehicles.

No headlights. Darkened windows that further destroyed any chance of seeing into the vehicle. And it was so close she couldn't even tell what kind of car it was.

She slowed.

It slowed.

She sped up.

It sped up.

Then, as if perfectly timed for maximum horror, a new light exploded in her face. Blinded by what seemed like a thousand-watt bulb, she jammed on her brakes and with tires screeching, gripped the wheel as the car fishtailed from the sudden braking motion. Moments later, she brought the car to a stop.

Breathing erratically, she felt the sweat pour off her. She unclenched her fingers from the wheel and sagged back in the seat.

The other car was gone. No lights. No noise. No pealing sound of wheels. It had simply disappeared.

Amanda glanced at the digital clock on the dashboard. Eight minutes had passed. She opened her window and the scent of honeysuckle and lilacs filtered in. She took deep breaths of the cool air.

Finally she gathered her scattered nerves together and drove home. The house was dark and she knew there was no way she was going inside alone. It was silly, she supposed— whoever the maniac in the vehicle was, he was probably long gone. There was no sign of any cars parked nearby, strange or familiar ones.

Just the same, after what had just happened, she had no intention of doing anything so stupid as walking into a darkened house.

Ten minutes later, she entered the Sutton Shores police station. The officer on duty glanced up from a newsmagazine he was reading and asked if he could help her. After she explained what had happened, he called another officer over, who then went with Amanda to look at her car.

Amanda demonstrated how close the vehicle had been to her when he'd pulled up beside her.

"Not a scratch," the officer said after examining the left side of her car. He walked to the back and checked the rear bumper. "Nothing here, either." Peering at her skeptically, he asked, "Are you sure this vehicle was as close as you thought? I'd say he was taking a big chance. If you'd slammed on your brakes he'd have been in your trunk."

Amanda frowned. "Whoever it was obviously knew I wouldn't chance an accident with a stranger on a dark road at midnight."

His expression was bland. "I don't see what we can do, Ms. Delaski. You can't identify the vehicle and there are no scratches on your car to indicate anything happened."

"Are you implying I made this up?"

"No, but you may have exaggerated the closeness of the other car. After all, it *was* dark and you did say he had the high beams on. That kind of a combination can distort perception."

"What about when he shone the light in my face?"

His expression remained neutral, giving her the feeling that if she'd screamed "Fire!" he wouldn't have looked any more alarmed. "It's not a crime to shine a flashlight in someone's face."

"But this was some high-powered flashlight bright enough to light up a building." He nodded and Amanda sighed. "You're saying you can't do anything."

"We can do this," he said sympathetically. "I'll have an officer follow you home and make sure the house is okay."

"Thank you," she said tightly and wondered if he'd decided she was some paranoid woman who needed a few crumbs of reassurance. He had probably only decided to go along with her this far to show that the police were concerned for their citizens.

Her house was as she left it. After the officer had searched the yard and each of the rooms, he pronounced the area safe and said good-night.

Amanda watched him drive away, then locked all the doors.

She couldn't sleep and when the phone rang at three o'clock she sprang upright in bed. She grabbed the receiver, her hello husky and cautious.

No one answered and when she put it down, it immediately rang again. This time she left it off the hook.

Staring into the darkness, she lay stiff and uneasy beneath the light covers. The practical side of her, the side that had grown up as the daughter of a CIA operative knew she would have to tell her father.

Just days ago he'd called from his house in Barrington, located about a half hour from Sutton Shores, to warn her to be extra alert to anything unusual. He hadn't been specific, but Amanda knew her father was never cavalier about danger. Something had worried him.

But in the past ten years Amanda hadn't lived in the eerie world of bodyguards, sinister plots and death threats. She had her own life, her career in youth counseling and a new project that she was excited and enthusiastic about. The possibility of being sucked back into that menacing arena of guns and guards not only didn't appeal to her, but it also made her angry.

Rolling to her side, she watched the pink reflection of the soon-to-be rising sun. Maybe it had just been kids having some dangerous fun. Maybe her early life as Walker Delaski's daughter had made her more suspicious than most. And yet she couldn't dismiss the fact that the dark vehicle riding her bumper at—midnight and seemingly with every intent of terrifying her—was more than slightly suspicious.

Perhaps she would just be extra cautious the next few days; at least long enough to get some perspective.

After all, she prided herself on never overreacting, on being in control of her life and her emotions. If nothing else happened, then she could simply chalk this incident up as a fluke and put it behind her.

At five o'clock she drifted off to sleep. She never saw the gray vehicle drive slowly by her house.

Chapter 1

After two days of surveillance, Thorne Law adjusted his sunglasses and slipped out of his car.

There was just no subtle way to do this, he decided as he moved forward through the summery June shadows and approached the side door of the sun porch. Her back was to him, her head bent as she studied papers from file folders that were strewn across a buff-colored wicker table. Her hair hadn't lost its rich bourbon brown sheen, although from his vantage point, he guessed the sophisticated, but loose style indicated the polished distance Amanda had acquired and perfected in the years since their last encounter.

"Confrontation" would have better described those private moments on her twenty-first birthday, Thorne thought ruefully. Her innocent declaration of love had come right up against his jaded cynicism and his bluntly cold rejection. On the one hand, Thorne viewed those heated minutes as having been his finest hour; total control of the kiss they'd shared, dismissal of his carefully hidden desire for her, and the instinctive knowledge that he was doing exactly what was best for her as well as for himself. He'd been in true form, not allowing any weakness in his personal life just as he had never allowed it in his work. At least, he had endlessly told himself that he had no regrets. Truthfully, however, he knew he'd been brutal to Amanda on that special night, but he'd had little choice. His attitude, as a result of having grown up on the inner-city streets, had always been keyed to precise objectives. Take a stand. Make the move. Don't regret. Never look back.

Thorne stepped closer to her now. Silent motion was a trademark of his, but in the past Amanda had always been aware of him before he wanted to be heard. Apparently ten years had perfected his approach, he mused, for she didn't turn or give any indication she knew he was there.

"You know better than to leave your door unlocked," he said softly, his arms casually folded on his chest as he stood in the opening that led to the side lawn. Her sundress was a soft pink splattered with deeper pink roses and Thorne thought it showed off her tan magnificently.

Startled, she jumped from the chair and whirled around, the papers she'd been reading and sorting so intently scattered across the table. Her eyes were wide with surprise, and for a fleeting few seconds Thorne caught an open vulnerability, but then it was gone, replaced by indignation. Her eyes—a smoky, swirl of green—had just enough gray to warn of a brewing storm.

She glared and he noted her quick scrutiny of his shaggy dark hair, his carefully set neutral expression, his blue sweatshirt and the faded, worn jeans. Only his boots were fairly new; purchased in Italy, where he'd spent Christmas.

Her eyes came back to his, blinking once more as if he were either an illusion or a nightmare come true. "My God, where did you come from?"

"Like I said, you left your door unlocked."

"So you just walked in?"

He shrugged. "You know better than to leave yourself that vulnerable."

"I hardly need to be reminded of vulnerability from you," she said briskly, and then immediately clamped her mouth closed as if she'd regretted the step into the past. Turning away, she arranged the papers she'd been sorting into a neat pile. "Besides," she continued in a crisp tone, "Sutton Shores isn't some third-world city under seige. Here, thankfully, we're free of spies and—" She looked up, giving him a cool appraisal that Thorne found just a little unnerving. It did too much to rouse his curiosity about her as a woman and not enough to remind him she was the daughter of Walker Delaski "—murderers and terrorist types," she finished with a lift of her chin.

"And if I were either you'd be—"

She interrupted him by holding up her hand. "Please. Spare me the worst-case scenarios. I grew up with body-guards and wishing my father owned the corner grocery store instead of working as a CIA operative, so I'm well aware of all the dangers lurking about." She narrowed her eyes. "The main one, at the moment, being Thorne Law having the nerve to just barge into my house."

He straightened. And he'd thought this would be a mere confrontation. So much for simplicity. "You wouldn't have heard me if I'd knocked."

"A poor excuse. More than likely I wouldn't have let you in and you damn well know it."

"And here I'd hoped you'd be sweet and soft-spoken, not some female with an attitude," he said, grudgingly admiring her bluntness.

"I do *not* have an attitude," she replied crisply.

"Walker warned me—"

As quickly as her indignation had flared it vanished and the color drained from her cheeks. "You're here because of Dad? Something's happened to him, hasn't it?" She started forward, but Thorne caught her arm.

"Amanda..."

Suddenly the snappishness was gone, replaced by real concern. "Why doesn't Dad take his own advice? The same advice he's always giving me? Every time we visit, I push him to tighten the security around his place, but he always reassures me he knows what he's doing...." Her words trailed off and she pressed her lips together as if to stop herself from verbalizing her fear.

For a man like Walker, Thorne knew there were no days free of fear, no days when security could be totally ignored. Amanda had grown up in that atmosphere and yet Thorne guessed his own appearance was simply too much of a reminder of their past—both personally and professionally. With a start, he realized that, in an odd way, he sympathized with her and if he'd been just an old friend he would have stepped forward and drawn her into his arms.

But they weren't old friends. In fact, he wasn't sure how to define what they were.

She walked to the sliding screen door to stare at the sweep of lawn and the beach beyond. Flower beds, roses in particular, defined the property boundaries with a profusion of summer colors. Her family had summered here since Amanda was a child; the Sutton Shores cottage was about a thirty-minute drive from Barrington where Walker had lived since retirement.

Recently a series of ominous threats with seemingly no discernible pattern had been aimed at Walker. Alarmed, the retired CIA operative was seeking immediate protection for Amanda. Keenly aware of the scope of any threat, Walker knew that anything aimed at him had the potential to touch his family.

Thorne had gotten the urgent request from his mentor and friend just days after he'd concluded the exhausting and frustrating—but eventually successful—capture of a terrorist group leader in Europe. He'd been just hours from leaving on a well-earned vacation when Walker's call had brought him to Rhode Island instead.

From what Walker had told him, and his own rushed gathering of information, Amanda had moved back to Sutton Shores to work on a pilot project for troubled girls. She had worked and counseled in other such programs in the northeast since graduating from college. She was known to be especially effective at the organizational stage, when making the girls comfortable and willing to participate was so important. When Rhode Island Youth Services had decided they wanted to begin a center in the southern part of the state, Amanda had submitted a proposal that was quickly viewed as innovative and workable. A house on the beach had been refurbished with the help of private donations. The girls and their supervisors would be living just down the beach from Amanda's summer cottage. Walker had told Thorne that he'd been thrilled his daughter was back in Rhode Island and closer to him, but, since the recent threats, he was determined to make sure Amanda got protection.

Walker had also warned Thorne that she might not be receptive to his arrival, but as Walker had said in his gruff, but concerned voice, "Her safety and life are more important than a few weeks of annoyance with me and inconvenience for her."

Given their own past, such as it was, Thorne doubted Amanda would be happy to see him under any circumstances. Yet his own respect for and long friendship with Walker weren't the only reasons he'd agreed to do this. He'd witnessed enough horror as a kid when his mother was killed and again in his own work as an antiterrorist specialist both in Europe and America. Experience had taught him not to shrug off a request from a professional such as Walker. The past two days of surveillance had been as much for his own benefit as it was for Amanda's. He had wanted to observe and analyze both her acquaintances and the area.

Confronting her had given him a healthy dose of what he'd expected: resistance and annoyance.

Amanda turned suddenly and looked at him, her eyes wide and worried, her thoughts obviously still on Walker. Her composure, however, was firmly in place as if she disliked Thorne seeing her with any sign of weakness. "Aunt Dorothy and Dad's housekeeper, as wonderfully devoted as they are, know little about vendettas and revenge and getting even. He's practically a sitting target. Of course, if he insisted Monk move into the house instead of letting him stay in the apartment..."

"Monk is getting old and your father knows he likes his privacy. Walker has always honored that." Thorne knew that the personal bodyguard Walker had had for years had already stepped up security on Walker's estate. Monk had assured Thorne he would keep him informed if he saw anything out of the ordinary. To Amanda, he said, "I'm not here to discuss Monk. But before we go any further, let me assure you, Monk's made sure your father's well protected."

And your father wants to make sure you are, too, Thorne thought silently.

But instead of relaxing, she ignored his words and went over to the phone, dialing quickly.

"What are you doing?"

"I'm calling Dad."

"You don't believe me?"

She glared at him, her snap judgment of him apparent. "Let's put it this way. I don't trust you."

Instead of rising in defense of himself, he shrugged. "Good start. It'll definitely keep things simple and straightforward between us."

She scowled, but then turned her attention to the phone. "Aunt Dorothy? Yes, I'm fine. I'm calling about—what? Oh yes, the house for the girls is due to open in a few days. I'm going through the histories of those who will be in the counseling sessions. But the project isn't why I called. This is about Dad. Is he all right?"

As she listened, Thorne moved to the wicker table and glanced at the papers she'd been reading. The computer printout sheets contained background history belonging to the girls she'd be working with. All were teenagers. Some came from dysfunctional families and some were apparently just trying to cope with the problems of growing up. A quick scan of the information and Amanda's notes told Thorne that Amanda still embraced idealistic visions; she believed that love, sincerity and exemplary goals were all that were needed to make the world safe. Admittedly his own cynicism didn't allow for such lofty aspirations, but he grudgingly admired her tenacity. Thorne knew little about teenagers, but a quick read of the work ahead of her made him conclude that her counseling center was indeed an ambitious project.

He glanced up to find her regarding him with suspicion and annoyance. "So, you've been lurking around spying on me."

Her arms were folded and her head tipped to the side, her face set with just a touch of belligerence. Thorne guessed the explanation Walker had told him to give, "concern over anonymous threats" wasn't going to be enough. "Two days. Hardly time enough to polish my cloak-and-dagger approach."

She didn't smile. "Two days of just watching me."

"And, if I do say so myself, sweetheart, your social life is about as lively as a religious retreat."

"I'm sorry I was so boring. If I'd known I was supposed to add excitement to your Peeping-Tom vigil, I would have rounded up some men and done a sleep-in."

She still had that edge of spunk he recalled so well. "Nice try, but your reputation is spotless."

Her eyes narrowed. "You've been asking questions about me?"

"Of course. Questions get answers. Or, at the very least, raise more questions."

"Damn you," she said softly.

Thorne gestured to the chair. "Now that we've dispensed with the preliminaries, why don't you come over here and sit down and I'll tell you how things are going to be."

She didn't move. "Might I remind you, Thorne Law, that your cavalier approach isn't appreciated. You are no longer in charge of telling me anything."

Thorne swore under his breath. He understood her anger, as well as her resistance to having him around, but neither had anything to do with why he was here. "Since I know Walker didn't mince words with you, I won't, either. Your father asked me to come down here and make sure you live to see your thirty-second birthday. Coming up soon, isn't it?"

She glared at him. "June 29."

"The precise date slipped my mind." It hadn't. He remembered the date, the night in the garden when she turned twenty-one, the feel of her mouth under his, the press of her young breasts against him. And the scent—too innocent and at the same time too damn alluring. Masking those too dangerous feelings, he said, "This isn't about having a choice, or even your hating the fact I'm here, this is about your father's fear that threats made against him might extend to you."

"The operative word being 'might.' "

Thorne scowled, then shook his head in frustration. He'd always believed in preventing problems rather than trying to deal with them when it could already be too late. Pulling out the chair she'd been seated on when he'd arrived he gestured again for her to sit down.

"I prefer to stand," she said stubbornly.

He narrowed his eyes and said tightly. "You want it straight and unvarnished, is that it? Suits me fine. Your father got some phone threats that strongly hinted you might be in danger. Given the number of enemies he's made in the past, he knows better than to just blow off that kind of thing. He told me he'd called you and cautioned you to be alert to anything unusual. Of course, at that point he was still scrambling to figure out the source and seriousness of the threats. But, regardless, he didn't want to leave you unaware and therefore an easy target."

Amanda refused to look at him. He had hoped she'd willingly tell him what had happened to her on Town Beach Road. Thorne couldn't conceive that she would just have dismissed it as a fluke, especially given the kind of atmosphere she'd grown up in.

"How can I say this without sounding ungrateful," she began in a cautious voice. "I appreciate Dad worrying enough about me to send you, but I have a full schedule ahead of me and I have no intention of cowering off to some remote safe house on the basis of vague threats."

Thorne watched her, his gaze steady, his posture perfectly still.

Amanda shifted and fiddled with one of the file folders. A car passed by and the rap of a stereo filled the summer air briefly and then faded. In the distance the steady roar of the ocean rolling onto the shore was accompanied by the cry of sea gulls. The sunshine danced through a wind chime, sending couplets of light waltzing across the floor.

Without looking up at him, she said, "Stop staring at me."

"I'm waiting until you define what you call vague threats."

"I don't know what you're talking about."

"You're a lousy liar, sweetheart."

She lifted her chin. "Suppose you tell me what you want to hear."

"Town Beach Road a few nights ago about midnight? Sound familiar?"

She paled and then shuddered, just enough to let Thorne know that whatever had happened had terrified her much more than she wanted him to know.

"How did you find out?" Her voice was weary and a little bleak.

Thorne ignored her question and asked, "Why didn't you call your father immediately?"

She stood up and crossed the room. "It all happened so fast and I wasn't hurt...." She paused. "I didn't want to worry Dad needlessly and since nothing's happened since then, I decided it must have been some kids." Turning and glancing back at him, she asked uneasily, "How did you find out?"

"From your father."

"But how—?"

Thorne reached into his pocket and pulled out a picture. "Your father found this in his mailbox."

The picture showed a car of the same make, model and color as Amanda's. It had been involved in an obviously gruesome accident. The writing on the back of the photo read: *On June 10 a midnight ride on Town Beach Road could have ended this way.* It was signed *Watching and waiting.*

Thorne noted the shadow of terror that slid into her eyes. Studying her, he knew the moment she realized just how close she'd come to disaster. "Tell me what happened," he asked softly.

She drew herself up as if she wasn't going to allow herself to fall apart on the basis of some hideous threat.

"I was on my way home from spending an evening with Sally Roche. She's a friend and will be working with me on the counseling project."

"You were alone in the car?"

"Yes. It was close to midnight and the Town Beach Road is the shortest route to here. I use it all the time." She paused and then spoke slowly, as if she didn't want to leave out any details. She told of the car just appearing in her rearview mirror, of the blinding headlights riding her bumper and of her attempt to outrun it only to have the vehicle pull in beside her and blind her with some high-powered flashlight. By the time she'd finished she was shivering. In a shaky voice, she added, "I'd hoped it was just some teenagers goofing around."

Thorne shook his head. "Not from the sounds of it. The kind of control whoever this was had on the vehicle.... Driving on a dark night with no headlights takes a lot of concentration. So does riding a bumper, and doing a side-by-side takes skillful maneuvering on a road like that."

"You sound like you've had experience with it."

"I've seen it done and believe me it involves more than a teenager could handle behind the wheel. No scratches on the car or any evidence to support your story, right?"

She nodded.

"Further proof that it was a professional. What all did the police tell you?"

"You know I went to the police?"

"I asked questions about you, remember? Walker gave me the picture, and the station was the first stop when I got here."

"They were less than no help," she grumbled.

"In support of the cops, Amanda, there's really little they *could* have done. Nothing happened to you and without a witness or even a scratch on your car, they had nothing to investigate."

"I don't make a habit of going to the police about stuff that doesn't happen," she said defensively.

"I know that. But the cops work with facts and clear evidence. This was just your version of what happened."

"My version!"

"Settle down. Let's say they caught the other driver. His version might be that he thought he recognized the car and pulled up close with his high beams on to see if he could recognize who was in the car. Ditto the use of a flashlight."

She gave him an incredulous look. "And how do you explain his rushing up behind me as if he were going to ram into me?"

"He misjudged his speed and wanted to catch up before you turned off."

"That's ridiculous. You're putting an entirely new spin on what happened."

"*From another viewpoint.* You've just heard how two people can witness the same incident and have two entirely different versions. *I* believe you, but from a factual standpoint what happened could be interpreted in other ways."

"The picture settles that."

"No, the picture does what it was meant to do. Worried your father and turn what happened to you on the tenth even more frightening."

"But who would want to do such a crazy thing? And why?"

"That I can't answer, but in the meantime . . ."

She slumped into a chair and pressed her hands over her eyes as if she wanted to close him out and all that he represented. "This isn't fair. It's just not fair."

Thorne drew her up and into his arms. Just a human-to-human gesture, he told himself. Nothing he wouldn't do with any woman who'd just been thrust back into a world of guarded moments with villains and threats, both known and unknown. Surprisingly Amanda didn't object, but she didn't rush to embrace him, either. She simply stood as if trying to absorb the turn of events.

Finally, after a few moments, she pulled away and wrapped her arms around herself as if she were chilled.

Thorne stood observing her, silently cursing whoever this nutcake was who had decided to stalk Walker and Amanda.

"So what happens next?" she asked. "I know Dad sent you because you're thorough, precise and figure all the angles as well as make sure nothing will go wrong before you act."

"Something can always go wrong, Amanda," he said, thinking of his harsh treatment of her when she'd confessed she loved him. He didn't regret being truthful with her, but he wasn't pleased with how he'd handled it. Then again, it was too late now and in the end maybe his way had been the best. At least it had ended things succinctly and sharply. No fuzzy maybes or crossed wires or false hope.

"I'm sure it can, but I'm talking about when you've focused on doing something important to you like being hired to find a terrorist or smoke out some splinter group that plans an overthrow."

He arched an eyebrow, more curious and interested than he wanted to be. "Do I take that to mean you've been following my career?"

"Certainly not," she said briskly. "Dad's kept close watch on your progress and success. He mentioned a few things to me."

"Ah, and you never told him that you didn't care if I rotted in hell for a zillion years? I believe those were your words the last time I saw you."

She glared at him. "They were my exact words and you know it."

It was the closest they'd come to talking about that long-ago night and for a few surrealistic moments they stared at each other, their eyes saying more than words could express, their memories of that summer night too vivid, too volcanic and too much at variance with the problems at hand.

Thorne swore beneath his breath.

Amanda drew an unsteady breath. "But instead of my fondest wish of never seeing you again, here you are lurking around asking questions about me."

"At your father's request."

"Which, of course, means the possibility of you going away is moot."

"It would seem so. You'll adjust."

"Don't you understand? I don't *want* to adjust." She went to the wicker table and put the file folders into a box that she then covered with a lid. Lifting it, she started toward the interior of the house. "I have things to do, so if you'll excuse me."

He took the box from her hands and put it back on the table. "Not yet."

She instantly swept it back up in her arms and tried to get past him.

Folding his arms, he planted himself between her and the open door. In a soft, even voice, he said, "I'm not going away. Not now and not tomorrow. We can work this out with a little mutual cooperation."

She turned away, but not before he saw the flare of frustration and uneasiness in her expression. "I can't believe this is happening again. Most of my life I was hemmed in and smothered, but I understood the necessity of it. I've worked for years to break out of that sheltered protected habit of always looking over my shoulder to see if my bodyguard was still there. It was suffocating, Thorne. With you here, I'm forced back into that whether I like it or not."

In that moment Thorne felt a surge of something he couldn't define, something that boded trouble for him. Protectiveness of her as a woman rather than just as Walker's daughter? Anger at whoever this bastard was who had thrown them together? Perhaps even a deep terror at everything that was at risk. Sure he was good at what he did, but in all of his other cases he was objective and undistracted.

"This doesn't have to be complicated, Amanda, and I don't want to disrupt your plans."

"Just like in the old days. You're just there like some shadow, watching. Dad told me when I was a little girl that the guards he picked for me were like the Secret Service who guard the president and his family. Admittedly that was awesome when I was a wide-eyed kid and impressed that I was so important. Now I just want to be me." Then with renewed resolve, she whirled on him. "I don't want a bodyguard. I lived like that all my life and I'm not about to begin again. Mother is dead and Dad is retired. No one I worked with knew my father was with the CIA. Wherever I've worked it's been assumed I was a well-qualified counselor for young people. My credentials spoke for me. And for all these years the progress of the kids and the new challenges—like the opening of the center here in Sutton Shores—have made what I do very important to me. And damn it, I won't go back into some suffocating, sheltered existence where I have to worry that every stranger I meet might be a threat."

"Amanda, I understand your frustration."

"No, you don't. You're just saying that to pacify me so you'll get your way." She paused a moment, "All I want is a normal life like everyone else has."

"Your father wants that for you, too."

"So he sent you?" She laughed derisively.

"When he saw that picture, he wanted you chained to me."

For just a moment she went still, as if these last words had destroyed all her arguments. She lowered her head and shook it slowly.

Thorne cupped her chin. "Is the reason you're being so stubborn about this because your father wanted me here instead of some security service?"

"I already told you my reason."

But Thorne caught the wariness in her eyes. "You're blowing smoke, sweetheart. Deep down, your annoyance isn't at being protected, but being protected by *me.*"

Almost as if relieved the real truth had been clarified, she suddenly said, "All right, yes! I don't like you. I don't want you near me."

He let her go. "So you'd rather risk God knows what because you hate me. Not smart, Amanda."

"Yes, it *is* smart, Thorne. Because nothing has changed. You want to lurk about, that's fine. But you are not going to be . . . well, chained to me."

"I think we can forgo the chain," he said sagely, then stepped away from her and started toward the door.

She planted her hands on her hips. "You're going to move in with me, aren't you?"

"Better than lurking about and getting accused of being a Peeping Tom."

"No, it is certainly not better! What am I supposed to say when people ask me who you are?"

"Why do you have to say anything? You're hardly a child." Despite his casual stance, Thorne realized that he hadn't considered the ramifications of simply moving in. To him, it was the natural thing to do to make sure she stayed safe. Years ago, all the time he'd been her bodyguard, he'd never been more than a few yards away from her. But now, despite the danger and Walker's having sent him, there were Amanda's feelings to consider. He shoved a hand through his hair. He'd barely started this and already it was complicated. "What about if you say I'm here to work with you?"

"Work with me as what?"

"How about your resident problem solver?"

"What is that?"

"Whatever you want it to be, sweetheart."

Chapter 2

Within an hour he had moved the few clothes he had into the bedroom next to hers.

Amanda tried to ignore him and busied herself with a few phone calls, although by the time she'd finished with them she couldn't recall what she'd said.

A distraction.

That's what he was; and what deepened her concern was the thought of days, perhaps weeks, of close quarters with him getting mixed with the unwelcome stir of attraction toward him that she felt . . . and didn't trust.

Scowling, she went into the kitchen and fixed herself a glass of sparkling water with a wedge of lime. She definitely didn't want any arrangement with Thorne—professional or personal—and yet knowing her father's confidence in her former bodyguard, she shouldn't have been surprised at the turn of events. Perhaps Thorne was right. At some level she'd known if she'd told her father of the incident on Town Beach Road, he would have contacted Thorne. Given the other threats, albeit vague, she would have been left with two choices: give up the project and go into safekeeping until the mystery man is caught or let Thorne move in to protect her.

In her opinion both were lose-lose choices.

But her father had never been slack when it came to her safety and Amanda knew that if she balked in a major way, she'd simply complicate her own life. So Thorne as a choice had been decided for her and now she was supposed to make the best of it.

The difficulty, she concluded, still too aware of her racing pulse, was that she didn't have a clue how to act around him. Prim and cool was certainly better than losing her temper or getting nervous. Thorne, on the other hand, seemed relaxed and unconcerned; but then he'd never given two hoots about her beyond the role of bodyguard. What she needed to do was to cultivate the same attitude toward him. After all, she was no longer a wide-eyed, twenty-one-year-old who wore her heart like some badge of love for him.

She sighed and listened to the sounds of Thorne moving around in the spare bedroom. A window being opened, a door closing, the slight creak of the bed. If someone had told her this morning that by nighttime, Thorne Law would be her shadow and sleeping just a wall away from her, she would have laughed at the outrageous suggestion.

A whole series of emotions had torn through her when he'd walked in with that sureness, that ability to tap her vulnerabilities whether they be fear or fury. Amanda wasn't sure who her frustration was directed at the most—the idiot who was making the threats or Thorne for making himself known. The daily contact, of literally living with him, of having her life complicated by a man whom she'd once thrown herself at in such a reckless frenzy, even now, ten years later, made her want to squirm with embarrassment.

Yet if that were all that she felt—just embarrassment— she could shrug it off. Young women often did humiliating things—it was part of maturing. She'd taught that in her counseling classes. However, shrugging off feelings for Thorne Law wasn't so clinically cut-and-dry. In fact her instant sweep of interest at seeing him had startled her. A totally ridiculous reaction, she admonished herself. It only revealed how big a fool she could still be about him.

She glanced up to find him standing in the doorway. "That didn't take long," she said in a pleasant voice, wishing she could ignore how sexy he looked in jeans so worn they should have been tossed out months ago.

"I travel light. Only the necessities. What are we doing for dinner?"

Surely he didn't expect her to cook for him. Amanda glanced up at the kitchen clock. It was close to five. "I usually just have some yogurt and salad."

He grimaced. "How about steak and grilled potatoes?"

Amanda's mouth watered. She didn't do much cooking; not because she didn't know how, but because she just never had the time. And cooking for one wasn't much fun. "I'm afraid I don't have either."

"Guess we'll have to go to the store." He was peering in her refrigerator and then checking the cupboard where she kept canned goods. Turning to her, he said, "I did notice a gas grill. Is the tank full or empty?"

"It's full. Dad had it done just after I moved in."

As though making a mental list, he said, "Okay, let's go."

"Go where?"

"To the store."

"Thorne, you know what you want. You hardly need me to go with you."

He lifted her glass from her hand, took a sip and handed it back to her. "Bodyguards tend to like to be close to the body they're supposed to be guarding."

She rolled her eyes and put her glass in the sink. For all the denial about being chained to him, she could easily substitute glued. "All right. I have a feeling arguing won't get me anywhere."

Thorne made sure the doors were locked while Amanda got her purse. He took her arm and steered her out the door, making sure it was locked behind them. His hand gripped her solidly, his fingers hot around her bare arm.

Amanda had already noted that he'd changed in a thousand ways that had nothing to do with physical looks. He still had the lean, muscular body that moved so silently that at one time she'd asked her father if Thorne had Indian blood. His dark, thick hair wasn't the tame style she recalled from his days as her bodyguard. Now it was shaggy and rumpled, as if a cut and a comb were distant memories. His face was craggier, his silvery-gray eyes too knowing and too chilly as if he'd seen too much of the base, less civilized side of life. He didn't frighten her as much as make her too aware of how different they were, how different they would always be.

They walked across the street to a parked nondescript dark sedan. He unlocked the passenger door.

Before getting into the car, she glanced up at him as he put on a pair of expensive sunglasses. "We could have taken my car."

With one hand braced on the edge of the car roof, he asked in a wary voice, "You want to drive?"

"Why do I have the idea that if I say yes, you'll cringe?"

"Women drivers make me nervous."

She slid into the seat, adding, "That doesn't surprise me in the least. It puts them in control and I imagine you wouldn't like that one bit."

"Cut me some slack, Mandy. At least credit me with making the offer." He closed the door on his answer and walked around to the driver's side. However, what sizzled through Amanda's mind was the way he'd called her Mandy. It made her feel young and defenseless and too aware of all those old feelings for Thorne.

Amanda gave directions to Bing's, a local market that specialized in superb meats and local produce.

A few minutes later Thorne parked in front of the meat market with its banner advertising the weekly specials. Inside, Thorne immediately caught the attention of the store's only female butcher. He mentioned steak and she reeled off the cuts and degree of tenderness. Amanda shook her head in amazement and grinned. Good grief, the man was absolutely lethal. Stand him in front of a female and before he had his mouth open to say anything they were drooling.

With a touch of dry humor, Amanda whispered, "I can see you're in good hands. Try not to break her heart by choosing pork chops."

He scowled at her. "What are you talking about?"

"Never mind. I'm going to get some vegetables." But before she could move away, he slipped his hand around the back of her neck and stopped her. Amanda felt a thousand sensations flow down her spine. He urged her forward and pointed to the variety of steaks on display.

"What kind do you like?"

"Whatever you choose is fine with me."

"Such cooperation," he said blandly. "I wonder if the same approach would have worked if I'd suggested we share a bedroom."

Amanda tried to pull away, but he tightened his grip.

"Am I supposed to get huffy with outrage at that?"

"Your pulse is jumping and your neck is hot. Did I hit a nerve?"

She tried to remind herself she had to be aware of her actions toward him, but all she felt was flustered. In a low, intense voice, she snapped, "Damn you."

"All you have to do is be yourself, Mandy. You're trying too damn hard to pretend otherwise. One minute you're cool and prim, the next in a huff about something. What happened ten years ago is history. You were young and honest about your feelings. That's nothing to be ashamed about."

Did he really believe that? she wondered. He'd certainly given little evidence of it at the time. In fact she'd been hurt and mortified. But she pressed her lips together, ordering her own silence.

Finally he released her. "Lighten up, sweetheart. If you're going to squirm every time I say something you don't approve of, it's gonna be a helluva difficult relationship."

He was right, of course. But on the other hand, easy banter was the first step in flirting and while she doubted Thorne was even remotely serious or interested in her beyond the reasons her father had sent him, wisdom urged her to stay on her guard.

While he asked questions about the different cuts of steak, Amanda walked over to the display of freshly made convenience foods. She was eyeing some marinated mushrooms when Olivia Follingsworth touched her shoulder. One whiff of the sweet, oily scent surrounding her told Amanda the older woman had purchased the perfume by the ounce, not by the bottle.

Amanda smiled. "Olivia, what a nice surprise."

"You look marvelous, my dear. I just arrived a few hours ago. The house was so stuffy that I left Clara to air it out while I did a few errands. You were on my list of calls to make. I'm sorry I wasn't able to get away soon enough to join the committee in welcoming you."

"They said you were concluding a fund-raiser in Boston."

"Yes, it's a new project of mine to get abandoned housing used for the homeless." Olivia Follingsworth had inherited a huge fortune from her late husband, but instead of investing in stocks and securities, she had wanted to finance worthwhile social projects. She was known for her generosity, but also a stickler for rules and order. Amanda knew that if Olivia put cash into a project, she expected a great deal of say in how it was run. Amanda didn't have a problem with that, but as Olivia stepped back and studied Amanda, she felt a pinch of sudden unease. "I'm very excited about the program for the girls, but I'm even more thrilled that Walker's daughter is going to manage it."

"I'm looking forward to it."

"You do know that the committee wants to privately fund it—totally—should this pilot project be a success? That way we won't be bogged down with any government paperwork."

"I'd heard that was the target."

"Of course, a lot of the pressure will be on you to make it work with minimal mistakes." Before Amanda could frame an answer, she added, "This means nothing that could cause difficulties in the good order of things or breaking any rules that would distress the committee."

Amanda frowned. She had no idea what the "good order of things" was, and she was unaware of any set of rules. She opted for a general answer. "I'll do my best to keep everything running smoothly."

Olivia smiled, but Amanda didn't get the impression it was out of approval or comfort. "I knew I could count on you." Then she leaned forward and lowered her voice. "My dear, I did see you with that disreputable looking man, but I assured myself that you had a perfectly good explanation."

Amanda stiffened, independence rearing inside her. She might not be pleased that Thorne was here, but she resented being told she needed to explain him. Obviously Olivia had seen Thorne cup the back of her neck, which from the perspective of observation could have seemed very intimate. But so what? Amanda took a deep breath. Like it or not, apparently what Olivia saw mattered a great deal. Explaining Thorne even to herself wasn't easy, but maybe that absurd job description he'd suggested was just silly enough to be believable.

Keeping her voice even, she said, "He works for my father as a problem-solver."

Olivia glanced in Thorne's direction. Amanda could only guess the confusion erupting in the woman's mind. Thorne did look disreputable, dark and sexy; more like a man who caused problems—especially for women—than solved them.

"How interesting," she said politely. "I don't believe I've ever heard of problem-solving as a profession. I had no idea Walker had come down for the summer."

Amanda debated on fudging the truth. But knowing Olivia, she'd be stopping by to say hello to Walker on the pretense of checking up on Amanda's story. Good grief, this was not what she needed. Never mind that she was old enough to not need her father's permission to hang out with King Kong if she chose to, but given the fragility of the project's funding and her own deep determination to make it a success, she felt caught. "Actually, Olivia, Dad isn't coming, which is why he sent Thorne."

She blinked as though trying to figure out just what that meant. "How odd."

Amanda knew she had to talk quickly and shift the emphasis from questions about Thorne to how she could work better with him there. "Now Olivia, you know Dad is very interested in this project and he wanted to make a contribution. Thorne is good at a lot of things and Dad thought that by sending him, it would relieve me of daily distractions that would take my attention from the girls and the project."

She appeared slightly mollified. "How very—"

"Innovative?"

"That wasn't exactly the word I had in mind, but—"

"But you will admit that total concentration on the project is best for the project."

"Well, yes, but—"

"Oh, Olivia, I knew you'd understand." Amanda gave her a bright look. "I'm so glad we had a chance to talk before the rest of the committee heard about Thorne. Now I can be assured that you will pave the way for any questions."

Bing, the head butcher and the owner, placed a wrapped package of meat on the counter. Olivia tucked her purse under her arm, "Yes, well, we'll have to discuss this further another time."

"All set, Mrs. Follingsworth," Bing said.

Olivia glanced up at him as if she'd forgotten why she'd come into the store.

"A half-dozen filet mignon fresh from the cooler, ma'am."

"Wonderful. Put them on my account, Bing," she said and took the wrapped package. Before turning to leave she said to Amanda, "I'm planning on being at the house in the morning. Perhaps you can meet me there at ten sharp."

"Of course." Amanda gave her a winning smile. "And it was so good to see you. I'll tell Dad you were asking for him."

Olivia studied Thorne as she exited the store and Amanda could just imagine the assortment of thoughts she was having. He did look disreputable and if Amanda hadn't been used to dealing with Olivia and knowing that she liked to know things before anyone else, Thorne Law might have sunk her counseling appointment with the project.

"Amanda, what can I get for you?" Bing asked. "Got some fresh-cooked jumbo shrimp that would make a great cocktail to go with those steaks your problem-solver is buying."

She pursed her lips, then grinned. She'd known Bing for years, from when he'd worked at a local grocery chain. On the few occasions that she or her father had any kind of summer get-together for friends and family, Bing made up the cheese and meat platters for her. "You heard."

"Yeah." He pulled on a pair of plastic gloves. "Don't sweat the Follingsworth dame, Amanda. Sutton Shores is all excited about the project with the girls. No one is gonna get steamed because you got a boyfriend living with you. Mrs. Follingsworth, well, she's got nothing better to do. Usually she's telling me how to cut my meat, so today, with you here, I didn't get the unasked for advice." He scooped up two handfuls of huge shrimp and wrapped them up. "Tell you what, just to say thanks, this is on me."

"No, Bing, that isn't necessary."

"Want to do it so don't give me no sass. Steak and shrimp will be a nice dinner. And some of those marinated mushrooms you was eyeing." He took a plastic container and filled it with the mushrooms. "Add some wine and candles...."

Why was it that a man and woman together always signaled a sexual relationship? "Bing, he's not my boyfriend."

"Whatever you say." He handed her the package and the container.

"It's not what I say, it's the truth."

"Okay." But his grin was wide as she turned to leave, as if they shared a secret.

Back in the car, Amanda sat rigidly, her anger at the position that Thorne's appearance had put her in making her madder by the minute. If she'd stayed home as she'd wanted to while he went to the store, none of this would have happened.

Thorne, however, seemed totally oblivious to her mood.

In a matter-of-fact voice, he said, "I'm going to stop and get some beer. You like wine with your dinner?"

"No, I do not want wine," she said tightly. The last thing she intended was to chance any light-headedness around Thorne. That had gotten her in trouble ten years ago. She noted his scowl and mentally dared him to ask what was wrong, but he didn't.

He drove to the liquor store's drive-up window, ordered a six-pack of beer and a bottle of chilled zinfandel wine.

After he paid for it and pulled away, Amanda said, "Didn't you hear what I said?"

"I heard."

"Then why did you buy it?"

"Because the plastic blonde with the door-knocker earrings got you all upset and when we get back to the house you're going to stamp around and screech—"

"I do not stamp around and I do not screech."

He took a left and headed down Town Beach Road. "Okay, complain furiously about how I'm ruining your life and that you hate me and that your wish ten years ago to have me rot in hell a zillion years wasn't long enough."

Amanda relaxed a little. To Thorne's credit he was trying to make her relax by saying he understood her frustration. "You saw her looking at you, didn't you?"

"Like she wanted to see the label on my underwear."

Amanda grinned. "You do look a little unsettling and Olivia is a bit snobby."

"When was the last time she got laid?"

"Thorne!"

"Isn't that what she wanted to know about us? If we were gettin' it on?"

"Olivia would never ask such a question."

"But she was thinking it."

Amanda sighed. She knew Thorne was right, for she herself had deliberately portrayed him as connected to her father—therefore an employee—rather than a friend of hers. It had all been to diffuse what Olivia was probably thinking. Amanda Delaski, the head counselor of a project involving teenage girls, sleeping with some stranger and setting a terrible example.

"Damn," she muttered to herself.

"Guess you'll just have to behave yourself around me in public." He said it so blandly she wasn't sure if he was serious or not. Then, as the meaning behind her words settled in, she scowled. Wait a minute. Olivia couldn't know how she felt about Thorne; that her pulse raced and she got all these funny sensations. All Olivia had was what she saw Thorne do to her.

Amanda glared at him. "In case you forgot, you're the one who touched me."

He turned and winked at her, then with enough sexual implication to send her mind on a fantasy, he added, "But I resisted kissing you."

She sat with her knees pressed together and stared straight ahead. He was teasing her, maybe even pushing her a little to see how rattled she'd get or to let her know that resisting her wasn't such a big deal for him. Resisting and then rejecting her certainly hadn't been difficult for him the night years ago when she'd thrown herself at him.

Since she had no intention of pursuing that subject, she decided to approach the original issue from another angle. "I just don't want you to ruin the project."

"And you're afraid me being here will do that?"

"She's the money tree, Thorne, and although she likes me and holds Dad in great respect, she's also rather narrow-minded about things."

"Like you having a man living with you."

"Well, you have to admit that from her perspective it does look a little odd."

"Then we'll just have to prove to her that I'm what we say I am, I am. A problem-solver."

Except you're the problem that needs to be solved, she thought silently. "What did you have in mind?"

He'd driven to the approximate area where Amanda had first encountered the crazy driver a few nights ago. "We'll work it out," he said dismissively. "At the moment, I'm more curious about that row of skid marks." He braked and backed up, opening his door and leaning low as he steered with his right hand. Amanda leaned over, too, trying to see what he did.

She watched as he straightened, slammed the door and pulled to the side of the road. "What are you doing?" she asked.

"I want to measure the length of the tire skids. You said the vehicle slowed and fell back behind you and then sped up, roaring toward you as if to slam you from behind."

"Yes."

"Well at that speed he had to stop or he would have hit you. If I'm guessing right, he floored it—peeled out, as we used to call it—and then slammed on the brakes. Therefore, there should be a double pair of skid marks where he braked. How long it took him to stop indicates how fast he was going. You drive and I'll follow the length of the skid marks."

Thorne got out of the car and came around to the passenger side. Amanda scooted behind the wheel. She turned the car around and as Thorne instructed, she drove back to where the marks began. Backing around, she again positioned the vehicle as if she were headed home.

Thorne said, "You're going to have to drive close to the middle so I can see the marks."

Amanda nodded, slowing to almost a crawl. Thorne opened the car door and once again leaned out. She'd driven for a few hundred feet when he signaled her to stop. He opened her purse and extracted an envelope on which he wrote a number.

"Okay, let's see if the peel-out speed matches the stopping marks." Again he opened the door and leaned out. "Easy, Mandy, slow it down. That's it...a little slower...slower...."

The car was barely moving when suddenly he sat up straight and slammed the door. "Where did you say those high beams were?"

"I didn't say. All I know is that they were blinding."

"Hmm, I wonder." Scowling, he shoved a hand through his hair. "What kind of car do you have?"

"A white Honda."

"So the headlights on a van or a recreation vehicle would be pretty high and could have blinded you easily."

"I suppose."

"And from the width of the skid marks, the tires aren't small like on your Honda."

"Which means?"

"That we should be alert if we see any vehicles hanging around that might fit that description."

"Sounds awfully simple. And how do you know so much about tire tracks?"

"Took some courses in police work before I got into the hunting-down-of-terrorists business. Comes in handy at times. I've learned that terrorists and your garden-variety criminal have the same goal—not getting caught. The tire track info may mean nothing, but then again . . ."

"Sounds iffy. There must be lots of those vehicles around Sutton Shores. Especially this time of year."

"Probably. But in the two days I've been watching you, I haven't seen any hanging around your street."

"Oh."

"That sounds as if you're disappointed."

"Maybe I am. If you had spotted one, we might be closer to finding out who this crazy person is. Then he could be arrested and—"

"I'd be out of your life...." he said in a thoughtful tone.

"Well, yes."

He rested his head on the back of the seat and closed his eyes. "Believe me, I want that as much as you do."

"So tell me about yourself. Any men in your life?"

"Not really."

They had finished eating and were sitting on the porch with only the light from the citronella candles. Amanda sipped from the glass of wine and felt about as lazy as she could remember. Thorne had cooked the steaks and she'd used the shrimp to make elegant appetizers. Thorne grimaced at the mushrooms so she'd feasted on those by herself. With the addition of foil-wrapped potatoes and a salad, it had been the biggest meal she'd had in weeks. They'd eaten on the porch and talked of little, simply enjoying the warm evening and the excellent food. Amanda couldn't recall a time when she'd been so relaxed.

At first, she'd staunchly refused the wine that Thorne had poured for her, but as the night progressed, she knew she was being unnecessarily stubborn. She rarely drank, and to be so uptight around Thorne, to deny herself a couple of glasses of wine, would indicate to him that she was too easily affected by him. That she definitely didn't want to do.

Thorne was sprawled in a chaise, a mug of half-finished coffee beside him. Amanda had opted for a second glass of wine and chosen a seat far enough away that she could convince herself he was just another body rather than the one man who could make the air crackle with tension no matter what the distance between them.

Now Thorne watched her and she was very conscious of his steady gaze. "No men at all? Odd, I would have expected all the eligibles in Sutton Shores to be competing for your attention."

"I'm very selective."

"Meaning you've already blown them all off."

"Meaning I don't think it's any of your business."

In reality, her social life was decidedly lacking in male companionship. Truthfully there had been a grand total of two in the past few years that Amanda had viewed as potentially serious relationships. Both men had been considered good catches by her friends, but they also tended to smother her. She'd concluded that growing up in a closely watched atmosphere had made her more conscious of privacy and a need for space and being in control of her own life. And there was the question of being in love; she wasn't sure about the emotion. She couldn't trust that her feelings would grow into a deep, abiding fulfillment; was fearful that what she might believe was love was actually a fleeting attraction as transparent and superficial as a teenage crush.

Finally she'd been honest with herself. She'd admitted her jitters, or cold feet or wariness of a forever kind of commitment, and had avoided serious relationships.

Now here was Thorne, who at one time she'd been positive would be her great love for all eternity, but instead he'd forced her to experience the hellish pain of rejection. Yet despite those bitterly embarrassing memories, she grimly noted that since his arrival her heart had been lurching and jumping crazily. She only wished that her apprehension just involved wariness of Thorne instead of anxiety about her own emotions.

Getting to her feet, she decided that before the evening got into any more personal questions, she would excuse herself. Thorne didn't move, nor did he make any gesture that he cared that she had.

She put her glass down, stood and stretched. "I think I should get to bed. I have to meet Olivia at the house tomorrow. I want to go a little early and check on some things."

"What time?"

"Thorne, it really isn't necessary for you to go with me. The house is just a few yards down the beach. I hardly think someone is going to try anything."

He got to his feet and made sure the outside screen was locked. "What time?"

"You are going to be a pain, aren't you?"

"Only if you continue to act like a fool and fight me every step of the way."

She planted her hands on her hips and refused to move when he tried to direct her into the house. "I am not a fool. I'm putting up with you because of Dad. I don't want him needlessly worrying about me. But there is no rule that says

I have to like it and act like some simpering child who wants to obey your every command."

"You wanting to obey me? By choice?" He shook his head at the foolishness of that hope. "Babe, I'll settle for low-level compliance." He turned suddenly and then in a flash, he gripped her arms and moved her into the darkened shadows.

"What are you doing?"

"Shut up."

"Thorne."

He lowered his mouth suddenly and kissed her and Amanda felt all the strength go out of her legs. It was a good thing she was against the side of the porch for surely she would have melted into the floor. Her arms were rigid and her heart thumping so hard it squeezed all the air from her lungs. He didn't deepen the kiss or show any inclination that he was all that interested in doing so, but Amanda couldn't have denied the pent-up race of sensation she felt if she'd wanted to. His hand slid into her hair, holding her head still as he braced his body in front of hers.

Finally he lifted his head and whispered. "Someone is watching us."

Chapter 3

Instead of moving away from her, Thorne leaned closer and whispered. "I don't want whoever it is to know we're on to him."

He could feel the shuddering in her body and her determination to stand still. "I know this is a dumb question, but if you know someone is out there, why don't you just go after them?"

Speakers from Amanda's stereo system piped music onto the porch, which helped to cover their conversation. Thorne, however, spoke close to her ear. "Not with you in here. Could be more than one person. Besides, I need a few moments to assess what's going on. I smelled the danger rather than saw it. How good an actress are you?"

She gulped, staring at him so that he could see the confusion in her eyes. "I don't know."

"If you handle yourself as coolly as you did with Olive Follingsworth, you'll be fine."

"Olivia not Olive."

"Whatever. Put your arms around my neck."

She complied, but her gaze shifted to the heavy darkness beyond.

Whoever was outside hadn't moved.

Since Thorne had walked in on Amanda earlier that afternoon, he'd been debating on the best type of relationship to establish for public consumption and still keep quiet regarding his real role here. An uneasy alliance all the way around, he acknowledged, and the addition of their turbulent past didn't make it any easier. Given her responsibilities with the counseling project, presenting themselves as lovers would definitely create social questions and perhaps raise the issue of her not being a good role model. Thorne had arrived at that conclusion when Walker filled him in on the details—especially those involving Amanda with the teenage girls. That incident in the meat store simply supported his theory—someone like snobby Follingsworth would expect above-reproach behavior.

And hadn't that been his intent? Don't touch her, don't do anything that could be taken personally, and yet the self-imposed orders were a hell of a lot simpler in theory than in practice. He pulled back a little, too damn aware of his own reaction to her—a response he definitely didn't want her to feel.

"How can you smell danger?" she asked and he guessed she was trying to distract them both from the closeness of their bodies.

He stared down at her, his hands framing her face, his thumbs brushing her mouth once then moving away. "Depends. Sometimes, it's an electrical smell that makes the nostrils flare. Sometimes it's a sudden stuffiness in an airy room. Sometimes, like right now, it's the scent of a woman who wants what she shouldn't have."

He felt her fists tighten on his shoulders and sensed she'd been caught off guard by his assumption of her. Swallowing, she shook her head slowly, saying, "You're wrong."

"Am I?"

"Yes."

Again, he brushed her mouth with his thumbs before tipping her head up and lowering his mouth. "Then kissing you won't matter, will it?"

This time he didn't wait for an answer, but crushed his mouth down on hers. Moving her just a little, his hands pulled her up against him into a provocative nestling position. He slid one hand beneath her right thigh and lifted it so that anyone standing in the shadows of the shrubbery would see exactly what Thorne wanted them to see. A man and a woman too involved with each other to notice anyone or anything in the bushes.

But kissing her soon proved to Thorne this wasn't an act or a role, nor was it even the instinctive male response to the closeness of a woman; what he felt was all too real. Her mouth was too soft, too sweetly fitted to his as it had been years ago, yet now the distinct promise had ripened. Thorne knew in that instant that this wasn't just a kiss, but more of a hot recklessness that had spawned between them. The wine had both cooled and heated her lips, creating a need to savor for some new experience in taste and texture. Concentrate, he reminded himself despite his desire to cherish her mouth, to draw her deeper until she clung to him in a drowsy haze. She wasn't exactly fighting him, but Thorne felt the barest of resistance, as if keeping a semblance of defiance against her own body's reaction to him was an absolute necessity.

Using her feelings to benefit the moment hardly showed him in a good light, but then given the claw of reaction he'd been having toward her all night, he didn't dare tell her that he, too, wanted what he shouldn't—no, couldn't—have.

Amanda.

Under him.

Wrapped around him.

Thorne didn't really trust himself to venture beyond the kiss, yet he reached down and lifted her into his arms without releasing her mouth. Carrying her into the house, he flipped off the lights and then immediately set her down and broke off the kiss. The idea of continuing on into the bedroom tore at him with a grittiness that had him instantly asking himself if he'd totally lost his good sense. Sex had never been a-should-he-or-shouldn't-he issue; for him the excess of satisfaction meant simply a time and place with a more than willing woman.

Scowling, he realized that what had worked in the past, with other women, would be a disastrous decision now. Thorne knew that later, despite her seeming compliance now, there would be hell to pay. Besides, he wasn't here to get it on with Walker's daughter. Ten years ago he'd had valid reasons to reject her; only a damn fool would put himself in that kind of precarious position again.

She swayed a little and he pressed his fingers against her mouth to indicate she should make no noise. Even in the darkened house he could see her tangled hair, her eyes just a bit unfocused, her body still too pliable.

"Stay here and don't move. I'll be right back."

She grabbed his arm. "No, don't leave me."

To his surprise she was trembling. "I'm just going to go into your bedroom and check if I can see anything from the window."

"I'm going with you."

He didn't want to argue and lose the advantage of spotting someone outside. "Stay behind me," he ordered softly, then stepped away and moved through the house to her room. He didn't turn on the light, but went to the window, where lacy white curtains were gently moving from the light breeze.

Concentrating, Thorne listened and stared. His ability to see into the almost total darkness and discern a barely moving object had become a skill honed from years of working in the blackest of nights. The key was to keep himself as invisible as whoever he was following wanted to be.

Seconds. Followed by a minute. Two minutes and still Thorne didn't move. His concentration was so total he felt Amanda against his back only in the most abstract way. Finally he stepped away and flipped on the light.

Amanda blinked at the sudden intrusion of light.

"He's gone," he said flatly.

He stepped around her and walked back the way they'd come. Out on the porch he released the screen's lock and went out into the yard, walking to the area where whoever had been watching them had stood.

Amanda followed and flipped on a flashlight. "Anything?"

"Not really. Grass is a little scuffed up, but he didn't leave behind any handy clues."

"What do you suppose he intended to do?"

"Just what he did. Look, watch from the vantage point of darkness, perhaps evaluate you and how to approach you the next time."

She wrapped her arms around herself as though to stop a sudden chill. "Then you believe there will be a next time."

"Yeah. There will definitely be a next time."

Hours later, restless, unable to sleep, Thorne stood on the porch and listened to the night din fidget around him. He swirled a tumbler of Scotch from a bottle he'd found that must have been Walker's. In the distance a lighthouse flickered.

It was close to two in the morning and Thorne was trying to fit together what he had so far. The bottom line had been the insistence in Walker's tone when he'd asked Thorne to come. Amanda had been, and always would be, a prime concern of Delaski's, but to call Thorne when he could have gotten a hundred security people in the flick of an eyelash revealed the raw edge of fear in the old man. He wanted it handled with thorough and swift silence, not a dragnet-type approach.

Thorough and swift silence, Thorne mused as he sipped. Just code words, sanitized to cover up the grisly reality. They simply meant kill if necessary.

He'd killed in the past—not a part of his work he particularly relished, but as in a combat situation, sometimes it was kill or be killed. A necessity when national interests and security were at stake, or his own life, or the lives of innocents. Yet terrorism was still in its infancy compared to the sophisticated wisdom acquired from its older sibling: war.

Terrorism, Thorne had been told years ago by a dictator now dead, was a dirty little secret that when the cold war ended, would show itself in a hundred hot spots and soon become the carnage of choice. He'd been exactly right. Splinter groups with their power-obsessed dictators viewed America as the hundred-pound gorilla that needed to be destroyed.

While the situation with Amanda was more personal, Thorne applied the same principle; she was targeted by some nutcake for God knows what kind of death. Whoever had her in his sights no doubt intended to terrorize, haunt, stalk, harass until the game became tiresome. Whoever had been on Town Beach Road, whoever had mailed the wrecked-car picture to Walker, whoever had been out in the bushes earlier would eventually grow restless with games of hide and watch. Eventually the game would end and Thorne knew that the watcher intended to be the winner.

Thorne drained his glass. Awareness of the complications with Amanda concerned him. Making sure she walked out of this experience in one piece and with as little disruption to her life and career as possible was the strategy he intended to follow.

Kissing her wasn't part of the strategy. As much as he wanted to tell himself that it had added credence to his wanting whoever was in the yard left unaware that he'd been seen, Thorne knew he could have used other methods.

And yet kissing her had seemed the simplest, the most obvious course to follow.

Hell, who was he kidding.

He wanted her mouth; he wanted to taste and touch and linger. He had wanted a viable excuse and the watcher in the yard had provided it.

Bastard. That's what you are, Law. You've been mucking around in the world of deceit and decadence for so long you don't know how to handle yourself around a woman who clearly doesn't need you to hurt her a second time.

He double-checked the lock to the porch and returned to his bedroom. Sliding his jeans off, he sprawled naked on the bed.

Stacking his hands behind his head, he stared into the darkness. In a low voice he muttered to the wall that separated them, "Mandy, babe, why couldn't you have been happily married?"

But another question probed deeper into Thorne. Would a husband have mattered?

He could ignore and deny and make excuses, but the bald truth scared the hell out of him.

He, who tried to avoid the most minor of complications with a woman, could lie here and honestly admit that when it came to Amanda, a major complication such as a husband wouldn't matter a damn bit.

It was a heart-stopping revelation that gave him new insight into why he'd rejected her ten years ago. He rolled, turning his back to the wall, and cursed fluently. She had too much power over him; a power she didn't even know she possessed.

But he knew. God, he knew.

"I have to say, I'm very impressed." Olivia Follingsworth nodded and smiled the following morning as she strolled through the recently renovated house where the girls would be living. Furnishings that Amanda had selected with comfort and casual in mind had arrived just a few days ago. She and Sally had decided on fabric shades and swag-type valances for the windows to keep the open-airy feel that the newly painted terra-cotta and cream walls gave the rooms. Olivia added, "You've done a magnificent job and in a very short time."

"I think the girls will like the house," Amanda said, her own excitement for their arrival evident in her voice. "I was very conscious that it not be an institution-type atmosphere. Fortunately, with only a small number of girls coming, we'll have lots of room to spread out." Amanda slid her hands into her pockets.

Olivia was dressed in what Amanda called summer estate casual: a picture hat, blue linen trimmed in white and spectator pumps. Amanda felt more like hot-dog stand casual, especially with her wrap skirt, a faded loose pink shirt with Rhode Island printed down the right side and her scuffed sneakers. She'd braided her hair, which had had Thorne commenting as they'd walked from her house to meet Olivia, that it would be hard to tell her from the kids.

Thorne wore jeans and a T-shirt and Amanda had been trying to figure out a way to suggest he get a haircut—not that she didn't like his hair longish, she did—but it did add to his dangerous appearance. She doubted that telling him what to do would be worth the words and the argument that would follow. It might have been ten years, but if she knew anything about Thorne, she knew he did as he pleased—including rejecting her in no uncertain terms.

She glanced around for him, but he'd gone outside. They'd said little this morning and she wondered if he simply wasn't a morning talker or if the darkness she'd seen in his eyes had been wariness. Unease, perhaps, that she might bring up what had happened between them the previous night.

Amanda had to admit to dwelling on that kiss detail by detail and, to her disgust, she relished each nuance. Maybe when he'd seen her in the kitchen he'd detected her thoughts and had concluded that kissing her wasn't at all smart no matter who'd been lurking outside.

He and Olivia hadn't formally met and Amanda knew the older woman was dying of curiosity even as she maintained a haughty distance.

Amanda said, "Sally and I plan to be here when the girls arrive and the rest of the staff should be in late in the afternoon. We wanted a chance to get to meet each of them individually and show them around personally."

"That sounds fine." Olivia glanced out at the wooden steps that led down to the beach. Earlier, Thorne had been standing on the top step as if to test the wood's strength. Olivia turned to her and said, "I do have another issue that needs to be addressed. That of this man with you. Thorne Law."

Amanda looked up sharply and to her own surprise felt all her hackles rise. Not that Thorne needed explaining, but that Olivia seemed determined to get one from her. Amanda didn't like justifying what she felt was clearly a nonissue as far as the counseling project was concerned.

"What would you like to know, Olivia?" she asked warily.

"What exactly is your relationship with him?"

Once I loved him and I'm terrified that those feelings haven't died, but I'm just as determined that I won't allow myself to be hurt the way I was before. Amanda shoved the painful thoughts away and said as blandly as she could, "We're friends. Like I told you yesterday, he works for my father."

"I know that's what you said, my dear, but—"

From across the room came the low, controlled comment, "I'm not sleeping with her, Mrs. Follingsworth. That is what you want to know, isn't it?"

Thorne stood near the door that led to the kitchen, his arms folded and his stance relaxed enough to indicate he'd been there a few minutes.

His words lay hot and alive like a gauntlet tossed down that Olivia obviously didn't want to touch.

Amanda turned to Olivia. "Would you excuse me just a moment?" Then, without waiting for Olivia to say yes or no, Amanda stalked across the room. Thorne neither came forward nor drew back, but simply waited. She gave him a stern look as if to say that for once his bluntness wasn't appreciated. On the other hand, Olivia's question to her had been even less appreciated. For Olivia to think that she had the right to question Amanda about any relationship simply showed that the older woman lacked confidence in Amanda.

She took his arm, but he shook free of her. "Better not touch me. She'll get the wrong idea."

"Then it's time we gave her the right idea."

"And what's that?"

"Stop looking so amused," Amanda muttered. "The right idea is that we're friends. Nothing more and nothing less."

"No more deep kisses on the porch, huh?"

"There was a reason for that. In fact, you initiated it," she said stiffly.

He leaned a little closer. "And you tasted sensational, babe."

She narrowed her eyes, debated exactly how to respond and then with a calculated boldness she didn't think she'd possessed, she said, "So did you, but it won't happen again."

He shrugged.

Amanda had expected a comeback, but when he just kept studying her as if trying to figure out whether her comment was serious or not, she decided that having the last word was enough.

She tugged him forward. "Please behave. Olivia is really very sweet, but she doesn't encounter men like you. She's used to the kind she can handle and slot into ordinary groups."

"Maybe I could tell her about the last man I killed."

Amanda swung around, her eyes wide with disbelief. "The last man you killed? You're not serious."

"Serious."

"But you didn't kill on purpose."

"Most definitely on purpose."

"Are you trying to shock me?"

"I'm giving you an option to my job description. Instead of problem-solver, you could tell her I'm a hired killer," he said sagely.

Scowling, she dug her fingers into his arm. The ten years that had passed had obviously brought a number of changes in Thorne's attitude. My God, to talk about killing as if it were just an everyday occurrence. Sighing, she realized how long it had been and how thoroughly she had put that "on guard, watch your back" life-style behind her. In some ways, she was ignorantly innocent. "I'm warning you, Thorne. I know Dad wants you here, but if you do anything to hurt this project..."

He actually looked contrite, which sent new confusion through Amanda. "Lead on, Mandy. I'll be on my best behavior."

Olivia smiled, but without an all-out enthusiasm. Thorne stepped forward and extended his hand. Olivia responded in subdued politeness. Amanda relaxed. She hadn't expected enthusiasm from either and had learned long ago to take the best from the situation and not sweat what she couldn't control.

Thorne motioned to the wooden steps Olivia had been looking at earlier. "I was on those steps a little while ago and they should be reinforced."

Olivia walked onto the deck and peered at the steps. "Is that the kind of problem you solve, Mr. Law? Unsafe steps?"

"Whatever Amanda needs me to do."

"Olivia," Amanda began, "I explained why Thorne was here."

"I know you did, my dear, but I have a few reservations. I need more information on him. He looks far too disreputable to be around all these young girls." She talked as if Thorne wasn't there. "You know they've come from troubled homes and having someone here that could remind them—"

"Now wait just a damn minute!"

Amanda stepped between them. "Olivia, that isn't fair to Thorne. I promise you he is no threat to the girls. Certainly you have enough confidence in me to know I would never deliberately allow problems for the project. My father has known Thorne for a long time and trusts him implicitly. Dad wants this—" Amanda moved her hand in a sweeping gesture "—to work and be successful as much as you and I do."

Olivia was clearly affected by Amanda's passion, but not quite sure she wanted to just accept Thorne.

Thorne stepped forward. "Mrs. Follingsworth, this project is extremely important to Amanda and the last thing I want to do is mess it up for her. Walker and I have been friends for years and I've known Amanda since before her twenty-first birthday, so it's not as if I'm just some guy who dropped in on her. You're welcome to call Walker if you have any questions. He, too, wants this project to be a success for you and Amanda and, of course, the girls it's designed to help."

Amanda held her breath and watched the range of emotion cross Olivia's face. Clearly she was impressed. But without comment she glanced at a diamond-encrusted gold wristwatch and said, "My driver was due at eleven o'clock, which I see it is close to. I must go. I have an appointment

in town." She walked toward the front door and then turned
to Amanda. "I'll be in touch tomorrow." She gave Thorne
a studied perusal, as if not quite sure what to think or how
to change the situation short of demanding his departure.
"Since you noticed the steps, Mr. Law, were you planning
to fix them?"

Amanda ducked her head and grinned when she saw the
flare of incredulity in Thorne's eyes.

To Amanda he muttered, "What in hell did she think I
meant? That I planned to make them worse?" He walked
forward and nodded. "With some of the rickety boards replaced, we can prevent accidents. I'm sure you don't want
the project to collapse because someone who gets hurt might
decide to file a personal injury claim."

"Oh God." Her face actually paled.

He held the door and then indicated a car in the driveway. "Go on to your appointment. I'll make sure the steps
are safe."

To Amanda's astonishment, she actually looked grateful. "Yes, that would be wonderful of you. I can see why
Walker calls you a problem-solver. A personal injury suit
would be a mammoth problem that the project doesn't
need."

No sooner had Olivia's driver driven away than a small
dark blue pickup pulled into the driveway and a teenager—
about eighteen—jumped out of the cab. He went around the
back and put down the tailgate, then hauled out a stack of
boards. Thorne went outside and directed him around to the
beach side.

"I brought you my toolbox, Thorne. I can let you use it
while you're here if you want."

"Thanks, Nicky. Tell Mike I appreciate you making this
delivery on such short notice."

"He said to tell you that if you need anything to just call." He glanced around. "Hey, this place looks pretty good. Hear there's gonna be girls here."

"That's what I hear," Thorne said, checking through the toolbox to see if he had everything he needed. "Did you bring the nails?"

"Nails? Uh...oh, yeah. In the truck. Be right back."

Thorne glanced up to see Amanda standing with her arms crossed and her eyes narrowed. "Can you hold down the shouting until Nicky is gone? The kid thinks I'm tough and I don't want to blow my image and let him find out you're the boss."

"I want an explanation, Thorne."

He stood and walked over to where she was. "Promise."

"This reminds me too much of those old bodyguard days when you were second-guessing me or paving the way before I even got to the problem."

"That was part of my job. Anticipating problems and solving them without making a big deal about it. It also makes for a more low-key operation and allows me to concentrate on the most important thing. You."

"Then why do I have the feeling you're running things—the project, Olivia and me?"

"You're making too much of this, Amanda."

Nicky came around the side of the house and dropped a bag of nails that landed with a *kerplunk* in the sand. Then he pulled an invoice from his pocket that Thorne scribbled across. He then handed Nicky a folded bill.

"A tip? Jeez, no one ever tips me for makin' a delivery."

"It's a bribe, Nicky," Thorne replied with a quick grin. "When I call you for help, I want you here fast."

"You call me for help? Yeah? Well, hell, sure. Anytime."

"That's what I was counting on."

Nicky looked over at Amanda as if seeing her for the first time. "Thorne says you're an expert with girls. Mind if I send my kid sister to see you? She's driving me nuts."

Amanda tried to be diplomatic. "Sibling rivalry, Nicky."

"Yeah, that's what my mother says. I say my sister is a pain in the a—"

Thorne gripped his shoulder. "Uh, Nicky, Mike probably wants you back at work."

He nodded, and Thorne walked him back to the truck. In a few minutes he returned. To Amanda, he said, "If you have things to do, why don't you go ahead? In the meantime, I'll get these steps repaired."

But she didn't move.

Thorne raised an eyebrow. "I know, you want an explanation."

"If it's not too much trouble, Mr. Law," she said in a businesslike tone.

"You're making too much out of the delivery of some lumber."

"Correct me if I'm wrong, but you're here because Dad is afraid someone will hurt me. I appreciate that, but adjusting to you as my bodyguard is not easy. Not to being protected, but to being protected by you." She took a breath. "I don't like you making decisions about the project over my head."

Obviously irritated, he asked, "What decision, for God's sake? The steps are rotten and I called Mike for some wood and nails. He said he'd send it with Nicky since he had another delivery in the area. Pretty efficient and it takes care of a problem that you don't have to worry about. You make it sound like I rescheduled the counseling appointments."

"My point is that you should have told me what you planned."

"And then what?"

She glared at him. "I don't know. I was never given the chance to decide what to do."

"Is it possible you might have asked me to call Mike's and order the stuff I needed to fix the steps?"

"Probably, but that isn't the point!"

"Then what is?"

"I told you. I don't want you making decisions without consulting me."

He looked at her for a long moment, holding her gaze for what seemed like eons. Then, with deliberate steps, he closed in on her.

She didn't move. "If you think I'm going to shudder and turn away from you, you're wrong."

"I'm counting on your stubbornness, Amanda."

"I hate it that Dad sent you."

"I know you do."

"And you don't give a damn, do you?"

"If I did, that might show I cared about you. And God knows we can't have that."

"Damn you."

He moved close, then closer still. For the sparest of moments he saw the need, the indecision and the subtle color change that revealed more than he guessed she wanted him to see. Thorne could have turned away and he almost did, but he became so caught in the span of emotions he saw in her face, he couldn't move. And in those fraught moments their gazes locked in a private interlude.

The thoughts spilled between them—unspoken, rife with sensuality, evoking fantasy and fascination.

Thorne cupped her chin. *Eye-contact is very dangerous, sweetheart.*

Amanda went still. *Everything about you is dangerous. Only the wanting.*

You don't want me. You never did.

Thorne released her and stepped away aware that his thoughts were scattering in too many directions. Without speaking, he could reveal himself, he could admit the lie ten years ago, he could tell her that wanting her had ceased be-

ing a question the minute he'd first seen her on his arrival in
Sutton Shores.

Wanting her isn't what Walker hired you for, he reminded himself. This was unprofessional and unaccept-
able. Just as it had been the night of her twenty-first
birthday.

Chapter 4

For the next few days Amanda and her friend Sally Roche spent the majority of their time at the house to finish the final details before the girls arrived. Thorne was there, too, but Amanda and he said little beyond surperficial conversation. In fact, Amanda thought, their relationship had been strictly professional, to the point that Amanda had begun to wonder if the kiss on her porch that first night and the heated confrontation the following day had been aberrations. Whoever had been watching her was either being deliberately sly and silent or—as she desperately hoped—had given up and gone back under the rock he crawled out from.

Contending with Sally's curiosity about Thorne wasn't as simple as dealing with Olivia. Amanda had concluded that Olivia still basically believed that a true lady—in this case Walker Delaski's daughter—would never get involved with a man who looked like Thorne Law. Amanda, of course, knew that the hard, dangerous, sexy, bad-boy persona—which Thorne had probably created and definitely had refined to a high art—held a kind of naughty appeal for some women. Even Sally, who usually dated men in gray suits and silk ties, with masters degrees in business administration, on occasion went out with "totally bad hunks" as she called them. Sally was short and boxy, but had a lively personality and a seemingly endless patience with the often withdrawn and mistrustful teenagers she worked with. Amanda had seen that same patience demonstrated when Sally had waited two days to ask about Thorne.

But now that the work was completed until the girls arrived, Amanda had only to watch Sally scrutinize Thorne to know that escaping her questions wasn't going to work.

"I'll say this much, Amanda," Sally commented after a full five minutes of staring and assessing. "If you aren't in bed with him doing sexy and wonderful stuff, you're crazy."

Used to her friend's bluntness, Amanda barely reacted. "It's always nice to hear such a straightforward opinion."

"He's yummy. Those jeans fit like he was born in them, the tanned chest, the muscles, the totally wicked smile and deep gray eyes and all that black hair...." Sally sighed, as if she couldn't think of enough good things to say about him.

Thorne was on the deck with a pair of binoculars watching some boats bob and plow across the water. Barefoot and wearing ragged cutoffs and no shirt, his deep tan made him look like a castaway just rescued after years on a deserted island.

Amanda had been particularly careful not to stare or pay too much attention to him. He simply had too much effect on her; an eventuality she neither wanted nor could her heart afford.

"Speaking of his hair, I've been considering asking him to cut it," Amanda replied as she closed up her planning book and put it aside. "Finally I think we're all set. All we need are the girls to get started."

Sally frowned, ignoring Amanda's attempt to change the subject. "Cut his hair? Why would you want him to do that?"

Amanda pushed her chair back and picked up their iced-tea glasses. "Because he looks—"

"Hot and sexy."

"I was thinking along the lines of sloppy and unkempt."

"You're kidding." Sally's expression was so incredulous Amanda might have been suggesting castration instead of a simple haircut. "Do you have any idea how much a woman gets turned on by men with hair she can tangle her fingers in?"

"Exactly the reason it should be cut. He's not here to turn women on," Amanda said staunchly, taking the glasses to the kitchen and intentionally ignoring Sally's disbelieving stare. She deliberately didn't glance out at Thorne. Just looking at his hair made her own palms sweaty. She'd felt the silkiness the night they'd kissed and found herself later dreaming of what it would feel like against her breasts. Even now, she felt her cheeks heat. Returning to the living room, she took a reedy breath, asking casually, "So how did we get on the subject of Thorne's hair?"

Sally walked over to where Amanda was putting things into the desk. "I have a better question. Why is he really here?"

"I told you—"

Sally shook her head, her eyes gleaming. "Come on, Amanda. You and I both know Thorne Law isn't here to fix steps and watch boats skim along the horizon."

Amanda turned away. She wanted to tell Sally the truth, but as much as she liked her, she knew her friend would be in near hysteria if she knew about the incident on Town Beach Road. She would flood Amanda with magazine and newspaper stories on stalkers and harassers, complete with grisly details, suggest Amanda buy a gun and heaven knows what else.

Admittedly Amanda's own past of living with a father in the CIA and having bodyguards all the time had made her view some of this with more perspective and less fear than the average person. The downside was carelessness, of not heeding the danger or as in her case, refusing to be intimidated by some idiot who got his thrill out of harassing her. Amanda knew that if her father hadn't been alarmed, she would have just shaken off the incident and forgotten it by now. But Sally wasn't her and what made it more complicated was that she had to give her some excuse for Thorne that at least sounded plausible. A reason that went farther than what she'd told Olivia.

Finally she said, "All right, but you have to promise me to keep this quiet. Thorne would be very upset if he knew you knew."

"Oh, I will, I promise," Sally said vehemently, leaning forward as if not to miss one word.

"I don't know the details, but it's stress-related. Dad didn't tell me, but Thorne hasn't had any time off for a few years and his work in antiterrorism is very pressure oriented. He needed some time to kick back and do nothing more serious than watch boats. He wanted a place where no one would bother him. Dad suggested he come here."

"And stay with you?" Sally asked, her interest intensifying.

"I've known Thorne for years, Sally."

"Then why haven't you ever mentioned him? My God, Amanda, how many women have a guy like that in their life and never mention him? And to boot to have your father allow and then send such a gorgeous hunk and never think—"

"Oh, for heaven's sake. I've never mentioned him because I've never had reason to. As for Dad...I am thirty-one and hardly in need of permission or a chaperon. But what's worse is the idea that an old friend couldn't come here without everyone assuming we were having some hot affair."

"Old friend or not, Thorne is hardly chopped liver or a science geek only interested in the mating habits of sand crabs."

"Did it ever occur to you that we're simply not compatible? He has a very jaded view of the world and would hardly be interested in a woman who counsels girls in Sutton Shores."

"Who's talking about forever? Haven't you ever heard of great sex? The kind every woman fantasizes about? He'd be absolutely perfect. And by the way, it's a great stress reliever—sex, I mean." At Amanda's scowl, Sally threw her hands up in futility. "Hey, I don't know. I have to admit that since I've known you I could count on one hand the number of men you've been involved with."

"Comes from learning a long time ago to be selective and careful. Two qualities I believe very strongly in. In fact, I think the girls would benefit from knowing they can be in charge of determining the direction of a relationship." Amanda had just read through a series of articles on intimate relationships and their pitfalls, especially for young women. She planned to use some of the more salient points in the counseling sessions. As she'd made her notes, she'd been struck by how automatically careful she'd been over the years. She knew, of course, that much of her caution was mistrust, a fear of being rejected. All thanks to her foolishness with Thorne. She shook away thoughts about him. Good grief, no matter what conversational road she went down he seemed to be waiting at some point. "Plus, given the increase in sexual diseases, I would be foolish not to be ultracareful."

Sally nodded. "Using one's own experience always makes for honest evaluations, but then you never did sleep around. You always seemed to be in control of your hormones."

Amanda shrugged. Except around Thorne, as I've managed to prove a few times since he arrived. "Just too busy working, I guess," she said, aware of how vague her answer was.

"So if he's here for R and R why is he helping you?" Sally asked, bringing the conversation back to Thorne. "Most men buy a few bottles and find a bed with a woman or two in it." Sally held up her hand when Amanda glared at her. "Let me guess. He'd planned to do all that, but when Follingsworth saw you two together, she put you on the spot. You had to come up with something, so you created problem-solver and then you had to give him some problems to solve. Fixing the steps for example."

Amanda felt a measure of relief. "Exactly."

Sally grinned. "Amanda, you're a terrible liar."

"Look, Sally..."

"Why don't you just admit you're involved with him? That's not so terrible."

"I'm not involved!" she said too vehemently. Evening out her tone, she added, "At least not in the way that you think."

Sally grinned, her eyebrows raising, showing she still wasn't convinced. "Okay."

"I'm not!"

Sally leaned forward and whispered. "Then you're a fool."

"I will say this. I'd be a bigger fool if I got involved."

Later that afternoon, after they'd returned to her house, she excused herself and went to take a shower. Mostly she didn't want to get into any conversations with Thorne. Thank God the girls arrived tomorrow and she could immerse herself in her work. After her shower she toweled herself and her hair dry, then creamed her body with a gardenia scented lotion. She put on a pair of white cotton eyelet trimmed boxer shorts and a matching cropped camisole top. Lowering the shades, she crawled into the middle of her bed and curled into a relaxed position.

Staring at the streaks of late-afternoon shadows along the windowsill, she admitted that with Thorne, she was playing with fire. She knew it and yet she felt as drawn to him now as she had ten summers ago. If she didn't know better she might think her free will and common sense had simply disappeared.

What was wrong with her? Was she in some stage of denial about her feelings for Thorne? Admittedly she hadn't dwelled on the past—both because it was painful, but more because it hurt her pride and badly wounded her heart.

Another woman would have chalked the experience up to youthful foolishness, and yet Amanda, by some inner refusal to put that night with Thorne firmly in the past—along with an assortment of earlier crushes—had elevated her impetuousness into a defining moment that changed the course of her life.

She'd loved him so desperately ten years ago; that summer night when her doubts were as scarce as her maturity and levelheadedness. She hadn't just thought she'd loved him, she'd *known* she'd loved him. But he hadn't wanted her and told her so in the most blunt and base way possible.

Now if she could stay focused on that rejection, she'd have no trouble keeping her heart at a distance. What she needed was strong emotional footage around him, not sweaty palms, a racing pulse and a need to touch him.

She got off the bed and went to the dresser. Opening the bottom drawer, she dug beneath jeans and sweats to pull out a small folder of photos. Her father had surprised her with them two weeks after her twenty-first birthday. He'd had them taken at the party, and among the pictures of her blowing out the candles, dancing with her Dad and opening her gifts was a picture of her with Thorne. They'd been walking into the garden. The photographer had been at a distance and their backs were to the camera, but Amanda remembered her excitement, her anticipation of how the next few moments with Thorne would change her life. Even now, after ten years, she could bring that night into her mind with crystallized precision.

She remembered the dangerous glint, as sharp as steel in his silvery-gray eyes when he'd noted she'd had a little too much celebration champagne. Feeling daring and bold, she'd coaxed Thorne into the garden. She'd been too starry-eyed to notice his reluctance and that he wasn't as pliable as the young men she'd known since childhood.

She'd ignored his stiffened posture when she slipped an arm through his. She'd disregarded his attempt to disentangle himself from her when she spontaneously hugged him. Nor had she heeded his muttered warning about being her father's employee, and even if he weren't, he was too old and too jaded for her to practice her flirting with.

Amanda had chosen to overlook the warning signs. She'd loved him desperately and had made up her mind that her twenty-first birthday was the time to tell him. She'd thought about the moment endlessly, had even practiced in front of a mirror what she would say and how he would respond. She'd pored through magazines that gave advice on how a modern, liberated woman didn't have to wait around for a man to make the first move.

Thorne, however, hadn't been cooperative or happy with her approach. In fact he'd been disgustingly blunt when she'd blurted out that she loved him.

"Love?" he'd growled as if it were a foreign word. "You think you're in love with me? You know what I think, Miss Amanda Delaski?" His tone was as brittle as flint. "I think you're wasted. Big time. Why don't you go and find some boys your own age to flirt with?"

Amanda hadn't backed down. After all, Thorne's not being a boy was exactly why she wanted him. His maturity, the dark, dangerous quality that drew her made her sure he was hiding tortured secrets and that she was the one woman who could make him happy. He'd been as her father had told her: a twenty-seven-year-old going on forty.

Instead of retreating with a girlish blush, she'd ignored Thorne's blunt dismissal of her and pressed on. "Age doesn't mean anything when it comes to love. I don't want anyone else, I want you. Oh, Thorne, I know if you would just give us a chance, we could be so happy...."

He'd stared at her for so long and with such a granite expression, she wasn't sure if he was in shock, furious or just at a loss for words. She'd looped her hands around his neck and tipped her head back, the dizzy deliciousness swirling through her; a combination of the champagne and the rush of love.

Licking her lips to make them more kissable, she felt as if she were drowning in the gray of his eyes. Still he made no move to put his arms around her. Her heart had leapt in anticipation and all her senses were alert.

He was tall, with a hard, muscular chest that she felt even through his suit. She wanted him to draw her into his arms and fulfill all her fantasies with a lover's kiss complete with sweetly spoken words and breathless promises for their future.

In effect, Amanda had drifted into her own romantic storybook. Roses drenched the warm summer night with their scent. Music for lovers played on the veranda where couples danced. She'd even chosen her clothes with great care. The black strapless georgette dress had a wrap bodice that tied in the back. It was more daring than her usual demure choices, but since she'd decided to spill out her heart and her love to Thorne, she had wanted to look sophisticated and desirable. If everything went as she'd planned, Thorne would be so taken with her, so overwhelmed by her maturity that he would tell her that he loved her and wanted her to marry him.

Yet when she'd pressed daringly closer, his eyes hadn't caressed her, they'd narrowed. The gray had deepened from silvery to a dull gunmetal that gave new meaning to the term raw and dangerous. Then with a deliberateness that even now caused her to shiver, he'd speared his fingers into her hair and destroyed the mass of curls wound with flowers. Holding her head, he had stared into her eyes and Amanda hadn't been able to decide if she'd been terrified or had drowned in excitement. It was a side of Thorne she'd never encountered.

Then he crushed her mouth in a kiss that was totally out of her experience. And for a fleeting few seconds, her breath evaporated and she hung limp with astonishment. No sweet virginal kiss, no coaxing of her mouth open, no soft touching of lips, but the kiss of a man who didn't flirt, who didn't move on a woman unless she knew exactly what he wanted. Tangled bodies, naked and taking their pleasure coupling in the most explicit and intimate way. His tongue, his taste, his boldness and his words, raw and hot and naughty...

Unexpectedly the bedroom door flew open, slamming back against the wall so hard a picture fell off the wall. Startled, Amanda's nostalgic musings flew from her mind as she scrambled into a sitting position against the headboard, her heart thumping, her lungs bursting to breathe.

A grim-faced Thorne loomed in the doorway, holding a gun with a naturalness that made it look less dangerous than he did. Legs apart, barefoot, low-slung, unsnapped jeans, his chest rising and falling all flowed up to his explosive expression: hard, cold and furious.

"What are you doing?" she barely whispered, the question immediately sounding foolish. She swallowed, trying to wet her dry mouth and throat.

Thorne glanced around, then checked the closet, moved to the window and snapped the shade so that it rolled up so fast it snagged the curtain. He peered out across the yard and toward the beach for an inordinately long time. Cursing, he turned, tucking the gun into the waist of his jeans. He closed the snap to tighten the waistband's hold on the weapon.

Awed and confused by the abrupt interruption, Amanda simply stared.

Glaring at her, his eyes narrowed. "Damn it, why didn't you answer me?"

Amanda jumped. His question came like machine-gun-fire. "What?"

"Didn't you hear me ask if you were okay?"

"No, I was...I must have fallen asleep." Had she? Or had she been so caught in her memory of him that she'd checked out of reality to sink into an old fantasy. Good grief, if he knew what she'd been thinking about; kissing him, wanting him to touch her....

Quickly she lowered her head and as unobtrusively as possible shoved the folder of pictures under the covers. Clearing her throat, she said, "Obviously there's something wrong."

He planted his hands low on his hips, his eyes slits of fury. "Wrong? What could possibly be wrong? I was just practicing a paramilitary stance to make sure I'm still in good form for after I get the hell out of here. In the meantime, I love standing outside the door of someone I'm supposed to be guarding and wondering if I should knock and hope she's alive or break it down to find out if she's dead."

Amanda glared back at him. Hope she's alive? Find out if she was dead? "Your sarcasm is in good form, I see."

He jabbed a finger at her. "You're just damn lucky I'm not trigger happy."

She gulped and was immediately grateful herself. "What are you talking about anyway? I told you I was going to take a shower and get changed."

"That was two hours ago and you're still in your under-wear."

"I'll have you know this is a new style of pajamas," she said, wondering what possessed her to think she had to explain what she wore or why. "I'm not in the habit of sitting around in my underwear."

He gave her an incredulous look that said he didn't give a damn what she sat around in.

She continued, "After I showered I decided to lie down for a while. Or is that a crime?"

"You should have told me."

"Told you? That I was going to lie down?" Now it was her turn to be incredulous. "Thorne, don't be ridiculous—"

He reached down and gripped her shoulders, hauling her up so that she kneeled on the bed. Shaking her, he said in a low voice. "Get this straight. There is nothing ridiculous about any request I make of you and I expect cooperation. I don't want to have to move into this room and take showers with you, but if necessary, you can be damn sure I won't hesitate a moment."

Appalled at his suggestion, she snapped back, "All in the line of duty, of course."

He hesitated only the barest of seconds. "You're damn right, babe. If it was anything more, I'd make a point of making you purr first."

Amanda's pulse took a leap and she grimly acknowledged to herself that Thorne had the ability to make her purr without half trying. For more reasons than she wanted to think about, that fact angered her. Maybe because he was so damn sure of himself and she was so *un*sure of herself. "You're a bastard, you know that?"

"I keep trying to live up to my reputation with you."

"Well, you're succeeding, Thorne. I'll be glad to follow your orders so you can accomplish your mission. That is what this is, isn't it? Doing as my father asks? Putting up with the upstart daughter who's too independent, too careful of her privacy to be sensible or sensitive to the slightest danger? So, without asking or even suggesting a local security service, she's suddenly stuck with the far too capable Thorne Law—Bodyguard Extraordinaire. Far be it from me to disturb such an ideal situation. Get the job done and then with any luck you'll be gone, Dad can relax and I'll be rid of you."

"Are you finished?"

Suddenly she was weary, tired of the inner tension she felt, concerned that all her energies weren't going to be enough for the girls and the project plus handling this constant exposure to Thorne. Truthfully he was the sticky issue. And as much as she hated to admit it, she felt some resentment toward her father for fostering Thorne upon her without preparing her. But then, she thought with some objective reasoning, her father didn't know she'd once loved and been rejected by Thorne. All he knew was that she didn't like bodyguards after so much of her life had been surrounded by them.

Thorne cupped her chin and urged her head up. She raised her lashes and saw a fleeting sorrow in his eyes that was quickly gone.

"Thorne, listen, I know we have to get along and—"

But he cut her off, pressing his thumb against her mouth. In a pure businesslike tone, he said, "Your father called. He got a call from this nutcake who made a rather personal reference to you."

"Oh, God." She felt her heart sink and then mire in guilt for her anger at him when all the two men had wanted was to keep her safe.

"Don't tell me you didn't hear the phone ring?"

She glanced at the extension beside her bed. "It didn't ring."

"It rang in the kitchen. Did you unplug this one?"

"No, why would I do that?"

"Hell, I don't know." He let her go, then sat down on the edge of the bed, shoving the rattan table aside and following the phone cord to the jack. He lifted the cord and dangled it in front of her. "This, babe, is definitely unplugged."

"I'm telling you, Thorne, I didn't unplug the phone. In fact I called Sally from in here before we went up to the house."

He plugged it back in and quickly punched out her father's number. Amanda sat frozen. Could she have unplugged it accidentally? It had to be that. It had to be.

"Walker, yeah. She's okay. No sign of anyone. She wants to talk to you."

Amanda took the phone while Thorne stood and walked to the window.

"Dad? I'm sorry you were so worried. I fell asleep and didn't hear Thorne call me." She deliberately didn't mention the unplugged phone. It was probably nothing. Perhaps when making her bed she'd snagged the cord and pulled it out. "Are you okay?"

"Now I am. When I get my hands on whoever this bastard is, I swear—never mind. As long as you're safe. I know Thorne has been sticking close."

"Yes, he's very efficient." She paused, her curiosity about who had called her father and what was said too much to ignore. "I assume it was a man who called."

"Yeah."

"What exactly did he say? "

"After the silence and some music that made me think of going to the dentist's, he went into a long description of you and how he watched you and you never saw him. He said, 'And when she does see me the next time she'll be so scared,' then he just stopped talking and laughed."

Amanda gripped the phone and felt the chilly beads of fear crawl down her spine. "Dad, honest I haven't seen anyone but Thorne and Sally. Besides, Thorne has barely let me out of his sight."

"Good. That's why he's there. I'm trying to lure this bastard toward me and away from you, but so far he's turned that into a game of cat and mouse. He seems to be dividing his time between Sutton Shores and here.'' He paused a moment. ''Honey, with your mother gone, you're all I have left. I admit to wondering if I was overreacting when I called Thorne, but now I know for sure I wasn't.''

Amanda felt a rush of love for him and no small amount of regret for her earlier annoyance. ''You always did have a knack for spotting potential trouble. I'm grateful, Dad, really I am.''

They talked a few more minutes about the project and then she handed the phone back to Thorne. After a few minutes of trying to piece together the sketchy phone call from the stalker, Thorne promised to get back to Walker within the next few days. He hung up, his hand lingering on the phone, his head bent in thought.

Amanda touched his back, the tanned skin warm and taut. ''What are you thinking?''

''Cat and mouse.''

''What?''

''This guy thinks he's the cat and we're a bunch of trapped mice not sure where he'll pop up next. When I was a kid, we had this big tomcat. I swear that cat knew every instinct of the mouse population in our neighborhood. He would watch them up close and then he would lie back, seemingly asleep, and make them think they had an advantage. Then, when they were too far away from their nest to run for cover, he would pounce. That cat had no morals, no sense of fairness. He was possessed with his need to win. To not let one mouse that he'd sighted get away. But what was really interesting was how sneaky the cat was. Sometimes he was out in the open, sometimes hidden. Once he'd curled up just inches from the mice nest. Poor things, they came out and were confronted with this huge orange cat staring at them.''

''So what happened?'' Amanda asked, finding herself on the side of the mice.

"The cat won."

"Oh."

"Yeah." He started to stand up, but she stopped him.

"Thorne, do you think someone came in here and unplugged this phone?"

He turned and stared down at her. "Let's not jump to conclusions."

"Don't sidestep what you're really thinking."

"What I'm really thinking is that someone is harassing your father with just enough detail about you to be cruelly frightening."

"Detail about me? Dad didn't mention anything specific."

Thorne reached around and gathered her into his arms. The gesture seemed more like a cushion of security against what he was going to say. Amanda, however, allowed herself to curl in, suddenly grateful Thorne was there.

Then, in a low, even voice accompanied by a bracing of her body, he said, "The caller told your father you smelled like gardenias."

For the first time, Amanda felt a fear that went into a numbing wrench. It didn't chill her or make her shake; it squeezed around her like an unrelenting vise.

"Babe, don't."

"Don't? Don't be terrified? Don't wonder if this jerk is watching me shower? Watching me put cream on my skin?"

"That's exactly the way he wants you to react."

"Well, how the hell am I supposed to react?" She knew her voice was rising to the level of outraged panic. Taking a few steadying breaths, she asked, "How else would he know if he wasn't peeking in the window?"

"One way might be how I knew the same thing."

Confused, she said, "I don't understand. If he was close enough to smell the lotion like you are, then I would have seen him."

"But he never said he smelled the lotion *on* you. He said you smelled like gardenias."

"Don't you think you're splitting hairs?"

"No. In fact, I think it's a major clue as to how this guy works. He's smart, and he gives just enough so that you'll fill in the appropriate blanks. In this case the assumption or conclusion he wanted both you and your father to draw was that he was so close he could smell you."

"But how did he know I use a gardenia cream?"

"I knew it before I walked in on you the other afternoon."

"How?"

"I watched you buy it in the drugstore."

Amanda was just too overwhelmed to be angry. Spies, Peeping Toms, a personal bodyguard and some jerk with a head game obsession. "I feel like one of those pinned butterflies under glass," she said sourly. "I can't believe you were in that drugstore, that I never saw you."

"I didn't want you to see me," he said dismissively. "If this guy watching you also saw you buy the cream, it's plausible he simply worded his comment to your father to sound as if he was breathing down your neck. Remember what I said about cat and mouse. He's playing head games with Walker and he would dearly love to get to you in the same way. Then he wins. That's the goal to win, to prove he's smarter, to prove he can intimidate you."

"You mean, you don't think he wants to hurt me," she said hopefully.

"I don't know what his idea of the ultimate win is. You or your father shaking with terror and begging him to leave you alone. Or something more final."

"Like killing us," she said flatly.

"Not if I kill him first."

Chapter 5

He slipped the key into the lock, turned it and pushed open the door slowly. He sniffed, priding himself on his sharp sense of smell. He'd once killed a CIA agent who had identified his hiding place by the stink of bay rum. He had little use for stupidity; a flaw he himself had never possessed.

He drew the apartment's air into his nostrils, and closed his eyes so as to concentrate and identify any obtrusive scents. Nothing out of the ordinary; just the lingering smell of air freshener to cover the ripe scent of dying roses.

Glancing around, he concluded nothing had been disturbed since he'd gone down the street to make the phone call. He had a phone, but never used it. Overcautious, perhaps, but a necessity to guarantee success.

He smiled into the silent room, allowing himself a moment to enjoy his own brilliance and flawless strategy at how all this was playing out so magnificently.

Making things right, making the bastard Delaski pay for his betrayal, making him watch his daughter die. So simple and yet to be accomplished with perfection, it required impeccable expertise.

He went to the kitchen and fixed himself a drink. Exactly two shots of imported Scotch over three ice cubes. He sipped and savored the expensive liquor. Then, listening intently, he swore viciously as footsteps approached his door. A line of sweat beaded on his mustached upper lip. Another rivulet clambered down his spine beneath his soft beige designer polo shirt.

He bared his teeth, then immediately relaxed. Rise to the occasion, he reminded himself. To accomplish this, you must always treat every obstacle as a toleration tool to be used as suits you.

He set the glass down, quickly checked the locked bedroom and resprayed the approach to the front door with the air freshener. He then arranged an appropriately polite expression on his face and pushed the spray container beneath a brocade chair. He released the lock at the first knock.

It was her.

Dressed in green lace she excited him as much as watching a motel sign blink. She smelled of some perfume obviously designed to enchant him, but that only succeeded in gagging and smothering him.

Nevertheless, he oozed his practiced charm. "Ah, my lovely neighbor."

She carried a casserole filled with something he was positive he wouldn't like. She glanced behind her, before whispering, "I hope I'm not disturbing you."

"I'm glad you came," he replied seductively.

"You are?"

"Of course. I would never be disappointed in having such a beautiful lady for company." The bitch actually blushed, he thought with some astonishment.

Again she glanced behind her, obviously hoping no one had seen her eagerness to be with him. "I shouldn't, you know. But I hate to see a stranger in town continue to be one. Why before you know it, you'll have lots of friends and then my checking on you..." She offered the casserole and a winning smile. "Or bringing you a little something to eat, won't matter."

He noted her attempt to curry a compliment, but deliberately ignored it. He smiled pleasantly. "Making friends with a stranger can be dangerous, especially for a lovely lady such as yourself." He loved to dabble between who he really was and who women like her thought he was.

Again her face flushed. "Well, I would hardly call you dangerous. I would call you interesting and different in a wonderful sort of way, and well..." She hesitated and he thought if she blushed once more he'd shove her out and slam the damn door. But instead, she added, "Unlike any man I've ever known."

He made a slight bow. "I'm honored by your compliment."

He opened the door wider to allow her inside, his fingers brushing the side of her breast as she glided past him. He felt the response and knew it wouldn't be long before her need to sleep with him would consume her. Of course, they would play this silly flirting game that he detested, but he knew. Eventually she would beg him. Women always did.

Women wanted him; a fact, he'd coldly and mercilessly used to his own advantage. They gave him cover and credibility and in some cases he actually found them amusing. Such as this one.

He touched a strand of her hair, then retreated. Since he'd gotten out of prison, he'd made himself learn his way around women. Nothing crude and jarring; soft music, polite conversation, an occasional gift, yet to his amusement his performances were so flawlessly brilliant that for a fleeting moment—irrational, actually—he'd considered forgetting about Delaski and his daughter and going into full-time stud work.

Shallow, bubbly bitches, all so desperate for the flimsiest of compliments. Charm, soft words, hints of the kind of sex they knew they shouldn't want, but salivated for. What, he wondered grimly, did this one want? He shuddered at the thought of a leather thong and a peach jam repeat. He'd always had a distinct distaste for peaches. With any luck, he'd be finished with his business and gone before he had to even French her.

"Did you have an interesting day?" he asked, putting ice into a tall glass.

"How sweet of you to ask." She beamed and preened, touching her hair lightly. "Yes, actually, I did. The girls arrive tomorrow and the project will finally get started."

He fixed the gin and tonic he knew she liked, added the wedge of lime and handed it to her. He raised his own glass in a toast. "Then here's to success."

She touched her drink to his and smiled winningly. "Yes. With Amanda running things, I know it will be."

"Ah, then here's to success with Amanda," he replied, his usual blank eyes gleaming.

The man drank and savored and later when the woman had finally gone, he went into his bedroom to celebrate the next step in his plan. He counted how many of the overripe roses would be dead enough for Amanda.

Thorne watched Amanda come down the stairs after checking the bedrooms for about the fifth time. She'd asked Sally more than once if all the foodstuffs had arrived, assured the Committee on Youth Services—the three women, two men had come to welcome the girls and the supervisors accompanying them—that everything was set to go. Also overseeing the entire morning was Olivia Follingsworth. The woman had eyed him speculatively, but Thorne had smiled as if his presence was a nonissue.

"Behave and be charming," Amanda had whispered after pulling him into a small passageway between the living room and the hall to the kitchen. It was cool and shadowed and out of earshot for the rest of those in the house.

"You mean my best jeans and shirt aren't enough?" he asked sagely, too aware of her scent and her softness. "I think my departure would be more effective with her than my charm." He wondered just how the late Buckner Follingsworth had dealt with his wife. She reminded Thorne of a militant activist on the hunt for debauchery and dirt. This morning, however, she had peered at him with what appeared to be a glimmer of concession.

"I pointed out the steps you repaired and she was very impressed," Amanda told him.

"Hardly heavy-duty brain work, babe."

"Apparently Bucky was never very good with his hands."

Thorne raised an eyebrow. "Hmm, then I was right all along. She needs to get laid."

Amanda tipped her head to the side and Thorne had to resist tangling his fingers into her pinned-back hair and tugging her mouth onto his. "I meant *working* with his hands," she said crisply.

He grinned, his gaze wandering down her with deliberate blatancy. "Yeah, so did I."

In that moment she reminded him of that night in the garden on her twenty-first birthday. Innocent, capricious and more than a little dangerous to his usually quick instincts about women. "Are you flirting with me?" she asked.

"Never flirt. I always cut right to the chase." This time, he took advantage of the shadows, of the moment alone and gave in to his own growing weakness for the taste of her. Drawing her close, and closer, he lowered his mouth to kiss her.

"No...you can't...." she whispered just a little frantically, though she didn't struggle to get away.

"Never say can't. Can't is for cowards and we both know you're not that."

"But..." Her eyes were wide, smoky green and alluring.

"One kiss...just for luck...." He touched her lower back and brought her against him, then dipped the tip of his tongue into each corner of her mouth. He felt her shiver. "For your success and all the successes that will follow today."

She rested her hands against his chest. "Thorne, how sweet."

"I never flirt and I'm never sweet. Just finding an excuse to do what I've wanted to do since the other night. Kiss you again."

No sooner had his mouth covered hers and he'd coaxed her tongue into a provocative tangle than Follingsworth called her. "They're here, Amanda, come and greet them."

She pulled away, but Thorne caught her to him, brushing her mouth once again. And she yielded a few seconds before pulling back once more. With a nervous laugh, she said, "Once for luck, okay, but two is definitely trouble."

In Thorne's opinion it was a long way from a "definitely trouble" kiss; too hurried, not deep enough, not enough of her against him, but with a sigh of resignation he decided it was a marginally safe kiss. If there was such a thing when it came to Amanda.

She patted her hair and smoothed her hands down the melon-colored linen dress she wore. "Do I look okay?"

He slipped his finger inside the slight scoop of her neckline and traced her skin. "Gorgeous."

She sucked in her breath. "I'll settle for open and friendly. Please come out and meet the girls."

He stiffened slightly, but in the shadows he doubted she noticed. "I was sort of thinking I'd stay in the background. Teenage girls can be a little overwhelming."

"You overwhelmed by some young girls? I find that hard to believe."

"Why? You overwhelmed me."

She blinked as if she hadn't heard correctly. Staring up at him, he saw her questions and her hesitation in asking them. Caution, no doubt, obviously from that night when he'd scoffed at her confession of love. He couldn't blame her—once burned, twice shy wasn't such a bad philosophy when it came to relationships. Thorne wasn't quite sure why he'd even made such a confession, tossing his feelings out as if they were confetti. Maybe because that was what they were really worth. Hell, it had been so long since he'd felt anything unconditional about a woman, he wasn't sure what the rules were.

"Amanda!"

"You better go, babe," he said when she didn't move.

"Yes . . . yes, I better." She swung her head in the direction of Follingsworth's voice. "Coming!" Then to Thorne, she said, "We'll talk later."

Thorne followed her to the door into the living room and stopped. She went on out the front door. The minivan had parked in front of the house and six girls had spilled out. To Thorne they all looked alike; baggy clothes and a kind of defensive, yet unsure posture. A redhead looked to be the most relaxed. Another had shaved her head, making him wonder just what kind of rebellion that was supposed to represent. He shoved a hand through his own hair, recalling that in high school, he'd worn his—rebellion and hair—well below his shoulders.

He turned toward the back of the house, determined to avoid a forced introduction. He knew little about kids, but he'd bet they were nervous, unsure what to do or say; no way did he want to make it any more difficult for them. Outside, he walked down the repaired steps, across the sand dunes that separated the house from the beach and worked his way around to the front yard.

Standing back so he could observe rather than intrude, he blew out lungfuls of air, unable to dismiss his increasing personal interest in Amanda. Despite the quickness of that kiss and the frustration of not having enough of her, Amanda's taste lingered in his senses. Her scent spiraled through him as if he needed both her taste and scent to draw his next breath. For the first time in a long time, he felt a sense of contentment. Odd, for certainly the circumstances of why he was even in Sutton Shores were a prototype for wired tension and constant headaches.

Thorne fought to deny any personal interest in Amanda beyond making sure she stayed safe and her project wasn't aborted because of this stalker. Making that denial work day by day, however, wasn't quite so simple. Touching her was becoming a need that he had to clamp under control every time he was alone with her. Once he'd rejected her for the best possible reasons; she was too young and innocent and he was too old and jaded. Now he didn't trust himself to test that resolve of ten years ago. In his opinion, if anything, the gap was now even wider. Maybe not in measured years, but a relationship with Amanda was out of the question.

After Jill's death in Germany—a woman whom he readily admitted, he'd taken far too much for granted—Thorne had concluded, he'd never be cut out for permanent relationships. In those weeks following her death, he'd felt nothing but regret that she'd come to teach in an exchange program to be near him and that for her dedication she'd wound up dead in a terrorist bombing. His antiterrorist consultant agency had offices in Frankfurt, where he'd been working to gather data on a new terrorist regime rumored to be spreading across Europe. After her death, he'd thrown himself into his work; the results of dedicated people who worked with him, they were able to crack the terrorist's inner circle and dismantle them. It had taken Thorne close to three years of unending, mind-draining work.

The first "real" vacation that he'd planned had been interrupted by Walker's call to come and guard Amanda. A simple enough request that he assumed he would handle as he did all jobs: concisely, quickly and objectively.

So far he'd failed on all three counts.

Now he watched as Amanda greeted each one of the girls as if the teenager was the most important contribution to the project. It was hard to tell from where he stood how they responded, but he remembered that when he'd glanced at the printout sheets on them that first day on her porch, he'd thought Amanda had her work cut out for her. The bald-headed one seemed the most withdrawn and when Amanda touched her shoulder she swung away as if she'd been burned. Amanda, however, took the rebuff in stride and even went so far as to step between the girl and one of the supervisors who tried to reprimand her.

Each of the girls carried a backpack and a plastic bag that Thorne presumed was their clothes. Follingsworth and Sally were taking the girls into the house while Amanda went to speak to the driver who had brought them. Thorne glanced beyond Amanda at a slowly approaching panel truck.

He straightened, his senses immediately alert. As the vehicle drew closer and slowed to a stop behind the minivan, Thorne moved.

Amanda swung around. "There you are. I wondered where you disappeared to."

"I want you to go into the house. Fast."

She scowled. "Thorne, what's wrong—"

"Move, damn it."

Amanda had heard that tone too many times in the past to argue. She hurried across the lawn and into the house just as the panel truck driver opened his door and climbed out.

The truck belonged to a florist according to the lettering on the side, but Thorne wasn't yet convinced. Perhaps because the trojan-horse approach worked far too well far too many times.

He walked up to the truck door where inside the driver was checking a clipboard. He was middle-aged, wearing a Hawaiian shirt with red suspenders and khaki pants. He glanced up at Thorne. "Hey, maybe you can help me."

"Maybe. You lost or looking for an address?"

"I got flowers for an Amanda Delaski at the Sutton Shores Youth House, but I don't see no sign. This is the right street. What's the number on that house?"

"Twenty-six."

"Yep, that's the one I'm looking for." He tossed the clipboard onto the seat, climbed out and walked around to the back of the truck, where he opened two doors. A number of flower arrangements and long florist boxes sat on the panel truck's floor. He reached for a vase of mixed flowers and a long white box tied with a red ribbon.

Thorne said, "Let me take those."

Confused the driver asked, "Take them for what?" Gripping his deliveries, he took a step away from Thorne. "Who are you anyway?" he asked, his eyes narrowing now in suspicion.

Amanda stood in the doorway flanked by Follingsworth, Sally and a few of the girls. Hell, somehow he'd lost control of this. A few more moves and he'd look like something out of the Keystone Kops and yet there was no way he was letting this stuff into the house without checking it out.

But he couldn't wrestle the flowers from the driver. That would look ridiculous, especially if they proved to be "just" flowers. For sure he would go back and tell his boss, who'd want an explanation. Not exactly the kind of publicity he wanted nor did Amanda want for her project.

Thorne reached into his pocket and pulled out a ten-dollar bill. Hadn't Amanda told him to be charming? Maybe extra accommodating would work just as well. "I meant let me take them inside and save you a trip."

The driver looked torn between the unaccustomed tip and letting his delivery be done by someone he didn't know.

Thorne added. "Don't worry, I work here." He pointed to Amanda and Follingsworth. "If I didn't, don't you think they'd be out here to see what was going on?"

The driver looked from Thorne to the two women and back to Thorne. "Yeah, I guess." Then he narrowed his eyes and asked, "Is that the Follingsworth broad?"

"It's her."

"Hell, from what I've heard she's enough to give the devil a headache. Don't care to have a run-in with her. Here, you take these." He handed Thorne the vase and the box. Thorne insisted he take the tip. "Hey, this is okay. Gettin' tipped for doin' nothin'. Good luck workin' for her, man. You're gonna need it."

Now all he had to do was think up an excuse for the commotion. Even from this distance, he could tell Follingsworth was beyond curious.

Amanda walked forward and Follingsworth followed. In a cheery voice Amanda said, "Thorne, why don't you take those around to the kitchen entry. I'm so glad you intercepted the driver. I want to make sure they don't have any of those tiny bugs the last flowers had."

Follingsworth said, "Bugs? Oh dear, we certainly don't want bugs in the house."

Amanda nodded. "Hmm, I'm sure Thorne is as capable of dealing with bugs."

Thorne rolled his eyes. Follingsworth visibly shivered.

Amanda patted her hand. "It's okay, Olivia, Thorne will take care of them just like he did the steps."

"Yes, well, that was going to be my suggestion." She stepped back into the safety of the doorway. "He is supposed to solve problems, after all."

"Yes, ma'am," Thorne said wisely.

He and Amanda walked toward the kitchen entrance. "You're a cool one, Mandy Delaski," he said with honest admiration.

"Guess one never loses her roots—lies and deceptions were as common around our house as milk and bread."

"Around my house, too, but for different reasons," he muttered as he set the flowers down on the tiny back porch.

"You've never said much about your family."

"No need to. They had nothing to do with my work."

"You know, that was one of the things Dad always said he admired in you. The ability to totally separate who you were from what you did." He made no comment, hoping that would end the conversation.

"Where are they?"

So much for that idea. "Dead."

"Oh, I'm sorry."

"My mother was an extraordinary woman, but the old man was worthless and shiftless. Died in some flophouse with a bottle beside him. His contribution to the world was not memorable."

"In a sense your father did contribute something," she said firmly. "He and your mother had you."

He'd opened the long white box, which held two-dozen yellow roses, but at her comment his hands, which had been carefully searching through the blossoms, went still. He glanced over at her, where she was seated on the steps, her legs tucked up under her. The envelope that came with the box lay untouched beside her.

"Why did you say that?" Then he waved his hand in a dismissive gesture. "Never mind. It's not important."

She reached over and rested her hand on his thigh. "I said it because it's true. You've made a tremendous contribution to not just people you know, but to the world. Dad relied on you heavily when I was growing up. The work you've done in the antiterrorist field is talked about and studied in Washington. And that commendation you got from the U.N. was very impressive."

He stared at her for a long time, feeling ridiculously pleased that she knew so much about his work, but more so that she'd taken the time to find out. In a way he felt like a little kid, hungry for recognition, which made him feel dumb and silly. He was thirty-seven years old, for God's sake.

In an even voice he said, "And you, Ms. Delaski, are a liar. I asked you that first day if you'd been following my career and you said no."

She shrugged. "I didn't want you to think my interest was anything more than it is."

"And just what might that be?"

"Admiration."

"Ah, a nice safe emotion."

"Admiration isn't an emotion. It's a quality."

"That comes from deep interest."

"In you?" She shook her head. "Now, Thorne, I know better than that."

"Hmm, is that why your hand is wandering up my thigh?"

She jumped, snatching her hand away as if it had caught fire. "You moved, damn it."

He chuckled. "I wasn't complaining."

She scooted a few inches away from him. He finished going through the flowers, but found nothing out of the ordinary. Not even a bug. He passed the box to Amanda and then went to work on the vase.

She touched one of the perfect yellow blossoms. "Yellow roses are my favorite and these are just beautiful."

"Why don't you open the card and see who sent them?" He brushed his hands off and set the vase away. "These seem to be okay, too."

"They're from Dad! 'To the most wonderful daughter a father could have. Much success with your project.'" She brushed her finger beneath her eyes. "How sweet of him." She lifted one of the long-stemmed roses and sniffed. "Oh, they're lovely. Fresh and fragrant."

Thorne handed her the card from the bouquet in the vase.

"These are from Bing, you know the owner of the meat market? How thoughtful of him."

Thorne stood. "Well, that takes care of that. By the way, your bug idea was brilliant. Olive strikes me as the type who would get hysterical at a bug."

"Olivia, Thorne. Olivia." She lifted the box of roses. "By the way, what were you looking for?"

"Nothing and anything. From what I've concluded so far, this guy isn't just some space-shot out to be a pest. Nor does he have some short-term agenda like knocking you off. In fact if that were his only intent he could do it or have done it fairly easily. Availability of guns—legal and illegal—and the fact that he's shown how close he can get if he chooses proves it. The night on Town Beach Road would have been an ideal place if murder had been his intent. Maybe he didn't pull the plug on your extension, then again, maybe he did. Sometimes, with a stalker or a harasser, it's the fear of what might happen, when it will happen and how rather than the actual act that's the most frightening and the most mentally debilitating. This guy is smart, calculated and determined. He also knows better than to do anything that would alert the police such as a garden-variety threatening letter. Also he made the phone call to your father, not to you. That tells me he really is playing head games—always unpredictable."

While he talked he noted she'd wrapped her arms around herself. "You're scaring me, Thorne."

"I don't want to scare you. That's what he wants to do. Get you rattled so you can't think straight. I want you to be alert and quick just like you were about the bugs in the flowers."

They carried the flowers into the kitchen, where Amanda asked Ginny, the head cook and supervisor, if she would arrange the roses for the living room and put the bouquet as a centerpiece on the long table where they would be eating.

In the dim hallway she paused before going to where the girls were. Thorne was behind her. "Maybe I haven't gotten so far away from all that suspicion and cloak-and-dagger living as I thought," she said grimly. "I'm not sure if I should be pleased or disappointed."

"Your instincts are sharp, Amanda. And that makes guarding you a helluva lot easier."

She sighed. "I suppose, but it seems to me there should be some sort of statute of limitations on living in a security web."

"There is. It's called being dead."

"Thanks. You're so reassuring."

"I call them like I see them. No one is ever totally secure. The problem for most is that they don't know how close to trouble they are. You're different. You've lived with danger. That makes you exceptionally alert, but in an odd way it also makes you safer."

"Knowledge," she said thoughtfully.

"Yeah."

"Which is exactly one of the points I want the girls to realize. The more they know, the more ready they are to face the problems that come their way." She grinned and in an impromptu gesture threw her arms around Thorne. "Sometimes, you know just the right thing to say." She stood on tiptoe and brushed her mouth across his cheek.

But as she pulled away, he gripped her wrists. "Not so fast."

"What?"

"Later—"

"Later, what?"

He shook his head, letting her go. Then before she could press him, he put his arm around her shoulder and squeezed. "Come on, you can introduce me to the girls."

Chapter 6

In less than an hour the first problem erupted.

Amanda introduced Thorne, who not surprisingly, had all the girls immediately making a variety of comments from hunky to sexy to hot. Fortunately Olivia and the committee had moved to the front door and didn't hear the giggled remarks. After a few last-minute suggestions to Amanda, they departed in a fanfare of good wishes and promises that they would be checking back often.

Sally had just taken the girls upstairs to show them their rooms when Thorne, watching Olivia's driver pull away from the curb, muttered with a grimace, "I thought we'd be rid of them after today. Are they gonna do daily check-ins to make sure the girls brushed their teeth and ate their spinach?"

"And your suggestion would be that they stay away?" In some respects she agreed with Thorne. No one liked the feeling of being graded, yet Olivia's interest in the project beyond just supporting it financially made her more personally involved and that could be a plus not a minus.

He shrugged. "I just know that when someone holds the purse strings and the power—in this case Follingsworth and the committee—they tend to think they know more about what to do than the grunts doing the work."

"Grunts?"

"Yeah, in the army the guys that do ninety-plus percent of the work are called grunts."

"What a lovely description of Sally and myself," Amanda said, holding her pique in check.

He picked up a newspaper he'd brought from Amanda's. "How about gruntettes?" he asked helpfully.

"Oh, much better," she commented with dripping irony. "Perhaps we could add the word to our résumés under previous work experience or qualifications."

He took a few steps closer to her, lowered his head and whispered, "Gorgeous gruntette."

"Even better."

He winked. "I thought it had a nice sound to it."

She folded her arms and glared as fiercely as she could. "Never mind that it's sexist and insulting. Anything else you want to add?"

He glanced around, obviously to make sure they weren't being observed by any of the staff. Satisfied they weren't, he brushed his mouth across hers. "You're a great kisser and I sure wouldn't put up much of a fight if you wanted to take me into a dark corner and hone your abilities."

She pushed him away, unable to stop herself from smiling. "Very funny, but I doubt you need lessons."

"Only in restraint, babe."

Amanda grinned again despite an inner sense that when it came to restraint, Thorne had probably invented the word and given lessons on its meaning. He sauntered out to the deck where he sprawled in a chaise longue and buried his nose in the newspaper.

She watched him a moment longer, considering some of her dangerous thoughts and feelings of the past few days that had taken hold and refused to let go. She liked the kind of naughty teasing Thorne was so good at, she liked looking up and seeing him nearby and she particularly enjoyed the rather domestic scene of him buying steaks at Bing's, repairing steps or simply reading the newspaper. If she closed her eyes she could almost picture them married; alone together on a summer Sunday morning enjoying coffee and sticky buns and the *New York Times*. Maybe walking on the beach, sharing their dreams, making love...making a baby...

She jerked her thoughts out of such foolish notions and shook her head at her own lack of willpower when it came to Thorne and those rose-garden fantasies she'd created in the past. This was the man who had rejected her and despite some teasing and a few kisses, he certainly hadn't given any indication he wanted a thing from her besides making sure she didn't get hurt by whoever was harassing her father. As soon as this jerk was either caught or no longer a threat, Thorne would be gone.

Memorize that thought, she reminded herself sternly as she turned to gather up her weekly planner book. Besides, if this project turned out to be as successful as she hoped, there would be many more projects in other places. She would have a full life and be far too busy for personal relationships.

Strong, loving relationships are a two-way proposition. And they certainly didn't occur when one person, namely Thorne, had firmly and coldly rejected the other, namely her.

"Amanda, could you come up here a minute?" Sally called from the second floor.

Amanda pushed her jumbled thoughts aside and hurried up the stairs. There at the far end of the hall she found Sally standing between two of the girls. Both teenagers were red-faced and furious. One stood with her hands clenched at her sides; the other with her fists planted belligerently on her hips.

"Julie refuses to share a room with Lisa," Sally said, glancing from Julie with the shaved head and haughty in-your-face attitude, to Lisa, a stunning redhead, who had been called a whore by her father since she was seven.

But before Amanda could say a word, Julie swaggered around Sally and close enough to Lisa to spit out a filthy name. Lisa countered, her language no cleaner.

Amanda sighed, no stranger to street language or first-day adjustments. "Besides a colorful vocabulary, what seems to be the problem?"

Julie sneered, "I ain't here because I wanna be, ya know. And you can't make me do nothin' I don't want to do."

"The purpose of the project is not to 'make' you do things," Amanda said calmly. "It's to allow you some free-dom to make choices, gain self-confidence and esteem in a relaxed atmosphere."

"Yeah? Then how come I gotta stay in the same room as her?"

"Because two girls are assigned to a room."

"She's a hooker. I hate hookers and I ain't gonna stay in the same room with her."

Lisa snarled back, "You know what? You couldn't get a guy if you paid him. Going to bed with you would be like sleepin' with a bowling ball."

"Better bald than being some dude gettin' it on with a coked-up p—"

"That's enough!" Amanda interrupted forcefully.

Both girls were glaring and sneering at each other.

"Julie, you go downstairs and get yourself a can of soda and cool off. Lisa, why don't you go on into the bedroom and finish putting your things away."

"Where's she gonna stay?" Lisa asked, jerking a thumb in Julie's direction.

"Not with you, that's for damn sure," Julie countered with a disgusted jeer.

"If you two could hold it down for a few minutes Sally and I will get something worked out."

Both girls stalked off in opposite directions. Amanda watched them go, Lisa into the bedroom and slamming the door. Julie stomping down the stairs in a huff.

Sally sagged against the wall. "Thanks for coming to my rescue. For a minute there I thought I would have to call Thorne."

Amanda tapped a finger on her mouth thoughtfully. "Maybe we could just switch one of the other girls."

"No dice. None of them wants to stay with Julie. Seems she was involved in some street gang and the girls heard that one of the initiation rites was that she had to kill another girl."

Amanda frowned. "Odd. There's nothing in her record that says anything about her killing anyone."

"It's all rumor and speculation, but the girls believe it so whether it's in black-and-white is irrelevant."

"As I recall from Julie's file, she's been in trouble for shoplifting and possession of drugs, but not for over a year. Her biggest problem is getting along in society. People are so turned off by her, which in turn makes her act with a more in-your-face attitude. I find her condemnation of Lisa curious."

"Curious!" Sally shook her head in astonishment. "How about hypocritical? Someone ought to tell her about being so high-and-mighty when she herself is hardly a candidate for sainthood."

"Hmm, but in the meantime, we have an immediate problem to solve." Amanda walked to the stairs and peered down, listening. Muffled voices came from the living room and she wondered if Thorne had gotten stuck with Julie. "Since Julie is the one complaining, she's the one we should move."

"But where?"

"I'm thinking."

Sally folded her arms and lifted her chin. "Uh, since Thorne is the resident problem-solver, why don't you ask him?"

Amanda didn't miss the more than obvious dig. "Now there's a good idea."

"Yeah, I thought you'd like it," Sally said with just the slightest smirk.

Amanda ignored it. They were both tired and Amanda guessed Sally was still reeling from her boyfriend's sudden plans to advance his career with an investment firm in Chicago—a move that didn't include Sally. Amanda had been greeted with that news the moment she and Thorne arrived at the house this morning and found Sally red-eyed in the kitchen. Thorne had disappeared, leaving Amanda to comfort her. She'd asked few questions, letting Sally say what she felt comfortable sharing.

From her own experience, she certainly knew the pain of rejection, but after listening to Sally's version of Ross's departure, Amanda had to credit Thorne with being up-front and honest rather than devious about his feelings. He'd flatly said he didn't want her before he resigned from her father's employ and went off to Europe. How much easier it would have been for Thorne to have accepted her confession of love, perhaps making a promise or even sleeping with her before just disappearing. He definitely hadn't taken the easy way out. On the other hand, Ross, from what Sally had said, had accepted the career move without giving her any clue as to what he was doing. And then not asking or even suggesting that she accompany him had smacked of a coward's way to end a relationship.

Not wanting to get into a discussion of Thorne or where it would invariably lead, Amanda suggested, "You go on in and make sure Lisa is all set and I'll take care of Julie."

"And Thorne, too? Seeing as how you're just—how did you put it the other day?—just old friends?"

"Sally, please."

"Please what?"

"You know what. I'm deliberately ignoring all the tiresome innuendoes so give it a rest, huh?"

"I just don't like being treated as if I was born yesterday."

"Just because—"

Sally held her hand up and interrupted. "I mean it, Amanda. You're obviously nutty over the guy and every time I see him look at you it's obvious he's not thinking about what problems need to be solved, unless it's how fast to get you into bed."

"You're wrong."

"Then tell me the truth."

"Why, for heaven's sake, does it matter what's between Thorne and me? Or for that matter, what isn't?"

"Because we're friends and, well, friends...good friends like I thought we were—they share things and tell the truth to each other." She gulped and swallowed, then glanced down at the floor as though suddenly gripped by embarrassment. Finally drawing a breath, she said, "I'm sorry. Here I'm taking my anger out on you. God, I told myself this split with Ross wouldn't dominate my thoughts. I would hold my head up and remind myself that no modern, independent woman wants a man who doesn't want her. But, it hurts so bad, Amanda."

"I know," she said softly and honestly. "Sometimes the rules we women make for ourselves, the very ones we think are building blocks of independence, aren't very strong or comforting when our hearts are being broken."

"So what do I do? I just feel so down and useless and angry. This is worse than if he'd just flat-out told me the truth."

Is it? Amanda wondered thoughtfully. She'd had ten years of living with the truth and it still hurt.

Giving Sally a hug, she smiled encouragingly. "I know the girls will keep you busy during the day. Maybe you should think about dating some other men. Not seriously. Just for fun and to prove to yourself that you can survive this and be a better person as a result."

"Sort of like if someone gives you lemons, make lemonade?"

"That's pretty simplistic, but makes a point. The lemons remain lemons no matter how much we might want them to be something else, so we have to be creative with what we have." As she spoke, Amanda realized that in her own situation she'd wanted her confession of love all those years ago to be some magic key to having Thorne; instead it had set up the perfect situation for him to reject her. But in some ways she *had* made lemonade, so to speak. She'd gone on to college and into a satisfying and successful career in youth counseling. She'd gained independence and self-esteem, combined with an inborn promise to herself to never again be so vulnerable with a man.

"Amanda? Did you hear me?"

Amanda shook away her musings. "Oh, I'm sorry. What did you say?"

"You suggested I do some dating. Maybe I could con Thorne into a night on the town."

"No!" Immediately she knew she'd reacted too impulsively and too emotionally.

Sally stepped back. "Well, that was forcefully put."

"It's just that Thorne—"

"Is off limits because you care about him more than you want him or me or anyone to know. Maybe you're even trying to fool yourself. Am I right? Come on, Amanda, don't try to deny it."

Amanda sighed and finally nodded. "Okay, yes, I'm attracted to him, but there's no future in it and he doesn't feel the same way."

"That's questionable." Sally smiled knowingly. "I've seen him watching you a few times when you were busy. Something is definitely going on and it sure isn't indifference."

Before she could come up with a response, Thorne shouted from downstairs.

"I'm coming," she called back.

"Go ahead, I'll take care of Lisa." Sally hesitated a second. "And thanks for the pep talk."

"Sure."

"Amanda? It wasn't so hard telling me how you feel about Thorne, was it?"

She shook her head. "It just isn't very smart to want someone who doesn't feel the same."

"But you don't know how he feels."

Yes, I do, she thought sadly, *I know far too well.*

As she hurried down the stairs, her mind replayed Sally's words: "Something is definitely going on and it sure isn't indifference.... You don't know how he feels." But Amanda knew what Thorne felt and it didn't include the path Sally was convinced existed—that of an intimate relationship. Protective, yes. Loyal to her father, definitely. Consumed with doing his job and doing it flawlessly, obsessively so.

Amanda acknowledged even a mild sexual interest—after all, they were male and female, literally living together and alone a lot of the time. Sexual interest wouldn't be all that unusual and probably even healthy, but beyond that, she knew better. She knew because of her own heartbreaking experience with Thorne. Despite the quick banter, the teasing, she couldn't allow herself to attach any serious meaning to them. To keep herself safe from another broken heart, she couldn't allow herself to fantasize or hope or even toy with the hope of an intimate relationship with him.

Yet mulling over how Ross had treated Sally gave her an entire new perspective on Thorne's rejection of ten years ago.

Painful as it had been, he'd told her the truth. Perhaps the old axiom of "the truth hurts" was at the core of her humiliation? A man rejecting you has a certain victim-type comfort to it and provides tiny slots that can always be filled with excuses and rationalizations. Truth, she realized insightfully, can't be manipulated. Happy or sad, it's there to be accepted or not.

Outside on the deck, Thorne straddled the chaise and used the newspaper as a brace for a pad of paper, making a list of items he wanted to have delivered. Amanda had no idea what items. Julie had gone into the kitchen, passing by Amanda with a broad, and yes, a victorious smile, as if she'd pulled off some major coup. Amanda was still focused on where the teenager was going to sleep—she couldn't just let her take the couch. Providing a certain degree of privacy for each girl was one of the basic working tools of the project. So many of the girls simply had none at home and it was worse if they were under state care.

Now Amanda was intrigued both by the mysterious list and the obvious rapport between Thorne and Julie. Given that Thorne hadn't even wanted to be introduced to the girls a few hours ago, finding the two of them talking as if they were old friends was indeed curious.

"Okay, so what happened?" Amanda asked, pulling a chair up beside him.

"We made a deal."

"A deal?"

"Yeah, if she promises to let her hair grow, I'll get mine cut."

"Cut as in short?" she asked, reminding herself that even though she liked it long, he would attract fewer stares from Olivia if it were short.

"Cut as in trimmed."

She nodded. "That sounds pretty harmless. What else?"

"I told her to quit talking like some loser with an attitude and to use the time here to learn. I also told her that life is gonna throw her if she snarls at every opportunity that comes along."

"The opportunity to learn to get along in a situation whether you like it or not."

"Yeah. You and I are a good example of making the best of a difficult situation."

Startled, Amanda asked, "Good grief, you didn't tell her about us, did you?"

"Come on, Amanda. What do you take me for? If you're talking about your twenty-first birthday, that was between you and me. If you mean the stalker situation, you know better."

But there are other things, she thought silently. The kisses, the tension, the sometimes unbearable need to touch. Have you forgotten those or do they mean so little they don't even come under the category of difficult situation? Amusement, perhaps.

Finally, when she knew her voice was steady, she said, "After the words she and Lisa exchanged, I don't think even an apology by Julie would smooth things over."

"You're right. Besides that would be a smoke screen. The kind of anger they feel isn't going to be forgotten with a mere apology."

"So what did she say?"

"She's willing to try."

She frowned, confused. "Try what?"

When he turned and looked at her, Amanda found her confusion slipping away for the fascinating allure of his gray eyes. They had a depth that drew her in; a ceaseless tugging that mystified her and confounded all her common sense. She licked her lips not with any intent to flirt or be coy, but in what was becoming an all too common dry-mouthed, powder-keg reaction to him.

Thorne wanted to tug her across his lap, slide his hands from her hips to her breasts and bury his mouth in her neck, hear the rush of pleasure, the shaking desire from her he knew would be there for him. He wanted, and his instinct told him she wouldn't refuse. A simple straightforward sexual relationship, and yet he'd done little more than kiss her and tease her. Maybe he was testing himself—how far could he go and not do what was eating at him. Maybe he wanted her to come to him so he could complete what he had walked out on once before.

For he'd wanted her the night of her birthday.

He'd wanted her and had thought of her numerous times in the years since.

And for damn sure he wanted her now.

Sex, he knew, didn't have to be so compelling—it was too easy to get, too easy to find enough women, enough pleasure to blank out serious thoughts about love and commitment—two areas he didn't trust in his own hands.

So what in hell was he worried about? She wouldn't trust him with her heart and she had good reason. Why in hell was he so hung up about this? He wanted her; he guessed she might feel the same way. Take that and leave it there.

A clatter in the kitchen shook them both from their thoughts. Amanda glanced down at her lap and Thorne shifted his gaze back to his list.

"So what's Julie going to try?" Amanda asked huskily.

Thorne cleared his throat. "Being cooperative."

Amanda eyed him speculatively. "How did you manage that so simply and so quickly? Upstairs she wouldn't have given a convent full of nuns a break."

"Well, we sort of made another deal."

Puzzled, she said, "This is quite amazing. You said you were overwhelmed by teenage girls and here you've struck all sorts of compromises with the toughest one of the lot."

"She's not as tough as she acts."

"None of them ever are."

"And I like her. She's had it tough, but she's a survivor. Maybe not in the way Follingsworth would call acceptable, but hell, Follingsworth and most women haven't got a clue what street living—if you can call it that—is all about."

Amanda acknowledged that, as much as she'd worked with problem kids, it never ceased to amaze her how resilient they were. Overcoming incredible odds, pulling themselves out of horrendous living conditions and, as Thorne said, possessing a gut-need to survive. "You struck a bargain about hair. What was the second deal?"

"You won't freak out?"

"Uh oh, that sounds ominous."

"It'll mean some work and, of course, you saying it's okay."

"I have to know what I'm saying okay to."

"Fixing up that room off the kitchen into a bedroom for Julie."

Amanda blinked. "The storage room?"

"Yeah."

She shook her head. "No, Thorne. That room is too small, it's dark, has just one window and it's away from the other girls. Besides part of this project is social interaction and if Julie is downstairs and the rest of the girls are upstairs it could cause other problems. Like jealousy, accusations of favoritism."

"Jealousy and favoritism when Julie is in a small dark room with one window? Seems to me if there is going to be jealousy and favoritism, it would be against Lisa. She has the big bright room upstairs and all to herself."

Amanda's eyes widened in sudden realization. "Oh, my God, you're right. What's the matter with me? Why didn't I think of that?" She stood, turning to leave.

Thorne caught her wrist and pulled her back. "Listen to me. One of the pluses of the work you've done was the requirement that the girls have a certain amount of privacy, a sense of their own personal space. That's why you've always insisted on no more than two to a room."

Amanda stayed very still, staring at him. "How did you know that?"

"I just know," he said vaguely, meeting her gaze for a few poignant seconds before continuing. "This confrontation between Lisa and Julie could work for the project and for the girls. In other words, by fixing up the storage room, all the girls would have a chance for a few days in a room all by themselves."

"Let them rotate rooms, you mean."

"Sure, why not. It's not like each has fifteen years worth of junk to move. It would give them an opportunity for a few days of privacy and the chance to room with all the girls instead of just the one they were originally assigned to."

Amanda's mind began to work through the concept and the more she thought about it the more she thought it just might work. It would certainly provide some innovative choices for the girls that would add to their social interaction.

"By the excitement I see in your eyes, I gather the idea appeals to you."

She grinned. "It's different, that's for sure."

"Well?"

"Let's do it."

He grabbed her up in a hug, swinging her around. "Oh, babe, I had a gut feeling you'd go for it."

She pulled back a little as he put her back down on her feet, not quite letting her go. She'd have to let Olivia and the committee know about the change. Not that she thought they'd object, but Olivia, especially, liked to be in on what to most seemed like everyday details. She did decide, however, not to mention Olivia to Thorne. No point in throwing cold water on his enthusiasm.

He reached down and picked up his list. "If I call this in right now, Nicky can probably deliver the paint and brushes this afternoon. In the meantime, I'll get the room cleaned out and washed down."

"Back at my house there are some extra curtains that should fit the window. Also a rollaway bed we could use."

"Why don't I get Nicky to help me bring the bed I'm sleeping in over and I'll use the rollaway? That geometric designed headboard is beginning to give me a headache."

"You're sure you want to give up your bed?"

"If I get lonely, I'll come and keep you company."

"To test all that restraint you mentioned earlier, huh?" Amanda quipped, so caught up in the excitement she forgot the wisdom of not flirting.

Thorne grinned, then traced a finger around her neckline, ending at the center just at her cleavage. "I was thinking more along the lines of testing the way you'd feel on top of me."

As if choreographed, he dropped a quick kiss on her aghast mouth, picked up his list and went to use the phone.

Amanda stared after him, her heart thumping, her skin still sizzling, her mouth still imprinted with his fleeting kiss. Surely he hadn't been serious. He'd been teasing or flirting or even doing what he did entirely too well—throwing her emotions into a chaotic tangle.

Or maybe he *wasn't* teasing or flirting. Maybe he *was* serious and using some bold words to test her reaction. Sure, she concluded pessimistically. As if Thorne Law would ever have to use any tactic beyond a straightforward one to get a woman.

As she walked back into the house, she reminded herself of one truth she knew for sure. He'd rejected her a long time ago and not one time since he'd arrived, despite the softer moments, had he given any indication that he wouldn't do exactly the same again. Already she knew he intended to leave. Already she knew that if he'd really wanted more from her than fleeting kisses, he could have more.

My God, was she that pliable? Was she that much of a wimpy woman who would just melt at the slightest encouragement? Where was all her determination? All the coolness that other men she knew accused her of having in abundance?

Where, damn it, was her pride!

She drew herself up and lifted her chin. She did not want him. She did not want to wonder what it would be like on top of him, feeling him against her and inside her.

"Babe, what about tonight?"

Warmth flared in her cheeks as she jerked around to face him. He leaned against the door into the dim hallway. His arms were folded, his face nearly hidden by the afternoon shadows.

"What did you say?"

"Tonight. I thought we could work on the room tonight. Nicky is coming in about an hour. The staff said they would give me a hand cleaning stuff out and washing things down. If we get the painting done, then tomorrow we could move the stuff in and get Julie settled."

She drew in a long breath, unsure if it was disappointment or relief. "Sure, tonight sounds fine."

"You okay?"

"What? Oh, yes, I was just thinking about all the things that need to be done."

But the most important thing she needed to do was not allow herself to fall into the trap of loving Thorne Law again.

It was after midnight by the time the last wall was painted. Amanda had sent the staff to bed and Sally home hours earlier. Ginny had volunteered to let Julie sleep in her bed and she'd take the couch in the living room. Thorne closed up the empty paint can, angled his hands low on his hips and gave the room one final inspection. The single window had been opened and the screen washed earlier. A cool wind off the water blew in on the newly painted daffodil yellow walls.

"Asking Julie what her favorite color was was a good idea, babe."

Amanda pushed a stray wisp of hair off her cheek. "It seems that at one time she was in foster care at a country house and they had masses of daffodils outside the window of her room."

"Must have been a good memory."

"Yes. She was also eyeing the flowers from Dad and the bouquet from Bing. I have a feeling she just might enjoy arranging some of the garden flowers. We'll see."

When Thorne didn't say anything, Amanda drew closer. "What are you staring at?"

He dropped an arm around her neck and slid her against him. She slipped her arm around his waist. "See that light over there?"

Amanda nodded. "It looks as if it's on the beach below my house."

"Yeah, that's what I was thinking. Flashlight, perhaps."

"Probably just someone taking a walk. That's not unusual."

"Maybe."

"What are you thinking?"

"That the stalker might be checking out your house."

"But a flashlight is a little obvious, isn't it?"

"Not if he wants you to know he knows where you live. Not if he wants you to know he's watching you."

Chapter 7

Moments later, Thorne reached into the back of an unused closet where he'd hidden his gun. He tucked it into his jeans and pulled his shirt down so that the weapon wasn't noticeable. In the kitchen, Amanda pulled on her Windbreaker and got her purse.

To Ginny, who had stayed up to help them finish the painting, Thorne said, "Ginny, we're gonna split. I left the window open to keep the paint fumes at a minimum."

"I just took a peek in," she said, smiling wearily. "It looks like a brand-new room."

Amanda added, "It does look terrific, doesn't it? By this time tomorrow, Julie will be settled and you'll have your bed back. We should be back here about eight in the morning. The deck doors and the front door are locked and everyone is asleep. You go and get some rest and thanks for all your help."

Thorne took Amanda's arm and they went out the kitchen door with Ginny locking it after them.

"Why can't women just say goodbye," he muttered in a way that obviously wasn't a question.

"That's all I did say."

"Ten more seconds and you would have been explaining how a key works in a lock."

"I just wanted her to know that I had double-checked everything."

"Why? You're the one in charge. You shouldn't have to do their job."

"Why are you making such a big deal out of checking a few doors?"

"Because you worry too damn much about what everyone else is doing and thinking and get damn little concern from anyone else in return. Like Sally blubbering about some boyfriend who dumped her."

Amanda halted. "How could you know that if you weren't eavesdropping?"

"It was obvious from the minute we got there this morning she was upset about something. I just wanted to make sure it didn't have anything to do with you."

"What would it have to do with me?"

"I don't know. That's why I listened."

They resumed walking; Thorne with his mouth set in a grim line and Amanda scowling.

"Then, on top of Sally," Thorne continued, "there's Follingsworth judging your relationship with me as if it were illicit or illegal."

She sighed. "Why in the world does it matter what she thinks? She's accepted you being here. Although I admit she gives the appearance of being somewhat disapproving."

"Appearance? A sledgehammer would be more subtle," he said bluntly.

Amanda smiled to herself, and gripped his hand a little tighter. For no reason that made sense, she liked that he had this overriding need to see to her welfare. Probably not a very modern outlook for a nineties woman, but she believed that strong self-esteem meant not getting uptight and indignant whenever someone else didn't see things exactly her way. In this case, Thorne.

"You're not like most men, you know. You're far too sexy-looking for women like Olivia to dismiss you as part of the furniture. Besides, she might have her eye on you for herself. Maybe she's hoping you'll leave me for her. She's very rich and maybe what you said is true. She needs a man."

He made no attempt to hide his distaste. "Not me, that's for damn sure."

"And Sally's looking for a new boyfriend. She even suggested she might like to go out with you." She slid her gaze sideways to catch his expression.

He looked down, raising an eyebrow. "I hope you told her I was taken."

"Of course, I told her I was too hot for you to allow you out of my sight for even a minute."

He studied her for a long time, then chuckled. "You're quick, you know that?"

She gripped his hand tighter. "I have a good teacher."

They walked for a few more minutes, then Thorne asked, "Did you really say that to Sally?"

"About being hot for you?"

"Yeah."

"Actually I told her 'no' when she suggested going out with you."

He turned now and faced her, sliding his hands into her hair and tipping her head up so that the moonlight illuminated her eyes. "Then I should thank you for saving me from predatory females, shouldn't I?"

Amanda stared into his eyes, wondering if she dared such boldness as saying she wanted him to kiss her. Given the back-and-forth conversation, she knew she could make it sound like a carefree idea. A nonchalant, breezy quip that, knowing Thorne, he would immediately seize upon. She felt an inner sense of jubilation. Not often did she feel so in control around Thorne and she liked the idea of keeping him a little off-balance. God knows she felt that way around him enough. There was certainly nothing wrong in turning the tables on him. And given the circumstances of why they were together, it added some much-needed levity. Otherwise she'd be a trembling mess. For despite growing up with bodyguards and the smell of danger too close for comfort, Amanda took this stalker very seriously. And deep down she was scared. Bone-chilling scared.

Touching her tongue to her lips, she put her arms around his neck. "You could kiss me."

If he was taken aback by her request, she didn't see it in his eyes or feel it in his hands. In a way that turned her insides liquid, he glided his thumb back and forth across her mouth. "Kiss you here?"

In the barest of whispers, she said, "Yes."

He slipped his hand down and cupped her breast. As though awakened from a long sleep, her nipple immediately tightened and nestled into his palm. She knew he felt it and yet he didn't increase his touch. In a low voice, he murmured, "How about here?"

Don't waver, she reminded herself and hoped he couldn't feel her pounding heart, but this time her voice didn't seem to work.

Continuing to hold her gaze, he slid his hand across her upper thighs, pausing just at the apex. "Here, then?"

She couldn't contain the tiny gasp. Deep inside, her stomach felt as if it were in free-fall and she knew the game she'd encouraged was no longer a game for her, but dangerously serious. Her very silence more than adequately answered his question. She wanted to say yes.

And from the long, intense silence between them, she knew he read "yes" as her answer.

Thorne brought his hand up and cupped her face. "I owe you a kiss, okay?"

Confused, and because she didn't know what else to do, she nodded.

It wasn't until they turned into the walk at Amanda's that it occurred to her they'd never returned to her house from the Sutton Shores House via the road. They always used the beach because it was shorter. Had that conversation about Sally and Olivia been to distract her or keep her from thinking too much about what they might find at her house?

Thorne lifted his shirt and retrieved the gun.

Amanda's heart raced, but she didn't flinch. "Where did that come from?"

"You didn't think I'd leave the gun at your house, did you? Sure wouldn't help if the stalker had the gun and I had nothing but an acute sense of ineptness. Don't worry, the girls haven't seen it. I found a closet no one was using and a nice dark place to hide it."

"I wasn't worried about you being careless with a gun. In fact, I'm glad you have it."

"Yeah, me, too. Let's hope I don't have to use it," he muttered grimly.

"What do you want me to do?"

"Exactly what I tell you."

She nodded. "You don't honestly think he'll try to confront you, do you?"

"It's not me he wants, it's you. But since he'll have to get through me first, yeah, I think if the bastard is stupid enough to still be around, he just might try something."

"But that light we saw might not have been him. It could have been just someone walking on the beach."

"Maybe."

"But you don't think so."

"In my business you assume the worst and hope for the best."

"But your business deals with terrorists."

"And who said terrorism is limited to people who like to blow up airplanes and buildings? This bastard is terrifying you and your father. Killing someone in a bombing or sticking a gun in their gut and pulling the trigger makes them just as dead.''

She shivered and realized the depth and extent of the fear her father must have felt to call in Thorne. ''That's how Dad views this stalker, isn't it? A terrorist with a single-minded agenda.''

''When it comes to you, babe, Walker views anyone who would try to hurt you as a terrorist. Don't you think not being able to protect you himself is tough on him? But he knows that the chances of getting this guy are greater if the two of you *aren't* together. It makes the stalker have to work harder because he has to watch you both at the same time. He has to keep Walker worrying by making phone calls about what he's done or will do to you, while at the same time figuring out ways to scare you. You're not Sally or Ginny, who would freak at harassing phone calls or threatening notes—'' Thorne drew in a deep breath. ''God,'' he muttered in a low voice.

''What is it?''

He shook his head.

''But you look as if you thought of something.'' When he still said nothing, she quickly added, ''Listen, maybe we should go back to the other house and call the police.''

''And tell them what? That we saw a weird light on the beach? That should get the chief out of bed at the least,'' he said with weary irony.

Amanda scowled. ''You're right. I had no evidence but my word when that car terrified me. I guess a flashlight on the beach isn't any more illegal than someone shining one in my—'' She halted, tugging Thorne to a stop. ''The flashlight. It's him. It's got to be. The flashlight is too coincidental.''

''Maybe.''

''Is that all you can say, 'maybe'? For God's sake, Thorne, it's obvious.''

Thorne drew her to a stop in front of her house. Silence poured over them, too much silence, Thorne thought grimly. And then there was the light inside—

"Babe, when Nicky and you and I came to get the bed, did you leave a light on?"

"Yes, as a matter of fact, I did. I knew it would be dark when we got back and—"

"Which room?"

"The living room."

"Not in your bedroom?"

"No. I did change clothes to do the painting, but I'm sure I didn't leave on a light."

"Hell."

"You think he was in the house? And if you say maybe..."

"How about yeah? I definitely think he could have been in the house."

"Oh, God."

Thorne approached the front door, while Amanda got her keys out. He took them from her suddenly shaky fingers and unlocked the door, immediately reaching in and flipping on the outside lights and the interior ones.

He held the gun close, his gaze sweeping the room with the expertise of someone who knew enough to check the dim corners and leave nothing to chance. One by one they checked each room, finally coming back to her bedroom for a final look. The light beside her bed was indeed on, but nothing else seemed disturbed.

Thorne crossed to the window and looked out into the dark yard while Amanda checked for anything that might have been disturbed or stolen. But the extra cash that she always kept in her top drawer was still there. Some jewelry that was fairly valuable lay on the dresser in plain sight where she'd left it when she changed from the melon dress to jeans and an old shirt. She went to the telephone to check if it had been unplugged, but it hadn't.

"Anything look different?" Thorne asked, moving away from the window.

Hands planted on her hips, she gave a final sweep of the room. "I don't think so. If someone was here, they weren't after cash or jewelry. We could be blowing this all out of proportion. That light really could have been someone just taking a late-night walk on the beach."

"But that doesn't explain the bedroom light."

"I might have flipped it on by habit."

Thorne shoved a hand through his hair. "Look, why don't you go on to bed. I'll lock up."

She nodded, about to argue, then realized there was little more to be done. The house seemed safe, nothing had been stolen and sitting around rehashing the evening's questions and events probably wouldn't accomplish much. Besides, she was tired and in a few hours she would be returning to the house to organize the first session with the girls. She sighed wearily. Definitely she would need to be rested and on her toes.

Then there were those heated moments on the way home. To stay up could very likely be inviting a repeat and more. What, she wondered reflectively, had happened to her resolve to have nothing to do with him beyond allowing his protection? Nothing had actually happened, and yet far too much of her fortitude around him had wheedled away. It was almost as if a deep-seated part of her would always want him; never mind will or logic or just plain good sense.

Shaking off this new possibility, she took clean pajamas from her drawer and turned to him where he was staring down at the table lamp beside the telephone.

"I'm going to take a shower." She was about to go into her bathroom when she stopped. "Oh, the rollaway is in the hall closet and there are sheets and pillows in the closet off the other bathroom."

"I'll be fine. Go take your shower."

Thorne waited until she closed the bathroom door and he heard the water go on before he lifted the receiver and called Walker.

Monk, Walker's full-time security man, answered.

"Amanda is fine," Thorne said when Monk immediately asked. "I know it's late, but I need to talk to Walker."

Thorne waited, his mind sliding back to their walk on the way back to her house. No longer could he deny, or for that matter explain, to himself this growing restlessness he had regarding Amanda. Thorne had never gone much for sexual teasing—mainly because it either boded trouble or gave the impression of shallow flirting that meant nothing beyond the moment. Yet with Amanda he had engaged in a round of sexy banter that had him touching her and seducing her with moves such as the "where do you want to be kissed" scenario of a few minutes ago. Maybe it was simpler to tease and keep it light, then face what he really wanted....

And perhaps it was because the last time he had allowed himself to be serious with her—at her twenty-first birthday party—he had not only kissed her in a way that was out of bounds, but he had flatly rejected her avowel of love. All the years since, he'd told himself that the clean break was best; she needed a nice guy with Ivy League credentials to marry her, not some jaded, cynical bastard who didn't trust the concept of forever whether it was a woman, an institution or his own willingness to commit to anything beyond the next job.

And commitment to the job was what had happened when Walker asked for his help. Get it done, clean up any stray problems and make an exit. Concentrate on the goal, he reminded himself, and stay clear of the side trips—namely one Amanda Delaski.

Walker's voice was husky from being awakened. "Thorne, for God's sake, it's almost two in the morning.

Something has to have happened for you to call at this hour."

"Sorry to have awakened you."

"Monk said Amanda's okay."

"She's fine. We were at the house late." He quickly filled Walker in on Julie and the circumstances of fixing up the room for her.

"Good. Glad to hear that you've blended right in."

"I could live without Follingsworth."

Walker chuckled. "Yes, I can imagine. She called here to see if I was aware of the danger in leaving poor Amanda at your mercy."

"Poor Amanda?"

"I assured her it was riskier leaving *you* at Amanda's mercy. That my daughter was perfectly capable of dealing with you."

"Your daughter could give lessons on handling trouble. She's gone ahead with the project, kept her head in a couple of tricky situations—she's quite amazing."

"I told you that you wouldn't have to nursemaid her. You recall how strong-minded she was when you worked for me."

"Yeah, I remember." He closed his eyes a moment, too many memories of the feel and taste of her washing over him. He cleared his throat. "Back to why I called. As we were getting ready to leave the other house, we saw a strange light on the beach—looked like a flashlight, but so far I haven't been able to figure out if it meant anything. But on the way home when Amanda and I were chewing it over, something occurred to me about the stalker's actions."

"Yes?"

"So far there's been the incident on Town Beach Road. Then the bloodied picture, the lurking outside and the call to you to rattle you about Amanda. This guy isn't following one of the more common patterns of a stalker—lots of harassing phone calls and threatening letters. I think he knows that those wouldn't be enough to freak you and Amanda."

"I'm not following you, Thorne."

"In other words, he started out with strong stuff. That little trick on Town Beach Road wasn't the ordinary first approach of a stalker."

"Hell, this guy is just more vicious."

"Or he knows what to do because he knows *you*. Or he knows Amanda's been exposed to danger while growing up and isn't so likely to be scared of the more ordinary approaches."

A long silence followed, then Walker swore. "Are you saying that this guy knows us personally?"

"Either that or enough about you to create a custom-made stalker's approach."

"Good God."

"My thoughts exactly," Thorne muttered. He knew this new conclusion could be of tremendous help, but it also made whoever this jerk was twice as dangerous.

"What's your best guess as to motive, Thorne?"

"Revenge for some perceived wrong is a possibility. Or if something was actually done to him, he may have let his mind feed on it until it's taken on a life of its own. No question motive is the key. If we can come up with some potential motives we could get a better take on who he might be. One of the things we look for in a terrorist incident is disgruntled employees. Fired or laid off, for some reason they lose it. I don't think this guy is randomly reckless. My guess, from what we've seen already, is that this is personal. His target is either you or Amanda—maybe both. I think we can now definitely rule out some random shooting spree."

"An ex-employee who wants revenge," Walker said thoughtfully. "Good deductive reasoning. I'll have to do some thinking and checking and get back to you."

"If we're not here, we'll be at the other house."

"I'll get on this right away. And thanks, Thorne. I knew it was a good idea to call you in."

He hung up the phone and settled back against the pillows. He felt good, a tired kind of good. This potential lead on the stalker made him feel as if they might just be making some headway.

Thorne drew in a satisfied breath, folded his arms and closed his eyes. He should get up and go get the rollaway. Just a few more minutes and he would. Just a few . . .

Amanda stopped in the bathroom doorway, her short, white nightie a whisper of lace and silk, her hair fluffy and warm from the blow dryer. Her heart raced and it occurred to her that if he'd planned some obvious seduction scene—him lying all dark and dangerous on her bed and waiting for her to emerge all warm and pliable from her shower—that she would have been disappointed in him. She acknowledged one of the things about him that had captivated her: he wasn't predictable.

"Thorne?"

But he didn't move and as she drew closer she could tell he'd fallen deeply asleep. Leaning down she gently shook him, but instead of coming awake slowly, he jerked upright, grabbing her and, before she had a chance to draw two breaths, pinning her beneath him.

In bare seconds, her hands were locked in one of his above her head. One thigh had forced her legs apart, and the other was positioned so that his knee pressed into her side. His face was just inches from hers and his eyes were so dark and intense Amanda felt the cold sweep of real fear rush through her.

"Damn it, don't you ever, *ever* do that again," he warned with a savage edge to his tone that she'd never heard before.

"I . . . I'm sorry." She swallowed, trying to find room in her lungs for some oxygen. "You'd fallen asleep and . . ."

"You should have said my name louder. You shouldn't have touched me."

To her astonishment his body felt solid and calm, not rigid and strained. In that moment she realized how tightly he could control and command not just his body, but the inborn responses. "I didn't know."

He gave her a long dark look. "Old street rule from when I was growing up. Touch a guy when he's asleep and you're dead."

"Oh."

He hesitated, his eyes locked with hers as if he expected questions. When she asked none, he loosened his hold. "Did I hurt you?"

The question held concern, but Amanda wasn't foolish enough to attach any meaning beyond the physical. She shook her head, the still-damp strands of hair from her shower clinging to her cheeks. She was too aware of all of him, and in ways she shouldn't even be considering. She didn't want him to move. Their position was undeniably provocative, but what sizzled through her was how well they fit together.

Staring at her, his voice low, he murmured, "I should get out of here."

Nod, agree, push him away, but do something! her good sense screamed at her. But she only studied him, wondering when and where she'd lost her will to resist him. Her breathing had slowed and evened out; she felt oddly relaxed and content locked beneath him.

"You're supposed to say get the hell off me and get out of here." When instead she moved compellingly beneath him, he shook his head in disbelief. "No teasing, babe."

"N...no." She licked her lips. "I mean...I'm not teasing."

His hand let go of hers and he braced his body so as to relieve her of its weight. "If I stay, it won't be to hold your hand or to go to sleep."

"I know."

"There are a hundred reasons why this is a hell of a bad idea." He brushed the strands from her cheeks, his knuckles moving back and forth in an evocative rhythm.

When he lifted his hand, she touched his cheek, loving the stubble, the lean tautness, the strong bones. "Two hundred reasons."

He lowered his head and touched his forehead to hers. "This isn't true love or some promise of forever."

She kissed his neck. "No...."

"Just sex."

"Yes ... just sex...."

He pulled back and looked at her. When she turned her head and lowered her lashes, he cupped her chin. "All you want from me is sex, is that it?"

Amanda steeled herself, making her next words sound cold and detached. "I don't love you, Thorne. I got over you a long time ago. You don't have to worry about me wringing my hands and crying when you leave."

Thorne wasn't sure if he bought her answer because of the fierce, stubborn look in her eyes or because it gave him a reason to do what he wanted to do without a guilty conscience. Either he could go with, but the tiny core of disappointment he felt at her words gave him pause. He didn't want her to love him or cry after he was gone. Or did he? Damn.

He shifted, drawing his knee into a more intimate position, but as much as he wanted her, as hot as his arousal would be in a very few seconds, he felt like an empty chasm wanting to fill himself yet knowing he wanted more from her than sex. He lowered his head and kissed her neck, moving to her ear and then to her mouth. Almost instantly her breathing got reedy.

When she pressed into him, her hips moving to better adjust him against her, Thorne felt her heat. Then as if some veil from the past drew apart he remembered the eager dewiness of the innocent young woman who had messed up his mind for years. Then it had been one kiss and a driving need for more that he'd managed to control. This time she wanted him, too. This time he could have it all—her mouth, her breasts, the sweet heat of her folding around him and tugging him into some opalescent oblivion. This time he could give her satisfaction, hear her breath stop and start, drink in the everlasting scent of her that was as familiar to him as the desire and longing she sustained in him by simply saying his name.

She's yours. She wants you so why in hell not just take what she's offering? Enjoy it and feast in it and stop trying to moralize it, he told himself fiercely. In fact, it's the best he could ask for. Making love without any promises or expectations beyond the moment.

Damn it. He couldn't. Damn.

He rolled off her and in one smooth motion got to his feet and stepped away from the bed.

She blinked in confusion, and Thorne mentally measured the length of exposed thigh, the peek of lace from her panties, the gap that revealed the swell of her breasts. Seeing her sprawled there, her arms extended, one leg drawn up, her hair fanned across the pillow, Thorne again cursed his own reluctance. His arousal, however, wasn't as disinclined and he was thankful for the shadows in the room.

Amanda scrambled up to her knees, her nightie revealing more than it concealed, her breasts rising and falling from her rapid breathing. "That's not fair."

Thorne blinked. "Fair?"

"I told you I understood it was just sex."

"I don't believe this. I backed off because you and I both know getting involved sexually will be messy and contradictory to the reason why I'm here. Most women would have agreed and said good-night."

"I'm not most women. I'm me. I wanted you and in case you've been living in some cave you should know that women are allowed to have sex with a man without dragging him into marriage."

"Mandy, listen to me..."

"Damn you!"

He tried to ignore the glisten of tears that she tried to hide. Shoving his hands through his hair, he said, "Look, we're both tired and a little uptight."

"I am not uptight."

"In a few hours you're going to be sorry you didn't get some sleep...."

"Sleep! How can you possibly think I could sleep after what you've done—"

"What in hell did I do besides stop us from making a helluva mistake?"

She planted her hands on her hips. "Thank you for that assessment of what we were feeling, Thorne," she said coldly. "I'm glad to know that—"

"Damn it, will you listen to me!" He roared so that the sound bounced around the room.

She gave no quarter. "Listen to what? You tell me you don't want me? Listen to you reject me just the way you did ten years ago? Then you didn't want me because I said I loved you. Now you don't want me because I said all I wanted is sex. That makes any feeling you have for me a big lie."

He stared at her for a full minute as the meaning behind her words bit deeply into him. Never had the need been so strong to walk to her and lift her into his arms, kiss her deeply and reassure her that he wanted her so bad. He wanted her. Desperately.

In a low voice that contrasted sharply with the earlier heated exchanges, he said, "Try and get some sleep."

But before he got out the door, he heard her last words. She whispered almost to herself. "I hate you and I hate myself for letting any of this happen."

Thorne closed his eyes and swore. Never had he heard such heart-wrenching pain. Going to her and taking her into his arms in a soothing way would at least show he wasn't a total bastard, but Thorne didn't trust himself to just hold her. Maybe later in the cool logic of dawn. But not tonight.

Chapter 8

By late the following day, Amanda and Thorne had reached a silent compromise of not saying any more to each other than necessary. The counseling and the cooperation of the girls was progressing nicely and she should have been so immersed that Thorne would indeed be nothing more than what he was intended to be. Her bodyguard. And yet she was haunted, preoccupied and distracted by him.

Olivia and the committee had stopped at the house with Olivia admitting that the idea of the new room and the other girls rotating so that each had a chance for a room of her own seemed to be working very well. Amanda had called her just before Nicky delivered the needed paint and cleaning materials.

Thorne merely shrugged when Olivia acknowledged his contribution. Amanda had expected a comment later, but he'd said little. Even Sally noticed how quiet he was.

That evening when they had dinner with the girls, Amanda was surprised and genuinely pleased with Thorne's participation in the conversation, especially with Julie. The teenager obviously had found a friend and Thorne was generous with his interest without trying to probe for information.

Seated next to him at the dinner table, Julie leaned closer to him as they were finishing dessert. "So where did you grow up?"

Thorne lifted a mug of coffee, glanced in Amanda's direction, then said, "Upstate. Outside of Providence."

"Yeah? Me, too. Bet it wasn't like the dump where I lived."

"As dumps go mine was pretty grim."

"But you're not doin' drugs or scammin' the cops."

His eyes darkened. "Believe me, Julie, I did enough stuff to disqualify me for sainthood. The one time I got arrested, the judge put me in community service. The guy supervising me asked me why I used my mind to figure out all the wrong angles when I could use it to do something legal and rewarding."

"Some guy gives you a pep talk and just like that you're a good guy?" she asked skeptically.

"Not quite," he said sagely.

By this time the other conversations had trailed off and all the girls were intently listening. Glancing at each of the rapt faces, Amanda was reminded of herself growing up with the stories her mother used to tell; stories that weren't grim or tragic, but that did just the opposite. They had dimmed the necessity of bodyguards and created a make-believe world where there were always happy endings and a sense that all was right with the world. Her mother had been avid on giving Amanda balance; creating for her a slice of time where she could dream and wish and marvel. Amanda had learned well; years later, after her mother's death, when Thorne came to work for her father, Amanda had promptly added him to her dream, wish and marvel list.

My God, she thought, resting her chin on her palm, it had been forever since she'd thought of those lists. Maybe because she'd grown up and hit the sharp wall of reality, where dreams and wishes were paths to pain, rejection and humiliation.

Sally leaned over and whispered, "Did you know that?"

Amanda jerked her mind back from the past. "Know what?"

"That Thorne's mother was shot during a convenience store robbery?"

Amanda turned immediately and looked at him. "No, I didn't. I knew his father had died in some flophouse when Thorne was small, but all I knew about her was that she'd died. I assumed it was an illness of some sort."

Thorne had pushed his chair back and propped one ankle on the other knee. She couldn't help but note the frayed edges of his jeans, the shredded threads among the tears on the denim. His shirt, a logo-free gray cotton, made the gray in his eyes more intense. His expression was so neutral, Amanda couldn't decide how he felt about sharing his past.

Glancing at Julie and the other girls with their eager eyes and total attention, he added, "I'm just here to give Amanda a hand when she needs it. My rather undistinguished past is irrelevant. Maybe Amanda would just as soon we change the subject."

He looked at her fully then for the first time that day. She caught no hidden motive in his comment, but more of a letting her know he knew she was in charge and this was her call.

She stood and addressed the girls. "I'll tell you what. The table needs to be cleared and Julie, you and Lisa are responsible for the dishes tonight. If Thorne doesn't mind waiting until the chores are finished...."

He shrugged. "Whatever."

"How about we all meet on the deck in about a half hour?"

As the girls quickly busied themselves, Amanda followed Thorne out to the deck. The sounds of giggles and excitement churned from the kitchen. Sally excused herself, telling Amanda she had a date and that she'd see her in the morning.

Now that they were alone, she asked Thorne, "Are you sure you don't mind?"

"I would have said so if I did. It's a boring story. Kid loses his mother and eventually gets the message that life owes him nothing. He straightens himself out with some help, gets some education and eventually goes to work for Walker Delaski guarding his daughter."

"And then leaves and starts his own consulting business in the antiterrorist field. I would say that's pretty impressive."

"Fascinating," he commented sarcastically.

"You sound as if it means nothing to you."

"Amanda, everyone has a story. Each of those kids in there could probably rewrite the manual on lousy lives."

"You're right, but they like and respect you, and best of all, they are obviously listening to what you have to say."

"Why does this sound suspiciously like you expect them to learn something from me? As Julie would ask, a guy gives you a pep talk and you turn your life around? I don't think so." He shoved a hand through his hair. "I'm not a counselor and what I know about dealing with teenage girls wouldn't fill a shot glass."

She slid her hands into her skirt pockets. She realized Thorne wasn't technically a counselor, but she also knew that life experience sometimes had much more impact than a textbook approach in a controlled environment. She'd talked with all the girls and one thread she'd found in all their histories was a lack of positive male influence. No, she didn't expect miracles from Thorne, nor did she expect all the girls to suddenly decide all men weren't jerks, but Amanda knew the power of positive influence. If Thorne's victory over his own past made a strong impression, the girls would never forget it.

To Thorne she said, "Then how about influence? Your supervisor had influence on you. Enough so that you never forgot what he said about using your mind. Oh, I know it didn't happen overnight, but it happened. People influence us in profound ways and sometimes it takes years before we know the extent."

He raised an eyebrow, the skepticism evident in his expression. "Ah, the bigger lemons of life are just there to make better lemonade, huh?"

She shook her head at him. "Why do you have to be so cynical?" But before he had a chance to say anything, she took a step closer, her voice lowering so no one would hear. "You know what I think? I think you're afraid to let the emotions underneath your past become your past. It's not where you went and what you did, but what drove you. In other words, twenty other people with the same background would have acted in twenty different ways. It's possible—"

He held his hand up to motion her to silence. "I don't need or want you in my head, Amanda. I'm not screwed up and don't need counseling. Every demon you can think of has been confronted and dealt with."

She drew closer and lifted her hand to touch his back and then changed her mind. She wanted to beg him not to be so cold with her, not to close her out, but wanting it and saying it were two different things. Those moments in her bedroom had been as much her fault as his; maybe more hers. In effect she'd called his bluff when she said she just wanted sex, too.

Face it, he doesn't want you and he never did. Perhaps he thought by keeping it purely on a sexual level, she'd back off in some feminine outrage. She, of course, knew her feelings were much deeper than sexual, but she couldn't tell him that. Knowing Thorne, she concluded bleakly, he'd remind her once again that there wasn't and couldn't be anything personal between them. Perhaps, if she steeled her nerve, she might just confront him and demand to know why.

In record time the girls had their chores done and streamed out onto the deck with the enthusiasm of preparing to be with a favorite rock star.

Thorne watched in some disbelief. To Amanda he said, "I can't believe this is all so fascinating to them."

"Maybe ten years from now you'll be the one mentioned by a few of these girls as having an influence on their lives. They like you and they relate because they come from a similar background and in some cases, like you, have seen some grim stuff. It's toughened them up, but it's also trapped them in a cycle that few escape. You've obviously escaped and maybe..."

"Maybe what?" he asked suspiciously.

"Don't look as if I'm trying to trap you."

"You already have," he muttered more to himself than to her.

"That's not my intent," she whispered.

"Then why in hell can't I get the taste and smell of you out of my mind?"

She swallowed, jarred by the slipping in of such an intimate comment into the conversation. He had to have been much more preoccupied with what had happened between them even if his outward attitude toward her had been cool and indifferent.

Not about to let him see how rattled she was, she said, "I was talking about the girls." She said quickly when he swore and turned away from her, "You telling them about your past could make them realize that they, too, have a chance."

"Some speck of light in a dark tunnel, huh?"

"We all need that, Thorne, or else we'd never find our way out."

"Exactly my problem with you, babe," he said succinctly. "Now that I'm in, getting out is like the decision from hell."

The stark fierceness of his words clutched at her, and she wished desperately that they'd been alone so she could ask what he meant.

Turning to the girls, who were sitting in a circle by now, Thorne perched on the deck railing, his hands gripping the wood, his face unreadable. In a slow, almost detached voice, he told of his mother's struggle against poverty, of his own rebellion that had made her determined to work harder to get him away from all the bad influences. He gave few details about his mother getting shot—a robbery one night when she was working. A few times he hesitated enough that Amanda realized how hard it was for him to relive such an excruciatingly painful event. She doubted the girls noticed how quickly he passed over the incident. Only the rigid set of his jaw and the tight control of his words gave any indication of his inner emotions.

She listened with as much interest as Julie and the rest of the girls. For him to reveal so much of his past so freely caught Amanda by surprise simply because he'd always been so reluctant to talk about himself. Even what little she knew of his work in antiterrorism had come from her father or articles she had diligently searched out at her local library. That he would use the example of his own past to show that poverty and the inner city could be steps to success instead of defeat were more powerful than textbook rules.

And the girls liked him. Oh, they thought he was sexy and cool and a few times they'd teased Amanda about what really went on when they were alone, but for the most part Amanda saw a real respect for Thorne. What she especially liked was the good example he set of a man who wasn't afraid to admit his own shortcomings while at the same time assuring each of the girls of their potential for success and self-esteem.

Later that evening as they returned to her house, she was disappointed that once again the strain was back between them.

As they entered her home, and as was their usual routine of checking for anything suspicious, Amanda commented on what was becoming the least stressful topic between them. "Maybe the stalker gave up and decided to go away."

"Not likely. The fact that he's been quiet and hidden worries me more than if he were making phone calls and lurking in the shadows. I'm still trying to figure out the light in the bedroom."

"I wonder how Dad is coming with his list of names," she mused. Thorne had told her of calling her father and the possibility the stalker might know them personally.

"I'll give him a call tomorrow." He walked past her, shutting off some of the lights. At the entrance to the kitchen, he said, "I'm going to get a drink. I'll see you in the morning."

She followed him. "I think I'll join you."

He shrugged. "Suit yourself." He opened a cupboard and took out a bottle of Scotch. "You want wine?"

"Scotch is fine."

He dropped ice cubes into two glasses and splashed the liquor on top. Handing her a glass, he lifted his and drank, then refilled it and turned to leave the kitchen.

"Thorne…"

"I don't want to talk, Amanda."

"All right, I'll just sit and enjoy the stars and the night with you."

"Why don't you go to bed."

"Because I don't want to."

He drew in a long breath, then swore.

"Well, aren't you going to ask me what I do want?"

Instead of answering, he swirled the liquor and took another swallow. Amanda, on the other hand, had been thinking a lot about what she wanted. She'd called herself crazy, a woman who must enjoy having her emotions shredded, a total fool for allowing feelings for him to emerge when she knew the result would be rejection. Sometimes she wished he wasn't so damn honest. Other men would say the words she wanted to hear, they'd engage in sexual teasing and know exactly what the consequences of that could be and gladly go right along. And not likely would they be so close when she was so vulnerable as she'd been the previous night and not seize the moment and the advantage.

Other men, yes. Thorne, no. She'd decided that he was too honorable, too professional and just too plain stubborn. Obviously he feared she would expect marriage or long-term commitment—the serious stuff. Well, proving she could be spontaneous might at least break this deepening tension between them.

He'd stepped around her without touching her and was already a few steps from the door when she whirled around, her voice rising more than she'd intended. "No, you're not going to ask me what I want, are you? You're afraid I might tell you? I might just say the truth."

"The truth? And what in hell is that?"

"That you're afraid if you sleep with me that I'm going to try to trap you in some relationship." She took a deep breath and added. "Isn't that what happened with Jill?"

He narrowed his eyes. "What do you know about Jill?" he asked in a deadly calm voice.

If ever Amanda had felt out of her element with Thorne, it was now. Gone was the slow, unwinding approach he'd used when talking to the girls. Now his body was motionless, his eyes so darkly probing she wanted to shrink into the shadows.

"Come on, Amanda," he urged dangerously. "You wanted conversation. Answer me. How do you know about Jill?"

Clutching her glass, she talked quickly before she lost her nerve. "I heard about her from Dad. He said that Jill adored you and followed you to Europe. She took a teaching position to be close to you. At first you tried to avoid making the relationship permanent, but then suddenly you changed your mind and agreed to marry her."

"So much for having a private life," he muttered, then said, "So what's your point?"

"Why did you change your mind and agree to marry her?"

"It's none of your business, you know that, don't you? Just because we've known each other for a long time and I have enormous respect for your father gives you no right to my personal life." Although he kept some distance between them, his voice was low, his words precise. "Or is the real question, why did I reject you and not her?"

Amanda stood rigid. She'd asked for this conversation. She was the one pushing to know him, to know about him, to learn not just what influenced him but what guided his decisions. And perhaps deep in her heart as much as she shrank from what the real truth might be, Thorne could be correct. She *did* want to know why he'd rejected her. She wanted to know what was wrong with her that she could have so loved a man who so obviously had not wanted her love in return.

"I suppose every woman wonders why a man chooses one woman over the other," she said briskly, glad he wasn't close enough to feel her pounding heart.

But as if he didn't care what her answer was, he said, "I decided to marry Jill because I loved her." It was the most distant, dispassionate tone she'd ever heard.

She took a deep breath and said softly, "I don't believe you."

"And how in hell would you know how I felt?"

"Because people don't 'suddenly' fall in love."

"The opinion of the expert, huh?" He gave her a cryptic look and drained his glass.

Not wanting to discuss her expertise or lack thereof, she plunged on to make her point. "I think you were fond of her and that you felt a certain responsibility because she came to Germany to be close to you."

He stared down at his empty glass, then walked to the counter, where he put it down. All the time Amanda's eyes followed him. When, without looking at her, he turned and walked to the door, her heart sank. He wasn't going to tell her anything and while she respected his right to *not* share his relationship with Jill, Amanda needed to know. Maybe to give her more insight into Thorne. Maybe to make herself, once and for all, face the fact that given the best possible circumstances, Thorne would never have loved her anyway.

Then, at the door, he stopped. Amanda held her breath.

He made a half turn so that his back was braced against the doorjamb. "Jill made too many assumptions about our relationship."

Amanda waited a few seconds before she ventured a response. "Probably because she loved you and thought you felt the same about her." She had the eeriest sense they were talking about their own reactions to each other rather than Thorne and Jill.

"I was fond of her and we had a good physical relationship, but at no time did I ever tell her I loved her."

"Sometimes women can be blinded by their own feelings and presume those same feelings are shared." In that moment she understood how Jill must have felt, for she, too, had made huge assumptions about Thorne when she was twenty-one.

He folded his arms and lowered his head, shaking it slowly. Suddenly Amanda regretted her probing.

"Thorne, look, you're right. This isn't any of my business—"

But as if he hadn't heard her, he said, "Actually I blame myself for not breaking off the relationship before I left the States. I just didn't want the hassle and the tears, plus I assumed that once I was gone she'd find someone else. She was a smart, attractive and passionate woman. But instead of going on with her life, she kept in touch by calling me and then she flew over and surprised me on my birthday."

His birthday was April 17. Amanda, too, had surprised him once on his birthday. The first year he'd worked for her father. She'd bought him a silly card and a dozen balloons. He'd been taken aback by the gesture and she'd immediately felt all the gaucheness of a sixteen-year-old.

Thorne continued, "I ended up taking her to Paris for a few days and it was during that time she told me she'd applied and been accepted into a teacher exchange program and would be moving to Frankfurt."

"Just like that? She didn't tell you she was involved with an exchange program?"

"Jill tended to do things and then assume they'd be accepted because her intent was good." Scowling at what he obviously saw as a bad way to handle decisions, he added, "She was so happy and excited that I didn't have the heart to tell her I didn't like the idea."

"So she moved to Frankfurt and began teaching?"

"Yeah. We lived together, although I wasn't there much. Work was frantic and I was doing about eighteen hours a day. Stress and pressure made me short-tempered. Now looking back, I have to wonder what was going on in Jill's mind. Instead of concluding I was an SOB to live with—which I was—she began to talk marriage and kids. Hell, the next thing I expected to see was photos of vine-covered cottages." He shook his head as if trying to understand female logic totally escaped him.

Amanda knew what Jill was thinking and to her it was very logical. "She thought you needed stability and permanency in your life. It's the nesting instinct."

"Nesting, hell. She figured I'd agree because she was there and had rearranged her whole life to be with me. But I never asked her to do that and...yeah, you're probably right in what you said earlier. I felt trapped. Anyway, I stalled. Then a few days later she brought up marriage again and I told her flat-out that I didn't want to get married to her or to anyone else."

Amanda couldn't help but recall his blunt words of rejection to her that night in the garden. She knew the pain Jill must have felt.

"Jill looked at me as if my saying no to marriage had never occurred to her. It was a bad scene and I felt cornered between worrying about her being safe because of some terrorist rumors in the area and wanting her to get the hell out of my life. Then some undercover work turned up several planned terrorists attacks—one close to the school where she was teaching. I knew then I had to get her out of Germany and if I had to marry her to do it, then so be it. But I didn't move quite fast enough. The terrorist attack took place the following day and Jill was killed.

"Oh, Thorne, how terrible."

He was silent a few moments, the tragedy obviously still painful to recall. "It was a number of months before I could concentrate on work without seeing what was left of her after that bombing. She didn't deserve that and if I'd gotten her out of there, she'd be alive today."

She touched his arm, her fingers pressing into the rigid muscle. "You can't blame yourself. You couldn't have known what would happen."

He slipped out of her reach as if he didn't deserve to be comforted. "I worked there and had a thriving business because of the existence of terrorist groups. I was paid a lot of money by those who wanted to know what group was building what kind of bomb and where they planned to detonate it. It was my business to stay one step ahead of them. It wasn't until after the explosion that we learned that a newly formed and secretive faction had moved just days before into an old building near the school. They were the ones the bomb was meant for. The passersby like Jill had the misfortune of being in the wrong place at the wrong time."

Thorne opened the porch door and stepped out into the night. Amanda stood for a few moments, still trying to digest all that he'd told her. In many ways he'd revealed more about himself than she was sure he'd intended. He'd gotten more deeply involved than he'd intended and then hadn't been able to end it easily. Then he'd had to live with the guilt over the consequences of that involvement. What struck her also was his adamant refusal, perhaps even fear, of being trapped. From what he'd said earlier about his past, Amanda felt sure his mother had felt trapped by the poverty of her own circumstances. No doubt she'd worked such long hours to provide a way to get herself and Thorne out of the inner city. Thorne's escape had come ironically after she'd died. And so it was with Jill.

My God, she thought, it's no wonder he was so leery of close relationships. Not only did his work leave little time for serious relationships, but the inherent emotional danger would always be a factor.

Amanda felt a certain empathy with Jill. She'd obviously loved Thorne and thought that their relationship was on the right track. Naturally she would assume marriage would be the next step. What puzzled Amanda was why Thorne hadn't broken the relationship cleanly when he'd had to know that Jill loved him. Certainly he'd had no qualms about being brutally honest with her when Amanda had confessed that she loved him.

Maybe he really did love Jill and just didn't know it or refused to acknowledge it. From her own experiences—as few as they'd been—she'd concluded that nothing she'd felt for any man came close to what she'd felt for Thorne. Either her feelings for Thorne were obsessively dangerous or true love wasn't anywhere near as thrilling as the books said it was.

Perhaps love came quietly, spreading around a couple like a scattering of rose petals. Or maybe it came hot and wild and bursting with untamed passion. Maybe it just grew and developed and in its time became full-blown.

She put her empty glass down and followed Thorne outside. Coming up behind him, she slipped her arms around his waist.

"Thank you for telling me about Jill."

"I had a feeling you wouldn't let up until I did."

"Was it so hard?"

"Actually it's the first time I've ever told anyone all of the story. In fact this seems to be the day for revisiting my past life. First Julie and the girls and now you."

In the warmth of the summer night they stood beneath the stars. Yards down the lawn and across the beach, the moon cast a long wavy light on the dark waters of the ocean.

She held him in a fierce hold, her cheek against his back.

He sighed, then tried to loosen her hands and pick up the thread of their conversation. "The less personal stuff between us the better, Amanda. Speaking of which, your hands on my belly is a bad idea."

"Not if I intend to unsnap your jeans."

"Cute."

"I'm serious."

"So am I. And the answer is no."

She stepped around in front of him, standing so close she could feel his breath across her cheek. "What if I seduce you? I could put on something sexy and sultry. Or maybe I could just take off what I have on. You know, do a slow strip?"

To her surprise a slight grin slashed his mouth. "You've done a lot of those, I suppose."

"Maybe."

"And you think that will be the way to get me to make love to you."

"Well, coming right out and stating it didn't seem to work."

He stared down at her for a long, languid moment. Then slowly, he slid his hands into her hair and held her head as he lowered his mouth. "Want to know something, Ms. Delaski? I haven't thought about much else since that first kiss. And you know what else? Wanting to take you to bed has little to do with what you have on or what you take off. All it has to do with is a cursing, driving desire that seems to have trapped me so that I can't escape."

Trapped?

Escape?

She felt an internal jolt. Once she'd been brutally rejected by him; this time he hadn't done that, but would this be worse in the end? But she wasn't naive. She wasn't a wide-eyed virgin with stars in her eyes and dreams in her heart. Unlike poor Jill, Amanda had no illusions of anything with Thorne beyond the time he was here. She wasn't trying to trap him. She had no intention of not allowing him to escape.

Take what he offers, she decided when his mouth covered hers. She tried to ignore the tiny wrench twisting around her soul. Don't make these moments forever ones and you won't get hurt.

His kiss deepened and Amanda felt all her senses slip from whatever restraints had held them in check. Her arms went around his neck as if having a life of their own and she pressed against him as if he were all the support and heat she'd ever need.

The kiss transcended any experience she'd ever had. Hot, volatile and so deep she knew she was drowning in a fantasy of sensation.

He tilted her hips against him, making her more than aware of his arousal. Then in a whisper of sound she almost couldn't distinguish from the pounding of her own heart, he said, "Still time to say no, babe."

"I don't want to say no."

"Thank God. I don't have the will to fight staying away from you."

Then he lifted her into his arms and carried her into the house.

Chapter 9

In her bedroom, he slowly lowered her to the floor, allowing his hands to skim down her sides, brushing her breasts, her waist, her hips. He kissed her again, leisurely, his hunger barely in check.

Since the night they'd parted angrily—for Thorne both frustration and self-derision had been beneath his own harsh words—he'd tried to keep his distance. As much as he wanted her then, he knew he couldn't and yet here he was. He wasn't sure what the difference between then and now was, or even if how he felt now would be justifiable later.

What a hell of a mess. Maybe he had no strength of character, no moral compass when it came to Amanda. For sure wanting her wasn't practical or logical and yet here he was, like a drowning man, reaching for the last life raft.

Admittedly she'd been a jewel. No pouting, an irksome characteristic Jill had, that, as fond of her as he'd been, had often made him wonder if it was more artifice to get attention than real. In the past few days, he'd learned Amanda had the maturity not to allow her personal life to dictate her attitude in her professional one. Not so himself, he realized, which gave him some insight about himself that he didn't like very much. Rather than putting their personal differences aside, he'd been silent, cool, barely civil at times. To her credit, Amanda hadn't allowed the tension between them to show in front of Ginny and the staff, or Sally, or with Julie and the girls.

"You're supposed to be mad at me, not seducing me," he whispered, touching his mouth to her neck before he reached over and switched on the bedside lamp.

Her senses swimming in hazy channels, she tipped her head to the side. "Mad at you?"

"Yeah. I haven't exactly been a prince the past few days."

"Is this an apology?"

"Just a confession that I haven't forgotten how to be a bastard. Then again, getting along *too* well gets us into trouble."

"Like now."

"Like always and definitely like now...." Without letting go of her, he moved to the bed and sat down on the edge. Tugging her between his thighs so her knees bumped the bed, he cupped his hands on her hips and tipped her forward. He positioned his thumbs so that they massaged the soft indentation just above the apex of her thighs.

Amanda closed her eyes at the instant response of her body. The fabric of her skirt and her panties should have decreased any reaction, any sizzle, any spiral of sensation, but the added hindrance that prevented skin-to-skin contact added a provocative anticipation. She drew in a ragged breath.

Thorne glanced up and she slid her hands into his hair. Even though their position allowed her to tower over him, she still felt uniquely under his spell. His gray eyes probed deep into hers so that she was mesmerized.

Slowly, and still watching her, he reached up and, one by one, opened the buttons of her blouse.

She shivered, the familiar old demon planting itself in her conscience.

Thorne rubbed her arms. "Cold or cold feet?"

"Just unsure."

"That I might hurt you?"

She shook her head vigorously. "Not sure if you'll like making love with me," she said quickly, saying it before she lost her nerve.

His hands stilled. "Sweetheart, believe me, that's the last thing that you should worry about."

"But you've been around and you're experienced and you know what you like in a woman."

"Is this conclusion coming from the comments the other night? That all that would be between us is sex?"

"No, this is coming from inside me. I just want you to be satisfied and—" She squeezed her eyes closed and felt the warmth climb up her cheeks. "Oh God, I wasn't going to do this...."

Thorne scowled, feeling as if he were venturing into some unknown territory. "Do what?"

She tried to back up, shaking her head.

"Mandy," he said gently, "since we already decided that we both wanted this out there on the porch—" He clamped his mouth closed at the direction of his words. Hell, what did what was said on the porch matter? That was then, this is now, he thought grimly. If she'd changed her mind, then that was that. Forcing her wasn't even an option and he sure wasn't going to seduce her and have her frantic with guilt in the morning.

"I know. You probably think I'm some tease."

More disappointed than he wanted to admit, he said, "Look, if you've changed your mind, it's okay."

"No! I haven't...that is, I want you. I want to make love...it's just that..."

"Let's back up. Either I'm confused or I missed something."

"I want you to be satisfied."

Again his thoughts tumbled in different directions. Something was going on and she was either too embarrassed or was just having a tough time getting the words out. She wasn't a virgin, shaky about the first time for Thorne knew from her father that she'd been involved with someone a few years ago. Walker had mentioned some executive in a few conversations with Thorne and had expressed worry that she might decide to marry. Some months later Walker had reported happily that the romance had ended. He'd given no details and Thorne had asked for none, recalling only his own rush of relief. It had been a hell of a reaction and at the time he'd tried to convince himself that he just wanted the best for Mandy, as Walker did.

Since virginity was probably not the issue, he wondered if there was something about her past she felt compelled to say? Admittedly, if this were any woman other than Mandy, he would give her a kiss, a regretful smile and say goodnight. He'd always avoided getting involved with intimate female musings and confessions when all he wanted was sex. Amanda, however, held some unique hold on him that he'd never understood, and in fact, had no intention of trying. If he ignored it, rejected it as he had when she was twenty-one, eventually it would fade and die.

Deciding to be as honest as he could with her, he gathered her into his arms and pulled her down on the bed beside him. Tucking her in close to him, she curled up as if collecting all the warmth she could get.

"Mandy," he whispered, blowing softly against her hair, "Satisfaction for me comes from being with you, not how innovative the sex is."

"But you don't understand."

"Make me understand."

"There's only been two other men and I didn't do very well with either of them."

Stunned by her admission that to him sounded outrageous, he wondered if she was being overly critical of herself. "Sweetheart, I think you're being too hard on yourself. You turn me on just by walking into a room and all that sexy talk about undoing my jeans had me thinking about your hands working . . ." He paused, considering his next words. No, better not. "Never mind."

She didn't pursue it. "That's just my point. Turning you on. Sexy talk. That's easy stuff, but here, when we're about to make love and you find that I can't—"

"Can't what?"

She buried her head deeper into his chest, her hands clutching him as if she was afraid he'd leap off the bed and run away. A clutch of fear raced through him and he didn't know why except that she was obviously worried about something far more serious than going to bed and having sex.

"Mandy, come on, babe, talk to me."

"Oh, Thorne, I feel like such an idiot." Then in a torrent of feelings, the words tumbled forth. "Maybe I was assuming we'd never get this far or maybe I wanted to think that you'd just sweep me away so that I'd be on some cloud of passion and magic would occur, but I'm scared it won't and I want it to, but it never has and even if it did, I probably wouldn't know because I don't know what to expect—"

He kissed her, stopping her midsentence, and felt the breathless catch in her throat. Lifting his mouth, he said in a low voice, "You've never had an orgasm. Is that what you're trying to tell me?"

She didn't move, wouldn't lift her lashes and look at him.

"Mandy . . ."

"I don't want to see the disgust on your face."

"Disgust! You're not serious." He drew back and looked at her, amazed she could draw a conclusion like that.

"It is disgusting," she said vehemently. "I'm not uptight about sex. I've read books and gone to seminars on sexuality. In other words I have answers for everyone else, but when it comes to me..." Her voice trailed off, then finally she added, "It's almost as if I'm afraid to let go, to allow myself to be that open and vulnerable."

Thorne stared at her for a long time. Was he responsible for this? Had his rejection of her years ago, his spurning of her confession of love and treating it as a girlish crush, had he set in motion some trapdoor that had snapped into place every time a man wanted more from her than compliance? He shook off the questions. Ridiculous. And yet that first day when he'd surprised her and told her how vulnerable she was by leaving her door unlocked, what had she said? Something about how he should be the last one concerned about her vulnerability?

Suddenly Thorne realized both the gift and the curse of this moment. Making up for his treatment of her in the past while at the same time digging himself in so deep, he'd be hurting her all over again when he left.

Amanda tried to pull away from him. "I know you don't want to hear all this. I should have stopped things on the porch. You're probably trying to figure out a way to leave and not hurt my feelings."

He shook his head. "Actually I'm trying to figure out how I got so lucky."

"Lucky? I don't understand."

"To be the first man to feel you climax."

Her eyes were immediately curious and cautious. "And if I don't?"

"You will."

"Thorne, how can you know for sure—?"

"I know." Then before she could say anything more, he kissed her. His hands cupped her breasts, feeling the fullness and the tightness of her nipples even through her blouse. And yet he knew that she needed more than physical arousal. The mechanics and the manipulation of sexual release were just the tip of satisfaction. He could give her that and she'd be grateful. Definitely the easy way out and one he should take and not get all bent out of shape about. Damn. This was what happened when he got involved beyond what he should be. With Jill, he should have broken things off before he left for Germany. He'd cursed himself a hundred times since her death, for assuming that she'd forget him as he intended to forget her. Maybe he'd been gripped by his harshness with Amanda and hadn't wanted to leave another woman hating him the way Amanda had. So what did you do, Law? You were indecisive, kind or just plain into avoidance—big time—and poor Jill ended up killed.

Personal decisions that should be cut-and-dried or even better, cut and run, ended up consuming him. Damn good thing he didn't operate his consulting business that way; he'd have been bankrupt or dead years ago. Cursing silently, he knew he was in too deep with Amanda—at least for tonight. For God knows what reason, he knew he wanted to give her more than good sex. More than just the physical. And that kind of messy emotional involvement scared the hell out of him.

She peered at him, her expression dubious. "You make it sound so easy."

"It has nothing to do with easy. It has to do with the guy being concerned about your needs, not just his own." He brushed his hand down her body. "Right now, you're tight and stiff. Why don't you get ready for bed. I'll go get things locked up and be right back."

He rolled off the bed, but she didn't move. He leaned down, bracing his hands on either side of her body. "I want you, babe, and you want me. I have a feeling that after tonight, our biggest problem is going to be keeping away from each other."

Her eyes were wide, still unsure. Thorne kissed her in a deliberately provocative way so that she had to reach for his mouth.

He grinned. "See, you're not shrinking away."

Finally she lifted her arms and twined them around his neck, tugging him down so that a longer kiss could go on and on. "What were you wanting my hands to do if I opened your jeans?"

He kissed her lightly again, then whispered in her ear.

She giggled, her fingers immediately moving to the waist of his jeans.

He held her hand away. "Eager, aren't you?"

She grinned. "Will you let me?"

"I'll try not to protest too much." He lifted her from the bed and stood her on her feet. Immediately he noted how relaxed she already was. He finished opening the buttons on her blouse and then drew it from her skirt. She looked tangled and disheveled and so enticingly impish that Thorne realized what he was about to enter into—both literally and figuratively—would be far different from past relationships. The fact that this was Mandy Delaski made it doubly complicated. Then, again, maybe it was vastly simpler than he thought. She wanted to experience sexual satisfaction. He could give her that. Maybe it would be enough.

A few miles away in the dimly lit apartment, the man shuddered through his climax.

His satisfaction came from concentration on his flawless plan and not from the woman beneath him.

He pulled free of her, sliding from the couch and getting to his feet, not looking at the provocative sprawl her body made on the cushions. No peach jam smearings, but he'd had to endure her perfume. Despite his distaste at the cloying smell, his performance had been more than adequate. He adjusted his clothes and checked his watch. In a few hours the delivery, or the gift as he liked to call it, would be made.

"It was so good...." came the pouty voice from the couch.

"You better leave. I have things to do."

"Leave?"

Like in get the hell out. Instead he said, "There's no reason for you to stay."

"I thought we'd spend the night together."

He glanced over at her, the idea so preposterous he wanted to laugh. He concentrated on buttoning his shirt. "No."

"Tomorrow? Could we see each other tomorrow night? Maybe?" she asked hopefully.

"I'm busy."

Still she persisted. "I know we haven't gotten to know each other too well, and frankly I'm usually rather cautious."

You were a bitch in heat, he thought, already bored.

"But I so needed tonight and the past few days," she said as if infused with new possibilities because of his silence. "It's been wonderful getting to know you and the enjoyment of making love..." She reached out and touched his thigh, her fingers brushing.

He stepped away, his eyes hard. "Of course, you liked it. You've been sniffing around for it since the day you did your welcome to the neighborhood speech," he snapped bluntly.

Her tiny gasp at his cruelly arrogant presumption didn't concern him. He could feel the raw-wired edge of impatience building. He hated after-sex talk. All the gooey platitudes, the soppy thoughts badly expressed. But making her angry or worse, inciting an emotional crying jag, would delay her leaving. Remember to charm, he reminded himself. Granting her a small smile, he reached down and extended his hand to help her to her feet.

She hesitated and he forced himself to say the words she wanted to hear. "Forgive my crassness, my dear." He added an even wider smile and a small stroke of his hand along her breast. Finally she took his hand, obviously taking his grin and touch to mean an added apology when none was offered.

Once she was standing, he quickly released her and turned away. He could hear her rustling into her clothes. He glanced toward the bedroom door, where the final preparations were waiting to be made.

She spoke softly, flirtatiously. "When will I see you again?"

He didn't turn and look at her, but he could feel his earlier impatience swell now beyond insulting her to a black demonic fury. "I'll call you."

"But you never call me," she whined. "I always have to come to you."

He swung around, his eyes filled with hatred and disgust. "Don't push me, damn it. I make the rules. *I* decide who I'll see and when I want to see them." He reached into his pocket and pulled out some folded bills. He'd pay her and that would get rid of her.

Crossing the room, his face gleamed dangerously and savagely. He forgot his practiced charm in his need to get her out of there, He jerked her toward him, then pushed the money into her bra. He was losing it, he knew it and at the same time the woman inflamed him with her soppy whining and blubbering need to be reassured.

She shrank back and he gripped her wrist harder, squeezing. So easy to break her flimsy bones. So easy.

"I'm not a whore," she cried, pulling the money from her bra and flinging it at him. "I hate you! You're a cruel unfeeling bastard...." Sobs gushed from her throat and she began to pound on him with her free hand, her voice rising from a cry to a shout to a scream.

The voice inside him shouted, *"Shut her up! Shut her up!"*

He clamped a hand over her mouth, his eyes fierce.

It should have been enough and for a few seconds he detected the terror in her eyes, but then it changed to anger. The demon inside of him snickered, *"You've lost control of her. She's no longer a mouse for the cat to play with."*

She brought her knee up and with a hard shove that he didn't dodge quick enough, she jammed his groin.

Pain exploded in his brain. Something inside him snapped and his hands coiled around her throat, squeezing, his face rigid, his hatred burning. Her eyes swelled, her face paling as she clawed to get free.

The demons cackled and cawed, urging him on.

"Damn you," he shouted in her face. "I just wanted you to leave. Why couldn't you have done as you were told. Why? Why?" As he rambled, he squeezed harder.

Let her go, boy.

She'll go to the cops. She'll say you raped her and beat her.

You're killing her, boy.

She's a whore, a bitch, just like you, Momma, just like the Delaski broad.

Remember the charm. Remember to be charming.

She hurt me. She had no right to hurt me.

She liked you when you charmed her, boy. She was useful. Now she'll just be dead and that won't be useful at all.

Her eyes rolled back and her knees no longer supported her. Suddenly he let her go, his hands flying wide as he backed away. She slumped to the floor, her body crumpled and still on the scattered twenty-dollar bills she'd thrown back at him.

He stared blankly. She lay like an abused and broken half-dressed doll that had been tossed aside. The marks on her throat flared like raw, red flames.

"Stupid bitch," he muttered, tears blinding his eyes. "Why didn't you leave when I told you to. Now, it's too late."

"Hi."

Thorne turned from where he'd been watching the lights from a distant boat. His thoughts were no more clear as to what he was about to do than they were when he'd left her in the bedroom. The enticement of her, and yes, the need to give something so special and so satisfying had overshadowed any realistic considerations of what would happen later. Right now, seeing her, wanting her and unable to deny his need to possess her, Thorne pushed aside the questions and fears about the tomorrows.

She wore a cinnamon-colored lace nightie that dipped deep and enhanced the swell of her breasts. It flowed down her body with a provocative ruffle that swirled at midthigh. Her hair was down and freshly brushed, the shade more a rich amber in the moonlight.

"Hi, yourself." He drew her close and slid his hand into her hair, loving the silky texture, fascinated by the waves that coiled around his fingers.

She reached up and brushed a coil of his hair back. "You haven't gotten it cut yet. Julie is going to think you tricked her."

"Hmm, but there's this problem of going to the barbershop. With being at the house all day, I haven't had time."

"You can leave the house to get a haircut."

"You going to come with me?"

"Come with you? Oh, the stalker."

"Uh, yeah. A minor problem," he said lightly. "Let's not make it easy for the guy. Since he's probably watching you, he'd think he got the break of a lifetime if he saw me go off without you."

"But he wouldn't do anything while the girls and the staff were all around me."

"Probably not, but if he lured you away...."

"Lured me away! You make it sound as if I have no will and would just walk off with a strange man."

"And you're presuming he would take that approach. He's much smarter than that. And as we've already determined from his actions, he's no ordinary stalker."

She grimaced. "Just what I needed—an extraordinary stalker."

"And deliberate. Don't forget we can't account for that bedroom light being on."

"You think he was in here, don't you?"

He sighed, wanting like hell to say no. "Yeah, I think he was."

"But if he's as smart as you say, then why would he leave a light on?"

"Could have been a misstep. Maybe he did it on purpose."

Amanda scowled. "On purpose? But why?"

"So we'd be standing here trying to figure it out. It's called diversionary tactics or it could just be more head games. I don't know, babe, but I do know that this seeming lull isn't the time to get careless."

She glanced beyond him to the beach. "Sometimes, it's almost surreal. With the project and being busy with the girls I almost can forget some jerk is out there who wants to hurt me. Then I look at you and I'm reminded that you're not here as a friend or a problem-solver, but as my bodyguard." She paused a moment, then added in a reflective tone. "Just like before, Thorne. Just like before."

Thorne watched the light wind swirl her nightie around her body. *Except this time I'm also about to be your lover.* Then his earlier questions about the wisdom of doing this slipped back into his mind. A bodyguard, yes, but one who is about to take you to bed, which has absolutely nothing to do with what he was hired to.

She turned back to him. "How much longer will this go on?"

Wanting you? Or finding the will to walk away a second time without hurting you? Neither question could he answer.

He shrugged. "As long as the stalker can make you and Walker sweat. Or if we get lucky maybe not much longer. The list of names your dad is putting together might identify him. This guy is particularly tough because in most stalker cases, the stalker is known. Star stalkers, those obsessed with celebrities, usually have a clear agenda. In one case I read, the stalker was in love with the star's sister. The sister was also the star's agent. The stalker believed that if he could get rid of the star then the sister would be out of work and he could step in and claim to be her savior from ruin. Weird, I know, but the kind of jerks that do this stuff aren't usually playing with a full deck."

"Do you think this guy has some sort of agenda?"

"Given Walker's past with the CIA, it doesn't take a rocket scientist to know he's probably got a lot of enemies."

For a few moments they both fell silent.

Thorne reached out and tugged her into his arms. Nuzzling his mouth into her neck, he said. "How did we get on this subject when I'm supposed to be getting into your pants?"

She laughed and tucked her fingers into the waist of his jeans. "Or me in yours."

"Hmm, a delightful dilemma." He touched her shoulders, taking the nightie along as he glided his hands down her arms. With the straps came the lace bodice.

Thorne could only stare. When her hands came up to cover herself, he gripped her wrists and stopped her.

"You're more beautiful than I could have imagined," he murmured, more awed by the shape and perfection of her than he thought possible. Her breasts were swells of rich cream, peaked pink and warm, a perfect delight when he lowered his head and lightly kissed each nipple.

Amanda gasped, her breath catching, her body arching. "More?"

"Oh, yes."

He lifted each breast, handling it with the treasured hold generally given to delicate masterpieces. He learned them, infused their softness into his palms, encouraged her nipples to burrow and nestle. Light touches. Feathery strokes. Intoxicating gentleness.

Amanda's knees began to sag. "Please . . ."

Thorne took her hands and raised them to his mouth, kissing each palm, then brought them once again to the front of his jeans. He tucked her fingers into the waistband so that the heels of her hands rested on either side of the zipper. She pushed her knuckles into his belly; her palms pressed against the swelled and hardening denim where moments ago was only a semiarousal.

He intended to take her into the house. He intended to be masterful in guiding her to the kind of excitement that would be the most fulfilling for her. He intended this to be slow and lingering with each touch and caress better than the previous one. Yeah, he intended a lot of things, but as her hands slipped deeper into his jeans and her mouth worked its sweet-tasting magic on his, Thorne felt something jar loose inside him. It was too powerful to call desire, too intense to label passion. It swept through him like some surge of power that scorched away all the hiding places where he'd put those feelings for her that he couldn't deal with.

Sex, arousal, turn-ons, teasing banter and even his rather bold statement that he could give her the satisfaction she craved—all of those were clear and easily defined in the light of day, in the objective distance of not being under her spell. Now to his astonishment, he was caught emotionally naked and more vulnerable than he ever wanted to be with Amanda.

She pressed tighter against him.

He took all her heat and went looking for more.

His hands slid beneath her gown to encounter a scrap of lace that somehow made her secrets even more erotic. He pushed the panties down and with some rather inventive wiggling she disposed of them.

Thorne pressed his hand against her, finding liquid fire. Touching her, he realized, was tantamount to lighting a fuse that flared beyond his ability to control. He wanted to sink into her, absorb her, taste her and more than anything feel the intoxicating high of release. Kissing her, feeling her, aching for her, he whispered, "Oh, baby, you're more than I bargained for."

Amanda sank into his touch, the heat of his mouth on hers, the exquisite press of his hands seeking out intimate places. When he backed up to the cushioned couch and dropped onto it, taking her down with him, she gasped at the hungry flames of heat that flared between them.

Amanda decided then that if she never found that elusive pinnacle that had always escaped her, these moments made up for it.

Thorne sprawled back against the plump cushions, settling her so that she sat astride him. The shadows were deep, giving the illusion of darkness while at the same time adding enough moonlight so that he could see her. Watching her with probing eyes, hot with need, smoldering with the heaviness of pervasive arousal, he worked his zipper down and loosened his clothes enough to free himself.

Swirling mazes of excitement wound through her and she shook back her head, laughing at the wonder of herself in such a provocative position.

Thorne took deep breaths, trying to rein in the roaring need to slide her onto him. "I think I missed the joke," he muttered.

"Oh, Thorne, this is so wild and wonderful."

"It's not what I intended. God, don't wiggle like that."

She leaned down and kissed him, her tongue doing things to him that should have been illegal. She wiggled again, this time her mouth was nibbling his neck. "What did you intend?"

"I'm supposed to be the one turning you on, remember? Instead I'm close to losing it."

She straightened, her nails lightly scoring through his chest hair. Her eyes danced teasingly and he didn't miss the obvious delight at his admission. "Oh, well, in that case I'll just move..."

"Don't you dare," he growled.

Then they both went still, their gazes locked, their bodies swaying, their need building.

Thorne touched her hips and lifted her, moving slowly against her. "You're so hot, babe."

"I want you. I want you to want me."

"I don't know if there was a time when I didn't," he murmured, using his hand as a guide to slowly enter her. "You're tight, babe. I don't want to hurt you."

"No... you won't... Oh!"

He rocked her gently as she slowly accommodated him. With each motion his own need roared, taking more power of concentration than he thought he possessed to hold back. Amanda's hips lifted and her back arched. He moved his hand against her, touching her, not breaking the rhythm of their bodies.

"Thorne... Oh, Thorne...."

"Shh, don't freeze. Just let it take you... Let it take you."

He ground his teeth together, determined to hold back. He wanted to see her, feel the impact against him, but his own release was rushing at him. Then she gripped him, her nails digging into his arms, her head thrown back, her eyes squeezed closed.

Nothing in her experience matched this.

Nothing in his experience was so incredible to watch.

She soared and reached and arched and climbed with such fluid glory, Thorne submerged into his own headlong rush only to tumble and explode into some mystical space where pleasure abounded. He sank into the opiate, finding a greedy richness of abundant satisfaction.

But the beauty that blew him away was that she'd taken him with her, not him taking her. He hadn't brought her release; she'd given it to him. It so boggled his mind he lay replete and boneless beneath her.

Amanda, on the other hand, hugged him with enough energy and excitement to last two lifetimes. "It was wonderful," she declared, kissing him again and again. "I never knew it was like that. Like spirals that build and build and then from inside burst like... I can't even describe it."

Thorne grinned. "I take it you liked it."

"Like it! Now I know what all the books are talking about."

"Babe, it's always better than what the books say."

He started to lift her up so he could move, when she went still. "Where are you going?"

He glanced at her and saw the confusion in her eyes. "I thought we should move. I'm tangled in these clothes and you must be cold."

She glanced down and then nodded. "I'm sorry. You're probably not very comfortable with me slung over you like this."

He touched her cheek, but she drew away. "Sweetheart, I'm not trying to get rid of you...."

"No, you're right. This is uncomfortable."

She scrambled off him and he immediately came to a full sitting position, then rose to his feet and adjusted his clothes. She'd turned her back and pulled her nightie back into place. Thorne touched her shoulders and felt her stiffen. When she turned she wore a forced smile.

She came up on tiptoe and kissed him lightly. "Good night and thank you."

"Wait a damn minute."

"It's okay, Thorne. Really. You did what you said you were going to do and it was wonderful."

"For God's sake, you make it sound like a vacuum cleaner demonstration that lived up to its guarantee."

She ignored him, adding softly, "I'll see you in the morning." And before he could stop her, she fled the porch into the house. A few seconds later he heard her bedroom door slam.

Hands planted on his hips he stared after her, trying to tell himself he didn't know what in hell had happened.

But he knew. He didn't want what invariably followed fantastic lovemaking—the languid touching, the words of pleasure, the lazy motion that invariably led to more lovemaking. Saturation and satiation. Rosy romantic repletions. Stuff that planted seeds of potential commitment.

So what do you do, Law? You could fake it or you could do what you did. Let her know that there's an infinite variety of ways to reject her.

He reached down and picked up the scrap of lace panties, the fabric cool and feeling as empty as his heart.

He cursed viciously. Good God, man, when are you going to quit being such a bastard?

Chapter 10

The following morning Amanda awakened and lay staring at the ceiling. Words like gullible, foolish, blind to reality or just plain stupid went through her mind. While they all might be true in some sense, she couldn't deny that she'd made love with Thorne quite willingly and with her eyes wide open.

He'd made no promise beyond making sure he satisfied her. And he'd done that far beyond her wildest expectations. So then why the emptiness? Why the deep disappointment those moments afterward when he cut things short?

She'd wanted more. No doubt about that. But more what? She turned her head toward the window, where rain clouds were gathering outside, and tried to stop the sheen of tears that glazed her eyes. More of him. More time to be intimate and more moments to hold him in her heart. She knew better than to hold out hope for anything serious with Thorne; she'd learned that lesson years ago and she should be pain-proof. So why was last night so emotionally different, more devastatingly painful, than that night in the garden?

Amanda squeezed her eyes closed as a new truth opened inside her. Ten years ago her expectations were unencumbered by reality or the possibility of refusal or, God forbid, rejection. Now she knew better. Now she was living and functioning around Thorne with the clear knowledge that this relationship was going nowhere. Reality was that he'd refused to give any ground on taking their relationship seriously. Maybe he hadn't been as cruel as he'd been when she was twenty-one, but the rejection hurt just the same. She knew she had no right to expect more and yet, she'd felt as if there'd been more between them than just lovemaking; she thought Thorne really cared for her in a deep personal way that had nothing to do with being her bodyguard.

Last night she'd instinctively responded as if their joining had been some great turning point. As if making love meant forever, as if it brought the contentment of revealed feelings and special touches, but instead of those lingering sensations this morning she felt twisted and confused and angry.

Amazingly not at Thorne, but at herself, for allowing herself to want the intimacy. My God, he'd given her ample opportunities to change her mind. She pushed the covers back and got out of bed.

Well, she obviously couldn't hide in her room, nor did she intend to act like she'd been swamped with morning-after regrets and embarrassment. Hadn't her original approach been a little flirty and coolly in control of her feelings and actions? Hadn't she called his bluff the other night by saying she didn't love him, that all she wanted was sex, too?

She went into the bathroom and flipped on the light, peering at herself closely. A few whisker burns on her breasts that immediately sent a shiver of memory down her spine. Her mouth was slightly swollen—the thoroughly kissed look, she thought grimly. But her eyes revealed new knowledge; a woman satisfied and a woman who wouldn't object too hard—no, truthfully would probably relish it—if he burst into the bathroom and swept her up in a grand kiss and took her back to bed.

"Fool," she muttered aloud and turned away to step into the shower. She'd be damned if she was going to let him see how much she hurt. In fact, she just might jar him a little just to see how *he* reacted.

Thorne heard the shower turn on just as the coffee finished dripping. He felt like hell and probably looked even worse. His head was pounding with the determination to justify his actions the night before, while at the same time his gut churned and clawed as if it had been denied something it craved. Thorne decided the weeks of celibacy before coming to Sutton Shores followed by that incredible experience with Amanda had his body all screwed up.

Keep the mind clear, he reminded himself. Stop blaming yourself when you did nothing underhanded. He'd made no promises except one and he'd delivered. Or rather she had. He still wasn't sure who had tipped who into that sensational sexual release, while at the same time he wanted to convince himself he didn't want or need her again.

He poured coffee into a big mug, added cream and took a careful sip. Walking over to the table, he set the mug down. He plugged the phone jack in by the counter. Sitting so that he could lean the chair back against the wall, he picked up the receiver and punched out Walker's number.

This not knowing who the stalker was and thereby forcing them into waiting until he made a move was wearing, Thorne decided, trying to justify his uptight nerves. *Face it, man,* he thought. *You aren't unraveling because of the stalker or tedium or the sense of not knowing what's coming next. If this involved anyone besides Amanda, you'd be cool, precise and as calm as cold steel.* God, if it were only that simple. Thorne was restless to get the job done, see her succeed with the project for the girls and assure himself that Walker wasn't getting grayer and older worrying about his daughter. Once accomplished he could split; he could get back to the simplicity of antiterrorist consulting instead of being mired in the complications of wanting Amanda Delaski.

Now Walker's brisk "hello" brought Thorne back to the purpose of his call.

"Good morning," Thorne said huskily.

"I was going to call you," Walker said with far too much chipperness. "I have the list of names you wanted."

Finally, Thorne thought, they were making some progress. He braced the pad of paper on his thigh and picked up a pen. "Shoot."

Walker rattled off names and Thorne wrote them down. "This is it? Just five names?"

"I already eliminated quite a few. Some aren't in the country, two are in prison and one is dead. I already started background checks on those that I gave you."

"As to where they are now, you mean?"

"Yes, and if they've been in any trouble. We might get lucky and find one is a stalker."

"That kind of luck only happens in the movies." Thorne looked at the list, reminding himself that five names worth pursuing were better than twenty dead ends. "I presume you know all these guys personally."

"Yes."

"From the phone call and the stuff our stalker has done so far, do you have any gut reaction to any of the names?"

"I have a gut reaction to all of them," Walker said, revealing a hint of the toughness that had made him such an outstanding CIA operative. "I wouldn't want to meet any of them unarmed and I wouldn't trust one of them within a mile of Amanda."

"I understand that, but I'm looking for similarities. A thread or something that might tie one of the names to this guy we're trying to ID. From what we have so far, the bloodied picture, the harassment of Amanda on the road, do any of these guys seem more suspicious than the others?'' Thorne wasn't sure just what he wanted to hear, but he wanted some way to sort these guys out. Some clue, some characteristic that made any one of them more or less likely.

Walker thought for a moment. "When we arrested Gus Gunther, he'd been making some obscene phone calls. That could come under the heading of harassment. Last address on him is the West Coast. No one there seems to know him so I'm presuming he's either using an alias or he's moved on. Monk is making some calls to check things out."

Thorne made a note beside the name. "How about this Bucco Whorton? Seems to me that name rings a bell."

"Worked for some fringe group intelligence organization in South America in the early seventies. I arrested him when he tried to claim he was a double agent. He made the usual threats about revenge and once he sent me a package that security confiscated. It contained some blood-soaked rags and a message about mopping me up and mailing me to hell."

"Oh, yeah. That's right. I recall you telling me about the bloodied rags."

"That sort of thing—threats, I mean—they aren't unusual and after a while you know which ones to take seriously and which ones not to. The old gut instinct, you mentioned."

"Yeah, but given the circumstances these days, with the caliber of viciousness working out there, every threat is doubly serious and worth following up on. How long ago did Whorton send the bloodied rags?"

"Fifteen years ago or more. Whorton disappeared and to my knowledge hasn't been arrested since. He's probably a long shot."

"If he's our stalker, it's a hell of a long time between threats."

"My thought, too, but you wanted names."

"Yeah, and who knows. Revenge probably doesn't have a deadline." He put a question mark beside Whorton's name.

Before he got to the third name, Amanda came into the kitchen. Thorne followed the easy flow of her body with a guarded curiosity. She wore jeans and a baggy black sweatshirt that hung to her knees. Her hair was pinned up and a few still-damp tendrils curled around her face and neck. She was barefoot, her toenails painted a coppery red. He stared, fascinated, but more than that, he realized that the confident demeanor with which she carried herself acted on his gut like a sucker punch. She looked relaxed, carefree, almost hedonistic when he'd been expecting her to be cool or icy, indifferent or at least delivering a lecture on his lousy behavior the previous night.

Just goes to prove that with Amanda the unexpected occurs more often than the expected, he decided. In fact he should be pleased and relieved she was so cool. That made the possibility of getting into an argument less likely.

Cool, maybe, but icy and indifferent? He scowled. Damn. How could she act as if nothing had happened between them? As if their lovemaking hadn't made any impact? *Can't have it both ways, Law. You hoped she'd be cool and not clingy, hysterical or expecting some promise you couldn't deliver. You got your wish and now you don't like that, either....*

"Morning," she mouthed softly as she passed by him and took the sugar bowl from the middle of the table. He watched through hooded eyes, his body leaning back in the chair, the phone anchored on his shoulder. She got a mug from the cupboard and he took note of the shape of her bottom when she reached up to the shelf. She then poured herself coffee, added two spoonfuls of sugar and slowly stirred while he memorized the soft mound of her breast where it swelled beneath the oversize sweatshirt. Her legs encased in the slender jeans brought back the memory of her warm thighs braced on either side of his hips. And the coppery-painted toenails. How had he missed those last night?

He stared, nearly hypnotized as she walked over and stood close to him to read the list of names. Her scent was fresh and evocative, magnetizing the air and making him instantly hard. Hell, he didn't need this.

"Thorne, you still there?" Walker asked and Thorne realized he'd been listening to Walker talk, but had heard nothing he'd said.

He swallowed, sliding his gaze back to the list and trying to concentrate. "Yeah, I'm here. What about this Harry Lake?"

She placed her hand lightly on the back of his neck, feathering her fingers into his hair. He closed his eyes, wondering how anything so light and ordinary could suddenly seem monumentally compelling. He wanted to drop the phone onto its cradle and drag her down for a deep, deep kiss.

"Harry's an interesting case," Walker said in typical all-business objectivity. His tone also indicated a complicated and long explanation. "For one, he used to be an agent and got into some trouble...."

Her body didn't quite touch him, but she stood so close that if he moved even a minuscule heartbeat she'd be brushing against him. Then as if desire could become reality on merely a thought, she pressed her thigh against his....

Walker was saying, "He had a hair-trigger temper, killed a guy under circumstances that couldn't be justified by the rules of procedure. There was an investigation and a hearing that I conducted concerning unbecoming conduct, reckless use of his weapon. He was found guilty and that, of course, ended his career with us. Although I tried never to let personal feelings mix with my work, I didn't like Harry. I had this sense that what he showed the world wasn't what he really was...."

Her thigh rubbed against his with a deliberate finesse. Thorne thought a rocket had gone off in his head. He gripped her wrist when she didn't back away. She lifted her eyebrows as if she had no idea what was going on.

Thorne said, "Walker, can I give you a call back in about five minutes?"

"And I was just getting into it." He chuckled and Thorne guessed that indeed he was enjoying "working" again despite the circumstances. "Five minutes. I'll talk to you then."

Thorne dropped the phone with a clatter. "Just what in hell are you doing?" he asked her in a low, deep snarl.

She smiled disarmingly, her fingers fiddling with his hair. "Oh, did I have the morning-after scenario wrong? I'm sorry. Did you want me to pout because you sent me away last night?" She made a face that reminded him of a kid who had missed the circus.

"Damn it, Mandy, I did *not* send you away."

"Or did you want me to follow up our, uh, how should I put this?" She tapped a finger on her cheek thoughtfully. "Our intimacy?" She brightened even more. "Or maybe you'd prefer I call it something more earthy. You know, talk dirty?" She leaned close to him, her breath warming his cheek, her mouth so light he barely felt it until she allowed her tongue to just brush the edge of his ear and then said some words about the most male part of him that sent a rocket of reaction straight to his already too-tight jeans.

Dragging air to his bursting lungs, he swore fluently. "Where did you learn to talk like that?"

"Around," she said with a breezy vagueness. "Hmm, does it turn you on?"

He scowled and debated on lying, but what was the use. The truth was too obvious. "You know damn well it does."

She boldly dipped her fingers, folding them over his zipper. In a far too controlled tone, she murmured, "Ah, then this is what you want to do the morning after. You want to do it again.''

Thorne snagged her wrist and plucked her hand away from him. "That's enough, for God's sake. You can stop trying to shock me."

She grinned, her voice dripping with honey. "Why, Thorne, isn't this much better than having me all pouty and red-eyed?" With that she swung her leg across his thighs and settled astride his lap, facing him.

Her scent enveloped him and he groaned.

In a low, sultry voice, she asked, "Want to know what color my underwear is?"

Damn it, he was not going to fall into this. "No," he said bluntly.

She wiggled against him in a provocative, slow grind, lowering her voice to a mere murmur. "Good, because I'm not wearing any."

He let his head drop, swearing under his breath. This was definitely a side of Amanda he'd never seen and in fact wouldn't have believed under most any circumstances. And yet here she was—hot, sultry, sexy and driving him crazy. He wasn't at all sure if he wanted to kiss her, open both their jeans and let passion play out its game or back totally away from her and demand to know just what was in her mind. Obviously, by the direction so far, Thorne concluded, she intended to go as far as necessary. But to prove what? That she could make him want her? Hell, he couldn't recall a moment since he arrived that he hadn't wanted her. That she could prove she controlled him when and if they made love? Perhaps being in control was the issue. He knew she resented his invasion of her private life, but more than that Thorne knew that his treatment of her years ago had made her wary of him. This approach had him off-balance rather than her.

She lifted herself off him, patted his cheek as if she'd made some important point and started to saunter away.

He reached out and grabbed a handful of the baggy sweatshirt. Maybe her intent was to prove some point. Well, maybe he'd just call her bluff. "Wait just a damn minute."

"Dad's waiting for your call."

"Another few minutes isn't going to matter." Winding her shirt around his fist, he dragged her back to him. He turned his chair so that he could pull her between his thighs. Then he settled her bottom against him, no longer caring if she knew how she affected him. Without asking, without pausing for a beat of hesitation, he tunneled his hands beneath her sweatshirt and cupped two very naked breasts. For reasons that defied explanation it turned him on like he couldn't believe possible. "Damn, you weren't kidding, were you? Lord."

She showed no inclination to stop his wandering hands, and, in fact, wiggled even deeper into the cove of his thighs.

"Want me?" she asked with just enough satisfaction that Thorne knew she was thoroughly enjoying this...this catching him by surprise. Perhaps even surprising herself with just how good she was.

He decided to disarm her a little, too. "Hell, no."

"I don't want you, either," she said loftily.

Thorne finessed both nipples and didn't miss the catch in her throat. He then slipped one hand between her thighs, and got an instant response. "If we don't want each other, then how come you're wet and I'm hard?"

"I am not wet."

"Prove it." The moment he said it, he regretted it.

She hesitated a split second and with what was left of his fast-disappearing good sense, he thought he may have called her bluff.

Instead she turned and faced him. Wetting her lips and keeping her lashes lowered, she reached for the snap of her jeans. Thorne's mind got hazy. Enough. If she was wet, it would be all over and damn it, he did not want this to happen again. His body did, but his body's reaction to Amanda wasn't always the most reliable. He placed his hands on her waist, intent on working her away from him. She had the snap open and her fingers on the zipper tab. With excruciating slowness, she nudged it lower and lower, proving without question that she wore no panties. Was she wet? He didn't want to know. Was he hard and wanting her with a fierceness that defied description? Yes.

With more regret than he cared to think about, he lifted her hand from where she was working the zipper down. "Baby, don't."

She shook her head, refusing to look at him, pushing away his attempt to halt her intention. "You wanted to know."

"I'll take your word for it."

As if she didn't hear him, she finished with the zipper and moved her hands to slide the jeans from her hips.

Again he tried to stop her. She reached for his hand to pull it toward her thighs. His raw wire of control sprang taut at its limit. A spectrum of emotions rolled through him that included regret and frustration as much as dogged determination not to be coerced into some seduction scenario that he hadn't expected, wasn't prepared for and knew with the little good sense he still possessed that if they did this again, it would be tantamount to injecting himself with some exotic opiate of desire.

He yanked back, rising to his feet, his eyes glittering with both arousal and fury at himself that this had gotten this far. "Unless you want to do it right here, right this minute, then don't go any further."

Her hands stilled, but she didn't shrink back. Then in a raw whisper, she said, "I hate and despise you, Thorne Law."

He drew in a long breath. The words hurt; he knew he deserved them and yet hearing them after watching this incredible range of emotions that she'd just displayed, he guessed the real kernel of truth was in the words rather than in the sexy come-on.

Not making a move toward her, he wasn't sure what to do. Gentleness could either make her furious or touch some vulnerable cord. And while a part of him wanted to soothe and reassure her that she excited him more than any woman ever had, he feared being that honest with her. Jill had always seized every gesture, every word and casually expressed thought as meaning ten times more than its intent. Except those words she didn't want to believe. Those she simply explained away or ignored.

Thorne had no take on Amanda. As long and as well as he knew her, this episode had proven to him her unpredictability. And using the words hate and despise might be overreactive, but he suspected they contained too much naked truth.

He shoved a hand through his hair. "Why did you do all this? The sexy talk, no underwear, coming on to me? This is all a little extreme for you."

If he thought she was going to suddenly blush and stammer, he couldn't have been more wrong. She glared at him as if he'd insulted her intelligence. "Why? Because you've never seen this side of me? You don't really know me except as either the body you're guarding or the silly declaration of love ten years ago that you dismissed as naive and silly. Now you're seeing a side of me that should appeal to you. Sexy and willing without expecting anything in return. Isn't that what you wanted? Isn't that what most men want from women? I certainly heard the same kind of story from the girls over the past few days. Be cool, be hot, be willing and then walk away. Isn't that some sort of code with the male population these days?"

He scowled. God, put that way, she made it sound as if they were all a bunch of animals. "I can't deny that much of what the girls have experienced has been just sex."

"And what about what we did last night?"

"Not the same."

"Why?"

"For one, we're both mature adults and we made love knowing what we were doing. Besides, we agreed that sex and desire were the issues."

"Exactly," she said with a touch of triumph in her voice. "I couldn't have stated it better myself."

Thorne frowned. Put that way he had to admit there was little difference, yet he wasn't amused by the way it sounded. Too casual, as if their lovemaking was of no more importance than indulging in any other pleasure.

"Do you want an apology for last night? Is that where this is heading?"

"No."

"Then what? A promise from me that it won't happen again? If that's what you want, fine." He stared at her for a moment regretting his next words, for in truth he found this openly flirtatious side of Amanda incredibly arousing. "But you have to promise no repeats of what just took place."

"Do you think I won't be able to stay away from you? Is that what you think? That because I told you a long time ago that I wanted you and that I loved you, that now, since you were the first man who'd satisfied..." She turned away, but not before he mentally recorded the pain in her eyes. "You're very good at exciting me even when my intent was to excite you. And I won't deny sex with you is fantastic, but that doesn't change the fact that if I could get you out of my life right now, I wouldn't hesitate a minute."

He rose, gripped her shoulders and turned her around to face him. "Did it ever occur to you that the feeling is mutual?"

"Oh, it occurred to me. It does every time I wonder what vengeful fate stuck us together again. I should have told Dad what happened between us years ago instead of trying to be mature and objective."

"He already knew," Thorne said flatly.

She blinked, her breath catching in astonishment. "He knew? But how?" Then her eyes widened. "You told him? You bastard!"

"Take it easy."

"Easy!" Her voice rose another octave. "Just where in hell did you get the right to interfere in my private life?"

"I was there, too, remember?" He deliberately kept his voice even.

"You rejected me!" She took a step closer, her hands balling into fists.

"For your own good."

"No, damn it, no!" She shoved him, her body trembling as she pummeled her fists against him.

Thorne grabbed her and shook her lightly. "Yes! Did you hear me? I said, yes! I had no choice, Amanda. *No choice.*"

"You didn't have to hurt me, to say all those things about me having a crush and being drunk and not knowing about love and what a man really wants from a woman."

Then with a bluntness his insides shrank from, a forthrightness he knew she didn't expect, he said, "It got rid of you, didn't it?"

His words lay between them with the scorching pain of a red-hot poker. The silence of the room thickened so that their breathing clamored in the quiet. Outside, the dark clouds brooded across the sky, releasing intervals of rain.

Amanda stood still, her head down, her arms folded tight around her body.

Thorne stood just inches from her, hands resting loosely on his hips. *Tell her the truth, man, tell her.* Yet he knew that the longer the silence dragged on, the more likely that her earlier words of hating and despising him would be true. What had he asked himself the other night? When was he going to quit being such a bastard? Now would be a start. He didn't have to tell her everything. Just enough.

In as even a voice as he could manage, he said, "I had to get rid of you because if I hadn't ... Hell," he muttered in frustration, but then continued, "If I'd stuck around, I'd have been no different than the guys Julie and the others talked about. I would have had your virginity, broken your heart and lost your father's friendship and respect."

Amanda studied him, obviously confused. "You're saying that you did me a favor?"

"You could say that. I was young, ambitious, too damn sure of myself and you were a major complication I hadn't expected. Fooling with the boss's daughter is always trouble. I had future plans for my own business and your father had been encouraging me. Winding up in bed with you would have sent some bad signals to Walker. Character stuff such as I fooled with young virgins, I can't keep business and personal stuff separated and worst of all I can't keep my pants zipped. I didn't want to be accused of any of those things. Once I'd kissed you I knew that I had to get out."

"But why couldn't you have explained it to me that way back then?"

"Get real, Amanda. You were wasted and horny. Hardly a combination fraught with the ability to comprehend reality. Besides, I didn't want any loose ends. I needed it to be very clear that I didn't want to be involved with you."

She stared at him for what seemed a century, before walking to the chair and sitting down. To his astonishment she didn't go into a litany of accusations or recite her own list of his less than noble character traits. "In other words you thought I was too starry-eyed to take you seriously unless you were blunt and cruel."

"In a nutshell, yes."

Amanda nodded. From the moment she'd made the decision in her bathroom to be seductive and breezy rather than appear at all affected by his dismissal of her the night before, she'd felt good and very much in control of her feelings about Thorne. She'd expected kisses and, yes, she'd expected they'd make love again. Instead she'd managed to make him furious. She knew he wasn't like other men; he didn't just take the obvious reason and run with it. In this case she'd been willing. No, *more* than willing: she had been seductively anxious to make love. She couldn't imagine most men refusing, but Thorne had. Perhaps it proved he was unreachable unless he wanted to be. Certainly that was true with Jill. He had agreed to marry her only when he'd feared for her life and wanted her out of Germany. He'd come here to guard Amanda from the stalker because her father had called him, not because she was the great love and desire of his life. Her approach this morning may have taken him by surprise, may have confused and even physically frustrated him, but Thorne never lost control of the issue or of what he wanted and didn't want to do.

She took a deep breath and laced her hands together. She had come out of this with something, however. She'd discovered a depth of honor in Thorne. Ten years ago when he'd rejected her, it had been for larger reasons than denying her what she wanted. And just moments ago, he'd refused to just tumble into making love. Oh, God, she thought, suddenly realizing she'd participated in this refusal by telling him she hated and despised him. Hardly the words a man wants to hear before he takes a woman to bed, she concluded grimly. In a way, she'd set herself up for this rejection.

He'd walked to the counter and refilled his mug. He did the same with hers.

"Thanks," she said, taking it from him. Their fingers brushed minutely. Hers were chilled and his were too warm.

Gripping the mug for its warmth, she spoke in the calmest voice she could muster, "So what did you tell Dad about your decision to leave? He never said anything to me besides you wanting to move on and get started on your own security business."

"That's basically what I told him."

"What did you tell him about us?"

"That guarding you was getting too complicated and too personal on my part. He understood. You weren't a kid and neither was I. He saw the wisdom in my resigning. That kiss in the garden... I went too damn far. It should have been sweet and virginal. I was older, I knew better and I should have kept things under control. But I wasn't going to tell Walker any of that. Hell, he would have had me arrested and probably castrated."

"So you took all the blame and handed in your resignation?"

"Walker was aware I'd planned to leave after you went off to college. I just moved it up a few months."

"When he called you about guarding me this time, did he bring up why you resigned the first time?"

"He asked me if I thought you'd be a personal problem for me."

"And?"

"I said no."

"And that was that?"

"Walker knows I wouldn't lie to him."

"Of course, you'd never lie to him, just as you haven't lied to me or made any promises. I guess last night was just a culmination of what we both wanted and didn't take that night in the garden, wasn't it?"

Was it? Thorne wasn't sure. That seemed too simple and the lovemaking too incredible. Yet, maybe that was all it was. It sure was a lot less complicated to leave it at that level. But instead of answering her, he said, "I better call your father back. He's going to wonder what happened."

She nodded, but didn't seem to be really listening. Thorne picked up the phone as she walked to the kitchen window. She stood still too long to be just staring out at the rain.

"What is it?" he asked before he punched the phone number.

"A florist delivery truck. Looks like the same one who delivered the flowers at the other house. He's stopping in front of the house." She left the kitchen, then called back, "It's even the same delivery person."

Thorne gave just half his attention while he listened to Walker's phone ring. He heard Amanda thank the delivery person and then he heard the front door close.

"Walker? Sorry for the delay. Amanda and I got to talking. Now where were we? Oh, yeah, Harry Lake."

He glanced up, expecting to see Amanda carrying a bouquet of flowers. Instead he saw a woman so pale and shaky that she had to grip the doorjamb. He dropped the phone and took the few steps to her in three strides, taking hold of her before her knees buckled. His eyes searched the area around the front door, but no one was there.

"What happened?" he asked.

"Th-the box of f-flowers ..."

He saw a long white box on a table, a red ribbon trailing off the edge. The lid was upside down on the floor as if it had been dropped hastily.

"What about the flowers?"

"They're dead."

"Dead?" He frowned. "You mean wilted or not as fresh as they should be?"

She shook her head vigorously. "No, dead, but more than that ..." As he started toward the florist box, she stopped him. "Don't l-leave me," she cried in a voice so terrified Thorne couldn't believe it was Amanda's.

"I won't leave you, baby. I promise." He slipped his arm around her and she clung as if he were a lifeline. He noted she stayed almost behind him as if she couldn't bear to see what was in the box again.

Thorne stopped and stared down at the contents. Then, slowly closing his eyes, he muttered, "Oh, God."

Chapter 11

Amanda clutched his arm and tried to turn away from the gruesome sight. "It's from him, isn't it?" Her voice was barely discernible, her question evincing more terrified resignation than curiosity.

"Yeah. A real psycho."

The long white florist box had been fashioned into a mock coffin. Lined with white satin, a dress had been stuffed with nylon stockings to resemble a miniature of Amanda's size and arranged in the position of a corpse. A recent newspaper photo served as her face. And scattered across the stuffed dress and the picture were dozens of dead yellow roses.

"He's going to kill me," she said with a numb-sounding voice. "This is some horrible warning so he can watch me sweat and shake and worry about when he's going to strike again."

"He definitely likes going for the grotesque," Thorne said in disgust, equally concerned. "Another reason it seems logical that he knows your father and perhaps knows you.

He knows freaking you out is going to take some original-
ity.''

"Well, I can do without the bastard's creativity," she
muttered, feeling her anger rise now that the initial shock
was over.

Thorne stared down at the box, picking up a pencil from
a holder and carefully moving the dead flowers away from
the stuffed figure. "Mandy, look at this dress."

She'd seen enough, but she did as he requested. After
staring at it a few moments, she gripped Thorne's arm
tighter. "My God that dress is just like the linen one—" She
couldn't finish the sentence.

"Not like it. I'll bet it's the dress you wore the day the
girls arrived."

She wanted to deny it, but a closer inspection indicated it
definitely was the melon dress. There was a dirt smear on the
shoulder; a swipe from Thorne's hand when he'd kissed her
for luck just before the girls arrived. She could only nod,
slightly nauseated by the knowledge that this creep had been
going through her clothes, handling her personal things.

"Where did you put it when you changed clothes?"

"In a basket with other things to go to the dry cleaner.
The basket's in my room."

Quickly they went to her room and she began to go
through the circular container woven of heavy straw.

Thorne stood behind her watching, his mind racing to fit
pieces together. His knee-jerk inclination was to get
Amanda away from here, but to where? And was running
the wisest course? In the end it could prove more dangerous if she was too isolated. If he followed his gut, it wasn't
even a question. He'd wrap her up and carry her around the
world if it would keep her safe, but the next question was
would she go with him? Probably if she felt there was any
risk to the girls or the project or anyone else involved. But
as far as he could determine, the stalker seemed to be to-

tally fixated on Amanda and her father to the exclusion of anyone else.

She sat back on her haunches, looked up at him and shook her head. "It's not here. He did steal my dress."

"I was afraid of that."

"Then he was in here. He must have left the bedside light on."

"Probably."

"Which means he was planning this for some time. He came here deliberately to get the dress to make up that awful box."

"Yeah."

She got to her feet. "You're not saying much."

"Just trying to figure out how this guy thinks."

"Well, I can tell you a few things," she said indignantly. "He likes to taunt and enjoys the pain of others. He's like a bully in the schoolyard. He probably works alone and doesn't have any friends and makes little effort to cultivate them." She paced the room, her hands fisted, her eyes snapping with outrage.

Thorne wasn't amused as much as relieved. He knew there was little that she couldn't handle and where Jill or Olivia would have been screaming or crying at seeing that mock casket and knowing how close this guy could get, Amanda had rallied her good sense and, more important, her outrage.

"You know what else?" She faced him, her cheeks flushed, her breathing just a little fast.

He folded his arms. "No, what?"

"He's probably the kind that when he's finally caught the neighbors will say—" she assumed a wide-eyed shocked look, her voice a mock tremble "—why he was such a nice man. Kept to himself, smiled a lot and even donated money to the local fund for the homeless. I just can't believe that he would do such terrible things. My, oh, my."

Thorne chuckled. "I shouldn't find it amusing, but you're right. The scary thing is the ingeniousness of a sick mind's ability to make the creep look ordinary, to look like a neighbor, to get that close and never be suspected."

"Well, in my opinion, he's warped and delusional. Coming in here, stealing a dress and leaving the light on is not a sane act. If we'd discovered it missing..."

"Even if we had, I doubt we could have concluded it was for a coffin made from a florist box," he said matter-of-factly. "Besides, I don't think he cared if you discovered the missing dress. He wouldn't have left that light on otherwise." Thorne thought for a moment. "No, I think he wanted you to know he was here, hoped you'd discover the missing dress and get scared enough to run. Then he could go after you. For example, if you'd stopped that night on Town Beach Road, he would have probably made his move then. When you didn't, he decided to turn up the heat."

"Oh, terrific." She grimaced. "Since I'm not running in hysterical circles, he keeps doing grotesque stuff until I go crazy."

"Santa Claus, he's not." Thorne paused. "Which brings up another issue. It's time to call in the police—"

"I'd rather not."

When he started to reinforce his argument, she interrupted him. "What can they do besides take my complaint and file a report? Then word will get out that I'm being stalked. The publicity will wreak havoc with the project. Besides, Dad has always dealt with these things without involving the local police. It tends to make the neighbors not at all sure they want you around if the police have to be called for every nutcake who makes a threat. And Dad has had plenty of threats in the past."

"Just the same, this little gift—" he indicated the box "—is pretty serious. The dress is proof of theft. In addition, there's breaking and entering."

She folded her arms in front of her as if she was reconsidering. "But we don't know who did this and neither will they. They'll ask a zillion questions I can't answer, snoop into my love life for disgruntled boyfriends and worst of all the stalker will probably disappear until the cops give up and then he'll be back." She scowled, annoyance in her voice. "Not to mention the fact that when I went to them that night the car or truck or van or whatever it was threatened me on Town Beach Road, they were less than no help."

"The officer told you why. There was no evidence then."

"There was my word for God's sake." Her tone very definitely showed her lingering frustration that the police hadn't acted. He knew there was no point in trying to convince her otherwise. "Damn it, Thorne, we could be close to finding out who this guy is. Then, of course, the police will have to be called in, but please not now."

Now, he thought with reluctant admiration, he knew one reason why she was so successful in her work. She never let anything in her personal life interfere—even a stalker playing head games. Odd, when he'd worked for her father, Amanda had done the opposite. Meshed the two and, too often, forgot he was her bodyguard. Her confession of love had revealed her attempt to personalize their professional relationship. He couldn't help but wonder if his rejection of her and her feelings had been the basis for what he'd just witnessed. She had her life at work—the girls and the project. And her personal life, which now that he thought about it, wasn't much. Hell, Law, you're hardly one to make the comparison. Your personal life could fit into a bullet casing and still have room for the gunpowder. Yeah, he'd take an occasional weekend in Paris or Naples or London with one of the women he'd known over the years. Maybe a trip back to the States to keep in touch with old friends like Walker, but beyond that all he did was work. Perhaps the brush with Amanda years ago and then the disaster with Jill could be the source of his own resistance to any kind of personal commitment, but of late he'd begun to wonder if there were deeper reasons—some he'd staunchly refused to think about.

So here they were, he decided speculatively. Together for professional reasons and fighting the personal stuff. Sexual, yes, but deep down he liked her. He admired her guts and her determination not to let anything or anyone stand in the way of making the project work for the girls.

She peered at him. "I hope your silence means you agree with me."

Thorne sighed. He didn't want to argue and he, too, doubted the local cops could do much beyond endless questions and paperwork. It would be entirely different if they knew who the stalker was. And Walker had experts working on the names on that list. "Most women would have taken one look at that box and wanted to call the local cops, the state and the FBI."

"Well, I'm not most women," she said tightly.

"Yeah, this would be a helluva lot easier if you were," he muttered in a low voice.

"Besides, if the stalker is watching me that closely he has to know about you."

"Know what? That I'm living with you?" Thorne shook his head dismissively. "If he was the one in the bushes that first night, then he saw the kiss. He probably concluded the obvious."

"That we're lovers."

"Yeah. No one knows who I really am, so if he asked around all he'd hear was that I was here helping you."

"Which may work to our advantage. He might not see you as a problem to be disposed of."

"Now, that's real reassuring." He took her arm and led her back to the kitchen. "I need to call your father. With two interrupted phone calls, he'll be frantic to know if you're okay." He paused a moment, then pushed the phone toward Amanda. "Better yet, you call him and then phone the house and tell them you won't be there until this afternoon. I'm going to take a closer look at that box."

"Wait. What do I say?"

"Tell your dad the truth. Maybe one of those names on his list has a fixation with gruesome games. As for the house..." He paused a moment, then decided why the hell not. Between their tension-filled talk earlier and the florist box, a little lightness was needed. He winked. "Tell them we decided to stay in bed for the day."

Amanda didn't miss a beat. She scoffed as she punched out the numbers. "I already tried that with you, but you weren't interested."

"Resistance, babe, is a lot different than lack of interest."

With a superior look, she said, "I didn't want you to resist."

He tangled his fingers in her hair and tipped her head back. In a low, meaningful voice, he said, "Believe me, it was about the hardest thing I've ever done."

Then he kissed her, hot and deep.

Twenty minutes later, she returned to the front hall, where Thorne had just finished working his way through the box.

"Any progress?" she asked.

"Unfortunately he didn't drop a business card by mistake. No fingerprints, either."

"How'd you check for fingerprints?"

He held up a small palm-size object that looked like a matchbook. "New gadget. It picks up any residue of oil from a fingerprint and flashes red. It doesn't do fingerprint analysis but it's faster and there's no chance of smearing. Our agency has been using it for about a year."

"Amazing."

"No end to the technological age." Thorne put the object back into a small black case. "What did Walker say?"

"He's upset and worried. He wants you to call him as soon as you can."

"Did you assure him you're okay?"

She nodded, staring at the pile of dead roses on the floor.

"What about Sally or Ginny? Did you tell them you wouldn't be over today?"

Indicating the dismantled box, she sighed. "It looks so harmless when it's all taken apart. Like a bunch of discards for the trash. Yes, I talked to Ginny. I told her I'd be there in about an hour."

He lifted an eyebrow. "Nothing much stops you from doing what you think needs to be done, does it?"

"Thorne, staying here and wringing my hands over this guy would be worse than going to the other house."

"I can see why you're the head counselor. Not even a stalker's gruesome gift is going to interfere."

"Would it if it were you?" she asked.

"Touché." He stood up, brushing his hands together. "Nothing else here," he said, disappointed. "Nothing notable and no labels on anything. Even the lid doesn't have the embossed logo of the name of the shop—" He stopped, a sudden thought occurring to him.

Amanda drew closer. "What? What are you thinking?"

"You said the guy looked like the guy who delivered the flowers the other day. Was it the same guy?"

"The van appeared to be the same and he looked about the right age and build, but I don't know for sure. Remember, you wouldn't let me near him?"

"Yeah, I remember."

"You talked to him so you got a close look."

"But I didn't get a look at him today." He cursed in frustration.

"You think the delivery guy—if it was the same man— might have seen the stalker?"

"Someone had to have seen him. That box didn't get into the truck by magic."

"Let's call the flower shop and find out." She hurried to the kitchen and pulled the phone book from the drawer. Without glancing at Thorne, she said, "What was the name of the florist?"

He frowned, trying to recall. The van had been gray and he recalled a flower design on the door, but he didn't remember a name. Then again, at the time, his concern had been more over the unscheduled deliveries. "I don't remember. Can't be that many florists in Sutton Shores. Call them all."

There were four plus a garden shop. Amanda called each one.

"But that's impossible," she said to the last florist she spoke to, then repeated what she had said to the others. "There was a box of two-dozen yellow roses and a bouquet of mixed flowers. Can you check your deliveries for that day once again?"

Thorne stared at the bag of trash on the floor. The meat market's name was stamped on the sack. "Mandy, did you ever call Bing and thank him for the flowers?"

She held her hand up to indicate he should wait until she finished. Then her shoulders slumped and she muttered, "Thank you for checking." She hung up, discouraged. "None of them delivered flowers here today and none made a delivery to the other house. They did suggest some names of florists in nearby towns. Apparently they often deliver down here. Now what were you asking?"

Thorne, who had walked over to the half-filled bag, picked it up and turned to Amanda. "Bing sent you that mixed bouquet. Did you ever call and thank him?"

"Certainly, I did. Later that afternoon. I tried to get Dad, also, but there was no answer. At Bing's, I talked to one of the girls—the one who thought you were so gorgeous—she said he was busy with a supplier, but she'd take a message. I told her to thank Bing for me and she promised she would."

"And your father?"

"I talked to him the night we came back and found the light on. I probably forgot all about the flowers, what with all that happened at the house and then wondering who might have been in here. Now that I think about it, I know he didn't say anything. What's your point?"

"That maybe the guy who sent the dead flowers and the stuffed dress also sent the fresh flowers and the bouquet."

Amanda shook her head. "But that would be crazy. There's too many chances he could have been caught."

"Doing what? Sending you bouquets of beautiful flowers and signing someone else's name? It could be assumed he was a shy secret admirer. You could be the one sounding paranoid. But more important, there's a chance you would have been more rattled than you are now if you had found out. Don't you see? The guy really is playing major head games. It doesn't matter if you find out what he's up to or not. He's set up his agenda so that either way you're scared. The more he can wear you down, make you crazy, the better he likes it. If you'd talked to Bing and your father and thanked them for the flowers and they said they never sent them, what would have happened?"

Amanda huddled in the chair with a shiver. "I would have wondered where they came from."

"Exactly. But more important, you and I would have figured out days ago that this jerk is gonna yank your chain just to see how you react. In fact I would bet he was disappointed that you didn't catch on to the other flowers."

"God, Thorne," she said, both scared and puzzled. "This is like working through some strategy game."

Thorne got on the phone and called Bing's Meat Market and then Walker. Both confirmed that they hadn't sent flowers to Amanda. In the meantime, Amanda excused herself to get ready to go over to the other house.

* * *

In her bedroom, she felt as if she were moving by rote. The elusive stalker was back with gruesome surprises. The project that she had such high hopes for was working nicely, but she felt as if her attention was divided into too many compartments.

Her feelings for Thorne, that while she refused to embrace them joyfully, made her heart leap with expectation and a need to just take whatever she could. That, of course, was a path to disaster and heartbreak. Yet, with any encouragement, she might have thrown aside good sense and her damnable pride and just gone with whatever he wanted to give. Sort of a can't-stop-the-feeling attitude.

Definitely the sign of a desperate woman, she concluded as she changed into a blouse and heavy sweater. She pulled on slacks and socks and sneakers.

Dressed, she slid her hands into her slacks pockets and walked to the window. She looked out at the rain splashing down the glass in silvery sheets. In the distance, the ocean stirred fiercely and the wind whistled through the trees. She had an odd sense of foreboding that she wanted to blame on the gray and dark day, not so much about the stalker, but about the direction of her own life—specifically a life without Thorne.

As much as she'd railed against him and as many times as she'd said she didn't want him around, she knew in her heart it was a lie. And just when she'd decided that no matter what her heart wanted, she would stick to what she knew to be absolutely true. He'd rejected her once and despite all that had passed between them this time, that basic fact hadn't changed. He didn't want her in the way she wanted to be wanted. Her common sense would tell her to accept that and stop looking for some sliver of hope, but then he would do something that excited her, or thrilled her, or just plain made her realize that the moment in the garden on her twenty-first birthday had indeed been a turning point.

She'd loved him then, she'd fought to forget him for years after he'd rejected her and she wanted to be coolly detached from any feelings for him now. Yet part of her yearned for him.

That part of her had allowed too many kisses and touches.

That part of her had made love with him willingly, gloriously, and had emerged so totally spent and satisfied, she'd wanted more and more.

And that part of her had made a last-ditch attempt earlier that morning to throw him off guard; a kind of backhanded seduction that now, in retrospect, did nothing but reveal how very affected she was by him and how unaffected he was by her.

She smiled ruefully. What had he said? Resistance wasn't a lack of interest? In a low, but resigned voice, she muttered to her reflection, "Well, in my opinion, Thorne Law, there's not a whole lot of difference."

"Whole lot of difference in what?"

She swung around. He stood in the doorway, dressed in jeans and a heavy gray-and-green striped rugby shirt with the collar flipped up. He'd pushed the sleeves up his forearms and was watching her with an intense curiosity.

"Hi," she said, suddenly flustered and at the same time annoyed at her instant reaction to him.

"Whole lot of difference in what?" he asked again.

That there's no difference in the pain of being rejected today and rejected ten years ago. In fact, it just may be worse. But to Thorne she said, "Oh, nothing, I was just thinking out loud. You ready to go?" She started forward and then stopped staring. "What did you do to your hair?"

"Nothing, it's fine," he grumbled.

"Thorne, you cut it."

"I made that deal with Julie so I decided I better not welsh on it. I just trimmed the ends."

"But it's uneven."

"Just a couple of places. I don't have eyes in the back of my head."

"That's why barbers open barbershops," she said logically.

"And since I doubt you want to go there before we go to the house, I figured this will do."

"Well, it certainly won't do. It looks terrible." At his scowl, she walked forward. "Turn around and let me see.'

He did, but reluctantly. After a close inspection, she said, "Come over here and sit down and I'll see if I can even it up."

He backed up as if she'd suggested a buzz cut. "No way."

"For heaven's sake, don't be such a baby." She gripped his wrist and tugged, but he refused to move. Sighing, she said, "You can sit in front of the mirror and watch every snip."

Still reluctant, he asked, "You ever cut a guy's hair before?"

She raised her eyebrows and gave him an affronted look. "You mean I forgot to tell you I have a secret life as a hairdresser to the stars?"

"Very funny."

She patted his cheek, ignoring his scowl. "Oh, Thorne, you're the one being funny. This isn't brain surgery and it will just take a few minutes."

"My mother cut my hair once and she swore she knew what she was doing. I looked like a plucked chicken when she got finished. Believe me at ten years old facing my friends was traumatic. I spent the hottest month of the summer wearing a hat."

She nodded somberly, then her mouth broke into a grin and finally she erupted in laughter.

Thorne glared at her for a few seconds, then chuckled. "Okay, it's a stupid reaction."

"Your reaction at ten was quite normal, but I was laughing at the paradox now. Here you are helping to stop worldwide terrorism, protecting me from some psycho stalker and the idea of me cutting your hair has you terrified."

"It's not getting it cut, but having it done—"

She pressed her fingers to his mouth as if to stop some bad language. "You weren't going to say by a woman were you? I already know woman drivers make you nervous."

"Sexist, huh?"

"And unfair."

"Noted, but is it all right if I object when they don't know what in hell they're doing?"

She grinned. "Then you've just gotten lucky. I've trimmed my own hair and Sally's and I even did Monk's once."

"You did Monk?" he asked with genuine astonishment.

"And he was very impressed."

"I'm impressed. He's very antsy about anyone touching him." Then he nodded. "I guess if Monk survived it... Okay, you can fix it, but just even it out enough to hide the hacks."

"Such unflinching bravery," she commented with teasing sarcasm.

"Do I get rewarded?"

"Depends on whether I have to tie you down."

"Now that sounds interesting. Leather or silk?"

Amanda laughed and considered the way she knew he'd look in leather.

Thorne grinned and considered the way he knew she'd look draped in silk.

She took his arm and led him to a chair that faced her dressing table mirror. He sat down and she went to the bathroom for a towel and her scissors.

Moments later, with scissors in one hand, she leaned down so that her cheek brushed his. "Just to let you know before I start. I love it long."

His eyes met hers in the mirror. "Yeah?"

"Yes," she murmured as she straightened and then slowly slipped her fingers through the silky waves.

She stood behind him, finding the uneven ends and feathering them into the rest. His head occasionally brushed her breasts and she felt the jolt all the way through her. His eyes never left her face and not once did he comment on the trimming that she was doing.

For Amanda it almost seemed surreal. The silence, the splashing rain, the snip, snip, snip of the scissors. Finally she finished and laid the scissors down. She removed the towel, careful not to spill the snipped hair. Reaching for her comb, she watched his reflection as she combed it smooth so that it fell into place. The waves were still the sexy shaggy style that she loved, the length now just below his collar.

Thorne pressed his head against her breasts and she felt an immediate leap in her pulse. She didn't pull away and in fact brushed the back of her hands down his cheeks to his shoulders. The placket opening of his shirt allowed her fingers to just pause on the trapped warmth of his skin.

"You feel good," he murmured. "But you've got too many clothes on."

"You should have taken advantage of it this morning."

"And last night."

"Yes. Now it's too late."

"Never too late, babe. They come off as easily as they go on." He reached up and pulled her around, seating her on his lap, her back to his chest so that they both faced the mirror.

He folded his hands over her breasts and despite the layers of clothes her nipples tightened. Pressing his mouth into her neck and taking kissing liberties with her skin, he lowered one hand with tantalizing slowness to the apex of her thighs. Amanda didn't move despite the clamoring inside her that made her want to arch and press her own hand over his. He cupped her, lightly lifting and sealing her against him so that she felt his arousal.

"I want you," he whispered with intoxicating intimacy. "I know I shouldn't. I know I should be strong and..."

"Resistant?" she asked softly, hoping he wouldn't pull away, languid in her need to feel him, to have him deep inside.

He pushed his hands beneath her clothes and unhooked her bra. "You've destroyed all my defenses. Being with you makes me want, baby, not just your body, but your heart and your soul."

His words were so profound, so startlingly honest that she wasn't sure she'd heard correctly. Maybe she'd imagined them, but her heart soared as if some mystical secret had broken open between them. She made no protest when he lifted her and carried her to the bed.

"Hurry," she whispered into the hush sweetness.

Quickly, their eyes never leaving each other, they disposed of their clothes.

He pulled her against him and with a groan took her down onto the bed with him. "This should be slow and easy," he muttered, his body feeling as if it was on fire.

"Oh, Thorne, please... I need you.... I need you, so much."

Thorne slid deep inside her, feeling her close around him as if she had been created especially for him. She arched high, her nails digging into his back. Thorne braced his weight, rising and then dipping deep; a feast of the senses, a banquet of heat.

In a perfectly timed, liquid rhythm, the glorious flow of wonder gripped them as Amanda arched into him, her climax showering down through her with such magic, she felt she'd shared a miracle with him. Thorne whipped his head up and back, a fuse of heat erupting down his body in layers and layers of profound pleasure.

As the rain splashed down the glass, they lay replete, satiated, both feeling wonderfully alive.

When the telephone rang suddenly, they both jumped and then collapsed on a burst of laughter.

"Are you gonna answer it or am I?" she asked, kissing his chin.

"You better." He nuzzled her neck, nipping playfully at her earlobe. "I can't move, never mind sound intelligent."

She reached the phone on the fourth ring. "Hello?"

"Amanda? Oh, thank God I got you."

"Oh, Ginny, I'm sorry," she said quickly, guilt immediately swamping her. Not for being with Thorne, but for letting her need for him distract her and make her late. "I know I said I'd be there in an hour. Something came up." Thorne muttered something explicit and she stuck her tongue out at him. He lifted his eyebrows and she grinned at his naughty inference. To Ginny, she said, "I'm on my way."

"No, it's not that you're late. It's—" She choked and gulped, making it obvious she was trying to control herself.

Alarmed, Amanda sat up, her face suddenly serious. "Ginny, take it easy and tell me what happened. Is it the girls? A fight? Is someone hurt?"

By this time Thorne had rolled off the bed and was pulling on his clothes. "What's going on?" he mouthed.

She looked at him and shook her head.

"E-everything here is o-okay." She sniffled and sobbed. "The p-police are h-here."

"The police!" She glanced at Thorne, who just shrugged, obviously as mystified as she was. "Don't tell me the girls—"

"No, no," Ginny sobbed. "It's...sweet mother of God...it's Sally."

Amanda gripped the phone, a cold chill rushing through her. "What about Sally?"

"She's d-dead. Murdered."

Chapter 12

Sally, murdered.

No! It's a mistake. A god-awful mistake.

Numbness drained her thoughts so that Ginny's words iced up her mind. Amanda barely recalled getting dressed and the frantic rush to the other house. The only reason she'd been aware that, instead of walking, they'd taken her car was that she wasn't wet from the rain. An inane thing to think about, but her mind's attempt to deny the horror had embraced the ordinary.

The police car, two officers, Ginny's sobbing, the confusion and tears of the girls all dispelled any notion there'd been a mistake. The house was chaotic and to Amanda's relief, Thorne quickly took control. Ordinarily she would have stepped forward and taken charge, but her mind kept going over and over Ginny's words. Sally. Murdered.

It was incomprehensible and Amanda desperately wanted to hope that Sally would rush in the door laughing and out of breath, her face animated, her enthusiasm high, her sometimes too-nosy questions bubbling from her lips. Oh, what she wouldn't give for some of Sally's too-nosy questions.

Thorne got everyone seated and quiet while the officers, clearly unsure where to begin, started their questions with Ginny, the staff and the girls. Once established that most of the information known about Sally was work-related rather than personal, the men turned to Amanda.

When the others got up to leave, Thorne said, "The police would probably like you to stay. Just in case you remember something when they question Amanda." The officers nodded, the younger one giving Thorne a grateful look.

Thorne sat down beside Amanda and she whispered to him, "Why would they send two such inexperienced officers?"

"Don't be too hard on them, babe. Murder isn't exactly an everyday occurrence here. My guess is that they're so afraid they might bungle things that the cool, brusque approach of most cops hasn't had a chance to be shaped."

The younger officer, who stood almost military straight in his newly starched uniform, said, "Ms. Delaski, you knew Ms. Roche well, can you tell us—"

"First tell me what happened to her." Amanda sat forward, her eyes wide. "Ginny said she was murdered."

"It appears to be a homicide."

"Appears! Don't you know?"

Thorne touched her arm. "Easy," he murmured.

The officer looked at the other one, who, after a scowl, nodded for his partner to answer. "The autopsy will determine the exact cause of death, but from the marks on her throat and the location of the body, we're proceeding on the presumption of murder."

Thorne said, "Marks on her throat? You're saying she was strangled?"

"The evidence indicates that, yes."

"Where was she found?" Thorne asked, giving Amanda a minute to compose herself.

"Near the Dumpster behind her building. One of the tenants spotted the body when she went to empty some trash. She later identified her as Sally Roche."

Amanda sat with her knees pressed together, her hands so tightly clasped her knuckles were white. "Who would do such a horrible thing to her? She never hurt anyone and I don't think she had an enemy in the world." She glanced up, her eyes misted with tears. "Could it have been a random killing? Or a robbery?

"We don't think so, ma'am."

Thorne folded his hand over her chilled ones. The two officers were notably uncomfortable with revealing the horrific details. From the exchanged glances between them, Thorne guessed dead women beside Dumpsters were definitely an aberration. Sutton Shores, by and large, was a safe community and fairly untouched by the violence of the cities. Thorne knew it was one of Amanda's reasons for having wanted the troubled teens project here to begin with. The almost idealistic atmosphere was just right and Amanda and the Sutton Shores Youth Group had especially sought a place without drugs and violence so that the girls could begin to believe they could have lives free of those things. Sure, the approach was utopian and the goals somewhat unrealistic, but Thorne had seen a change in the girls. Not gargantuan, but the positive images and surroundings *had* taken effect.

Then, with somewhat of an inner jolt, he realized that he, too, wanted Amanda's pilot project not just to marginally succeed, but to be held up as a model for more houses, as a reason to increase private funding and provide the kind of positive changes illustrated by the Sutton Shores project. He couldn't help but think that if there had been such programs in his own neighborhood things would have been different. He would have benefited from having a place where someone would listen to him, would care, where someone would have encouraged him to release the bottled-up anger he'd felt at his own mother's murder. Now Sally's murder only served to remind him of his own inner turmoil that had never quite gone away. Deeply entrenched anger that he'd allowed to devour that part of him capable of feeling love and commitment—anger that became a brace against getting hurt, a thick wall to keep him objective and distant, a binding vow to keep himself from feeling anything emotional.

And yet here with Amanda, from the onset, he'd fought getting involved to little avail. The stalker and his next move worried him, and wanting Amanda had become more than an obsession, a fierce need that involved not just making love, but wanting love with her. A need that he was fast losing the will to ignore and resist. And now this.

Thorne had little doubt Olivia and the committee would view Sally's death not so much as a tragedy but as a public relations disaster. And in most PR situations anything controversial or image-damaging was avoided as assiduously as a dozen roaming skunks at a picnic.

He squeezed Amanda's hands as the two officers tried to frame their questions in a delicate manner. Thorne said, "Mandy, the police need to know some personal things about Sally."

"That's right, Mr. Law. I know this is difficult, Ms. Delaski, but since Ms. Roche had no family here, the people in her apartment building all mentioned your name as someone she was particularly close to. They mentioned your friendship and that you and she worked here at this house. What about boyfriends? Did she have any?"

"She did have one, but he moved to Chicago recently and they ended their relationship."

"A friendly parting?"

Amanda drew a deep breath. Just a few days ago Sally and she had talked about how insecure and unwanted she'd felt. And now... "Actually, no. Apparently he wasn't as serious as Sally thought. He took the career change as a chance to move on and end the relationship. That's what Sally told me."

"How did she feel about that?"

"Hurt, angry, unsure of herself."

"So she'd been depressed and upset since she told you about the boyfriend leaving?"

Amanda frowned. "Sally was usually light and upbeat and believed in a kind of go-with-the-flow approach to problems. Within a day or so she seemed to be okay."

"Did you give her any advice? From what the girls and your staff here told us before you arrived, your job here is to advise and counsel."

"I told Sally that she shouldn't dwell on what couldn't be. That she needed to accept things as they were and move on. I also suggested that she not think in terms of a serious relationship. She should just have some fun and not get serious with anyone for a while." Even as she said it, Amanda realized that she'd given herself and acted on exactly that same advice about her feelings and nonrelationship with Thorne.

"Do you know if she took your advice?"

"I don't know, but she was more like herself the past couple of days. Yesterday when she left here she said she had a date."

The two officers looked at each other and Thorne wondered if this was the information they were trying to get at.

"Did she mention who she was seeing?"

"No, not by name." How she wished she'd been curious and asked questions.

The police officer made some notes and then continued. "Any details such as she'd known him from before? Where she'd met him? If he was from Sutton Shores? What she thought about him? Was he older? Younger? That sort of thing?"

Amanda shook her head. "No, all she said was 'thanks for the great advice.'"

"And that being just date and have fun without getting serious?"

Amanda nodded. Again, the officers exchanged looks. This time Amanda caught it.

"What is it that you're not telling me?"

They looked at Thorne for advice on how much to say.

"Trust me, she can take it," he said, tightening his hold on her hands.

"She may well have taken your advice, Ms. Delaski, but from what we have, it turned out not to be any fun. The body was partially undressed and money was stuffed in her bra. Preliminary examination revealed that she had sex shortly before she died. We have a number of possibilities we're investigating, but from what we have, it could be that she was paid for sex and the guy got rough and when she resisted he killed her. The murder probably occurred somewhere else and the body moved to where we found it. It could have been dumped from a car after sex or the killer could have taken it there to distance himself from the crime."

All the time they talked, Amanda shook her head back and forth as one shock after another washed over her. In a hoarse voice, she said, "This is a nightmare. Sally would never have gone out with someone who wanted to pay her for sex. I knew her too well. She wouldn't."

They nodded as if they'd expected that answer and added, "If you think of anything else, please call us."

The police left, but Amanda didn't move. Thorne put his arm around her, but she didn't sag back against him. Instead she sat stiff and still, her voice raw and shaky. "My God, I'm partially responsible for her death."

"Don't be ridiculous," Thorne said, his own concern for Amanda taking on new meaning. "You have enough to be worried about with this damn stalker, taking responsibility for Sally's careless behavior—"

But she cut him off, her tone brittle. "I told her to go out and have fun. Even the police made a point of emphasizing that."

"Cops look for reaction and they always know more than they're willing to reveal. Plus they're trying to figure out Sally's movements the past few days. If she took your words to mean pick up some stranger for fun and games then I'd say she pushed fun far beyond any limits of your intent. I know you and Sally were good friends, but no one can know what another person would do in every situation."

"You met Sally. Did she strike you as the type who would pick up some stranger? Or go out with some guy who paid her for sex?"

"I don't know, but given what the police said they found, it can't be ruled out."

"No. I don't accept that." She pulled away from him. "I knew Sally. You didn't, not really, and those two cops didn't, either."

Thorne frowned, his tone just a little edgy. "And if Sally were here she would swear she knew you," he said flatly. "But did Sally know we slept together? For that matter, did she know we have a past both of us would like to forget?"

"What does any of that have to do with her selling sex?"

"My point is that there were things about you that you didn't tell Sally. It's not inconceivable she may have done things she kept to herself."

"That's different. I didn't tell Sally because what's between you and me doesn't mean anything and I didn't want to take any chances on Olivia or the girls finding out. It had no relevance to the project and would have been a distraction."

With more than a touch of impatience at her refusal to consider she didn't know Sally, he took her shoulders and turned her to face him. He cupped her chin so she had to look at him. "I want you to listen to me."

"I won't listen to Sally's character and reputation getting trashed when I know none of it is true."

"You are one stubborn woman, you know that?" he snapped bluntly. Neither his words nor the fury in his eyes affected her; she glared at him, unmoved. Thorne continued, "That performance you put on in the kitchen this morning was out of character for you—in my opinion—based on what I know about you. If someone had told me you would do that I would have said no way. And yet you did. I can't deny it because I saw it with my own eyes."

"I don't see the relevance to what happened to Sally."

"We're talking about doing unusual things, doing things out of character, doing things that best friends and lovers would deny in a heartbeat if asked about that person's activities. My point is that circumstances, motivation and a hundred variables cause people to surprise us. Sometimes happily and sometimes as with Sally, sadly." At her defeated look, he added, "All I'm saying is that Sally may have done something reckless and she died as a result. I'm not saying she was a prostitute or a tramp or rampantly promiscuous and I'm not blaming her, but from what the police say they found, at least last night, she wound up in some major trouble that she couldn't get out of."

Ginny approached the couch where Thorne and Amanda were sitting. Her eyes were red-rimmed and she twisted her hands in her apron. "Mrs. Follingsworth is on her way. She heard about Sally and she's in a state. She wanted to talk to you, Amanda, but I told her you were busy with the police. I hope that was okay."

Amanda nodded and stood. "That's fine, Ginny. I expected Olivia anyway. How are the girls doing?"

"They're all worried about you and they're afraid the project will be canceled. Poor things, they feel bad for Sally, but they've seen Mrs. Follingsworth in action about Thorne so I think they expect a major meltdown when she arrives here."

Thorne grimaced. "The dragon lady from hell."

Amanda ignored his comment. "Thanks for the warning, Ginny. Tell Olivia to come into the counseling room. At least I can spare the girls her rantings or lecture."

"All right." Ginny turned away and then hesitated. "Was there something else?"

"Yes, but..." She shook her head in annoyance. "I'll think of it. Probably wasn't too important."

Amanda nodded, then walked toward the room she'd used for private sessions with each of the girls. Thorne started to follow her.

"No, Thorne. I want to hash this out with Olivia alone. Besides, since you technically have nothing to do with the project she wouldn't allow you in."

"Wouldn't allow me? I don't give a damn what she would allow. There's no way I'm gonna allow her to chew you out, blame you or God knows what else because Sally is dead. You're already carrying a load of guilt because of good advice that Sally obviously took to an extreme."

"Thorne, please. I know what needs to be done."

"What needs to be done? Keep the purse strings from knotting up? Is that what you're going to do?"

"I'm going to try to save this project, yes."

"And suck up to Follingsworth to do it?"

She stiffened, but held her ground. "If that's what it takes, then I'll do it. What these girls have accomplished isn't insignificant. I saw their horror at what happened to Sally. I wouldn't have seen that the first day. They're more aware that violent death isn't ho-hum stuff. They hurt because they lost Sally, because they've lost a friend. Maybe it sounds hokey and clichéd, but for the girls it's a tremendous leap forward. Olivia is the key to keeping this project alive and if I have to..." She drew in a breath and then turned away. "Never mind."

Thorne took her by the arms and made her stand still and face him. "If you have to what?"

"Whatever it takes."

"Damn it, Amanda, if you have to what?" he asked again through clenched teeth.

She sighed. "You don't understand. Seeing these girls mature, develop self-esteem, believe in themselves and what they want to accomplish was what Sally and I wanted for them more than anything. Olivia's influence goes far beyond her purse. She's the one the committee defers to and she's the one that future project developers will ask for opinions and critiques."

"So you're gonna kiss her—"

"Stop it! You have no right to interfere or even have an opinion. You're here to keep me safe from a stalker, not try to run my life or tell me how to do my job."

For long, tense seconds they glared at each other; their breathing in ragged tandem, their bodies close but not quite touching, his hands still pressing into her shoulders.

Finally Thorne released her and backed away. "Fine. You do your job and I'll do mine."

"My thoughts exactly," she said coolly.

Moments later Amanda closed the door to the counseling room, leaning against the wood as if she needed its sturdy support. Maybe in the abstract Thorne was right, maybe she was being too deferential to Olivia. After all if the project was a true success, then it should be judged on its merits and the outcome of the lives affected, not on how much money or verbal patronage would come from a particular backer.

But Amanda had been involved too long in privately funded projects to be that idealistic. While private funds provided the best in material needs so that the concentration could be on the emotional needs of the kids, funding also required a certain amount of "sucking up" as Thorne had called it. Amanda, too, hated it, and if it weren't for the girls and their potential she would have abandoned, out of personal distaste, a lot of the programs she'd been involved with in the past. That was one of her flaws, she decided grimly: she always tried to ignore the negatives and concentrate on the positives.

She'd done the same thing that night in the garden with Thorne—refused to consider that he might not be at all interested in her.

She'd done it when Thorne came here—accepting him because her father had sent him, because she believed a stalker kept at a distance via Thorne would give her the opportunity to continue her work.

Instead she found herself so tangled up with Thorne that she'd allowed the love she'd buried so many years ago to again intrude, and grow until she simply refused to think about his leaving.

My God, she thought suddenly, is it possible I'm glad the stalker hasn't been caught because as long as he's free Thorne will stay?

Is it possible love can make a woman that idiotic?

Her heart pounded. Yes, she was idiotic because once again she'd allowed herself to fall in love with him. Why was it so easy with Thorne and so impossible with other men she'd known. Nice men, who'd wanted her and hadn't rejected her. Men who wanted marriage and families and a togetherness that grew deep and strong. But, no, she was emotionally tangled, had been, for years by a man who had not only rejected her but was so upfront and honest about *still* not wanting her that she'd taken that on as a challenge in itself.

Her actions in the kitchen weren't as out of character as Thorne thought. Sure her original intent had been to throw him off-balance, catch him off guard, to get him to believe that making love with him hadn't changed her life; she could

be casual and nonchalant just as he was. And with some seduction thrown in for good measure.

She crossed to the window. At the front lawn's edge
Olivia's driver was opening the limo door for her. The rain
had diminished to a light mist. Her thoughts went back to
Sally and she pressed her fist against her mouth as her eyes
once again blurred with tears. Sally murdered and here she
was about to "suck up" to Olivia to convince her that a
murder shouldn't stall the project.

For one awful moment she wanted to run from the room,
out the side door and back home. Home where she could
curl up in bed and cry over the loss of her friend, cry that
once again she was about to lose Thorne, and, yes, even cry
that future projects would be lost without people like Olivia
Follingsworth.

She took a shaky breath and dabbed her eyes dry. Get
yourself together, she scolded. It's what Sally would want.
In fact she and Sally had both viewed the financial side as a
means to the end, a necessary factor to keep the project focused on results and not on funding.

That focus had been one reason Amanda had been so
adamant in terms of her feelings for Thorne. They had to be
kept out of any discussion. He distracted her enough, as
those incredible moments in her bedroom just before the
phone call had proved. She sighed wearily. Yet to have
Olivia and the committee or, worse, the girls and the staff
wondering if she was more interested in him than she was in
her work would have been a disaster.

Now she wondered at the wisdom of having kept her
feelings about Thorne from Sally. Perhaps if she'd shared
with Sally, her friend would have done the same about
whoever she'd been dating. Perhaps Sally had felt Amanda
was too career-oriented, too focused on being the serious
counselor to enjoy the give-and-take of two friends discuss-
ing the merits and faults of their love lives.

A knock on the door brought Amanda back to the present. Taking a deep breath, she opened it, expecting to see Olivia. "Oh, Ginny, I thought it was Olivia."

"She just arrived, but I remembered what I wanted to tell you."

"What?" Amanda peered beyond Ginny to see Thorne stop Olivia and say something. Damn him, she thought, annoyed and deliberately ignoring a sudden deep awareness and understanding of his sense of outrage. She had no doubts that Thorne Law would die rather than kiss up to anyone for anything. And for a brief few seconds she adored him for his concern about her and the project.

"...it's just something I thought you might want to know."

Amanda glanced back at Ginny. "I'm sorry, what were you saying?"

"Sally told me she was seeing a man named Harry. Rivers or Waters or something like that. I was showing the girls how to make bread and not paying a lot of attention to her exact words. Plus Sally said his name under her breath so only I would hear. I don't know if it's any help, but I thought you might want to know."

Amanda frowned, the name Harry rolling in her mind as she tried to connect where she'd heard it. She knew Sally hadn't mentioned him to her, for she would have remembered that instantly.

"Maybe it doesn't mean anything, and I sure wouldn't want to get this Harry person in trouble or anything." She glanced in the direction of Olivia, who was bearing down on the both of them. "Here comes Mrs. Follingsworth. I better go."

Olivia swept forward, regal and in charge; she was dressed in bright yellow and strings and strings of pearls. Her head held high, she wore a hat that reminded Amanda of an abandoned bird's nest. Feathers were stuck in the straw and the brim sagged from the dampness.

Ginny hurried away and Amanda held the door wide as Olivia entered the room.

She swung on Amanda before the counselor ever had the door closed. "I want to know everything that has happened."

Quickly Amanda explained what she knew.

"Well, have they questioned that man she was seeing?"

Amanda stared. My God, was she the only one who didn't know about this Harry? "You knew Sally was dating Harry?"

"Yes. Harry Lake, and from what she described, he was probably a replica of your Thorne Law. That dark, disreputable type."

Amanda felt the color drain from her face as the full name, Harry Lake, took on meaning. He was on the list of possible stalkers her father had given to Thorne.

Olivia continued, "I'll just never understand you young women. I saw Sally at Bing's late yesterday. She was all aflutter over having dinner with him. Worrying about how thick to get the steaks cut, and what she should wear and hoping they could have a meaningful relationship. Whatever that means," she said with a sniff. "Probably lots of sex and other things. And look what it all got her. Dead in an alley. What kind of example is that for these girls? And what is the committee going to say when they hear? My God, it's a smear on potential projects. And you, Amanda. You're the one who praised her to the skies when obviously she was more interested in dates and relationships than work with this project." She took a breath and with renewed energy, added, "It would seem to me—"

But Amanda was gone, already pulling open the door.

"I'm not finished," Olivia called.

"I'll be right back." She hurried across the living room, ducking into the different rooms, looking for Thorne. Finally she found him talking to Julie and Lisa. The two girls were nodding and exchanging comments, excitement on their faces as if they were the best of friends. In a fragmented moment Amanda saw all that she'd worked for in that one perfect scene. Enemies becoming friends; young women mature enough to put aside barbed words and find the best in each other instead of seizing on the worst. Amanda swallowed as the simplicity and the power of the image made its impact on her heart and conscience.

Thorne turned and walked toward her and just the sight of that easy stride, the lean hardness of him, of knowing she could count on him hit her hard. It made her realize that she loved him so desperately that letting him walk away was going to be the hardest thing she'd ever done.

"You okay?" he asked in a low voice, brushing his fingers down her cheek.

Suddenly she wanted him to hold her and let her bury herself in his warmth and protection and support. She touched his arm, her insides shaky and queasy.

"Baby, what is it?"

Then, not really caring who saw her, she slid her arms around his waist and gripped him as if every other anchor she'd ever had had disappeared. Thorne tugged her even closer, rocking her against him, uncaring who might look, who might criticize.

"The Follingsworth broad give you a tough time?"

"Yes, and no... it's not that...."

"It doesn't have to be anything, babe. You don't need an excuse to come to me. I know this news about Sally has been rough."

"But I could have prevented it, Thorne. If I'd done the reasonable thing, the thing any other woman would have done, Sally would be alive."

He leaned back a little so that he could see her face. "What are you talking about?"

She gulped. "I know who the stalker is."

"What?" he asked with genuine astonishment.

"It's Harry Lake, Thorne." She then filled him in on what Ginny and Olivia had told her.

Thorne drew in a long breath. "One of the guys on your father's list."

"Yes. Sally was dating him and I believe he killed her just to show he could do what he wanted with who he wanted in order to get to me. In effect, I put everyone at risk by continuing with the project. I should have told Olivia I was being stalked and that the best thing for the girls and the project would have been to get another counselor. Instead I counted on you being here and on my past ability to go on with my life despite some lurking danger."

"This is all after-the-facts conclusions. Obviously if we'd known days ago what we know now, we would have done things differently."

"You don't understand what I'm saying. Sally's dead, and if I'd been less concerned about what I wanted to do and more concerned about the risk here—"

"Risk, here? Hell! *Life* is a risk. You know that better than most. We have to weigh risks to ourselves and not deliberately put someone else in harm's way, but beyond that we can't do much. No one forced Sally to date this guy and from what you've told me, she wouldn't have listened if someone *had* told her he was a stalker who killed whoever got in his way. Trust me on this, babe. This guy is smooth and sophisticated and looks nothing like what we assume a killer or a stalker looks like."

Thorne cursed and then headed for the telephone. He punched out the police station number. "Yeah, this is Thorne Law. I have a name for you to check out. Sally was dating a Harry Lake." He quickly told them the information he'd gotten from Walker. Then he lowered his head and shook it slowly. "Hell, I was afraid of that," he muttered before hanging up the phone.

Amanda touched his arm. "What did they say?"

"Lake's disappeared. The police have been looking for him since they found Sally's body. They were hoping Sally might have mentioned his name to you, which is why they kept asking all those questions about the advice you gave her. Apparently she was seen going to his apartment last night around six so they naturally went to question him. The apartment had been cleaned out, but they found two dead roses in one of the bedrooms. Roses like the ones in the box the stalker sent to you."

"Then I was right," she said in a defeated voice. "The stalker killed Sally."

"Looks that way, but the bigger question is where is he now and when will he strike next?"

Chapter 13

Two days passed.

Three days.

By the morning of the fourth, Amanda felt as if she were functioning at the end of a tightrope. Thorne alerted her father to Sally's murder and Harry's disappearance, while keeping in close touch with the Sutton Shores police department. Amanda had officially dropped out of the project. Despite Olivia's protest, she'd taken the girls aside and told them why. Not because they had a right to know the truth, although she believed they did, but because she felt a bond with them and wanted them to know she wasn't abandoning them.

It wasn't the finale she'd envisioned when she suggested and then eagerly agreed to head up the first project of this kind in Sutton Shores. She was leaving with a sense of loose ends, of failed hopes and prospects, but worst of all of getting snarled up in what she'd tried so hard to avoid—letting her personal life interfere with her work. Ginny had sobbed at her departure; Julie and Lisa, now so open and distant from the angry young girls they'd been when they'd arrived that first day, had hugged Amanda so fiercely, it had taken all her composure not to burst into tears.

Thorne, however, had shown little reaction beyond urging her not to drag out the departure. Since they'd concluded that the Harry Lake the police sought for Sally's murder was probably the same Harry Lake stalking her, Thorne had become the quintessential bodyguard. He never let her from his sight unless he had checked and rechecked the area, speaking little beyond the necessities. He was all business, which was what she wanted. Or did she?

She wasn't even sure. Yes, she felt physically protected, but she also felt invisible and disconnected, just a job to him, a responsibility, a favor to be accomplished for Walker Delaski. She could almost believe that the closeness between them hadn't happened. Not just their incredible lovemaking, but the work with the girls, the silly teasing, the sometimes too-tight tension, his telling her about Jill.

But now here they were confined together in her home, barely speaking, marginally civil, waiting for something—for anything—to happen. Amanda had even had moments of wishing Harry would pop up unexpectedly just to get past the endless waiting and watching and wondering.

Now Amanda took a deep breath and checked her appearance in her bedroom mirror. Despite the solemnity of the next few hours, she was nearly giddy at the idea of getting out of the house and seeing anyone besides Thorne.

Wearing a fitted navy blue suit and a beige silk blouse, her hair pinned in a French twist, her makeup light, she dabbed English Lavender on her wrists and her throat. Satisfied, she picked up the dark blue straw purse, her short white gloves and walked from her bedroom into the living room.

Thorne stood by the porch doors dressed in a gray suit and white shirt, his dark tie knot loose. He looked sleek and magnetic, seeming to overpower the room. He glanced at her, his gaze hooded and exacting, missing nothing and making no comment. She noted the slight flare of his nostrils when she stepped closer.

"Nice," he commented warily. "Innocent and cool."

"It's always been my favorite," she said, refusing to be coy or feigning ignorance of what he meant.

"You smell like you did that night in the garden."

She halted in the process of pulling on her gloves. "I'm surprised you remember," she said on the barest of whispers.

"Remembering, babe, was never the problem, forgetting was," he said grimly, and before she could decide whether to respond or ignore him, he had moved away to double-check the house locks. Then in a maddeningly neutral voice, he said, "I still think this is a damn stupid idea."

She stiffened. "It's not an *idea,* nor is it a choice. It's Sally's funeral. After what's happened, I will not allow Harry Lake to keep me hiding in this house when I know I should be at the cemetery."

"Yeah, well, Lake might just be counting on you being there."

"But I'm perfectly safe. After all, I have you and that gun you're carrying beneath your jacket," she said with more than a touch of sarcasm. She knew she sounded petty and churlish, but she didn't care.

Thorne raised an eyebrow. "Don't be a smart-mouth. I don't like this arrangement any more than you do."

"Really," she said sweetly, her head tipped as though curious. "From what I could tell from the past few days, you seem to be right in your element."

"Amanda, back the hell off."

"Or what?" She planted her hands on her hips and glared at him. Her voice rose. "You'll quit? You'll call Dad and tell him to find someone else to guard his smart-mouthed daughter?"

He lifted his hand and she thought he was going to cup her neck and pull her forward to kiss her, but then he let it

drop without touching her. In a blunt warning that left little room for misunderstanding, he snapped, "Keep it up,
baby, and I might just say the hell with being a nice guy and
make you eager to get laid."

Amanda made herself stare at him directly. Desperate to
control her reaction, she nonetheless didn't lower her lashes,
blush or shiver. She ignored her slamming heartbeat, leap-
ing pulse and the clawing inner eagerness. "The only thing
I'm eager for is this to end and you to leave."

"On that we both agree."

In the car a few minutes later, she sat straight and still,
staring out the window. Thorne drove. Alert and focused,
his expression was the same as it had been for days; neutral
and unemotional.

At the cemetery, he took her arm, the first time he'd
touched her in days. Amanda walked with her head up and
her eyes straight ahead. She knew some of the mourners and
she nodded to them, but many she didn't recognize and she
found herself searching for someone who might look like
Harry Lake. Thorne had received a picture from Walker,
but it wasn't recent and Walker said he doubted it would be
of any help. As it turned out, when the photo was shown to
the residents of Sally's apartment building, no one could
positively say it was Harry Lake.

The sun beat down on them as they all stood in a semicir-
cle around the casket. Committal prayers were said by a local minister and then the crowd slowly dispersed. Amanda
walked up to the coffin and rested her palm on the warm
wood. "Goodbye, Sally, I'm going to miss you so much, my
friend."

Thorne put his arm around her and squeezed gently. The
reassuring and comforting gesture from him was such a
contrast to the past few days, it only made the tears she was
trying to hold in more painful. She took a step back and
started to turn away, but then she noted that Thorne hadn't

moved. He was staring at something that had been thrown off to the side.

Before she could frame a question, he took her arm, walked a few steps and stopped near the man in charge of lowering the coffin into the ground. Thorne said, "That box over there. Where did it come from?"

The man glanced toward the direction Thorne indicated. "Some florist didn't get his flowers delivered to the funeral home in time so he brought them directly here. I told him they probably wouldn't be acknowledged because the funeral director wouldn't have them on his records, but he said that was okay. He put the roses over there in the shade so they wouldn't wilt. He asked me to put them beside the grave after we fill it."

"Mind if I take a look?" Thorne asked.

He shrugged. "Go ahead."

Thorne walked over to the roses, a huge loose arrangement with baby's breath and feathery ferns. Each bud was perfect. He searched through the flowers for a card. After pricking his finger on a thorn, he pulled out a small white card and read the writing: "You were too special in life, not forgotten in death."

Amanda reread the card. "Why, what a lovely sentiment."

He slipped the card into his pocket.

"What are you doing?" she asked. "That should stay with the flowers."

"Who's going to read it? Not Sally, that's for damn sure."

She started to object, but then closed her mouth when he strode off toward the abandoned box.

He knelt down and turned the cover over. "Just as I thought."

Immediately Amanda saw what Thorne had seen. The box had no logo, nothing to indicate where the flowers had come from. "It's just like that gruesome mock coffin sent to me. God, Thorne, you don't think these were from Harry?''

''Yeah, I do.''

''But the sentiment on the card sounded as if it came from someone who cared about Sally.''

''Maybe he had a prick of conscience.''

''Or maybe despite what he did he really did have some caring feelings for Sally.''

''The misunderstood killer. Sure,'' he said cynically.

''What are you thinking?''

''That the flower delivery guy is probably Harry Lake.''

Amanda stared at him for a moment, her hands suddenly shaky.

''Think about it. Isn't it rather odd that he's delivering all these flowers to people connected or touched by Harry Lake?''

''But we both saw him, and the picture Dad sent didn't look like the delivery person.''

''No, he looked like what we expected. Nondescript, in a uniform, smiling and acting like a guy doing his job. The kind of face you forget easily and would be hard-pressed to identify if asked. You certainly wouldn't have expected him to grin and leer and act weird. That would have called attention to him. Harry wants attention, but he wants it as Harry, not as some delivery person. Unless I miss my guess, playing the role of the delivery guy was Harry's way of playing his old role of living at the edge of danger. He probably got some thrill or high out of being so close to you as he was on that day he came with the mock coffin, especially since you had no clue who he was. It put him in a position of power and allowed him to be the master.''

''Just another cat-and-mouse game.''

''Exactly.''

He glanced around and then took Amanda's arm, urging her toward the car. ''In fact, I bet Harry is probably watching us now, watching you and planning when to make his next move.''

Amanda glanced around, feeling very much like that proverbial mouse under the taunting eye of the vengeful cat.

A cat who killed for sport.

Minutes after midnight her eyes flew open.

The light blinded her, drenching her, exposing her as if she were illuminated, alone, on some stage surrounded by darkness, as if she were driving down Town Beach Road assaulted by penetrating headlights. She squeezed her eyes shut, but even the inside of her lids were seared by the laserlike beams.

"Thorne?" she cried, her instinct of needing him so natural, so quick, that she expected him to be there drawing her close and telling her she'd just had a nightmare.

But he didn't come, he didn't answer.

She moved, trying to sit up to find some darkness or shadows or even the relief of some color, but all that surrounded her was white. Greedy, burning, macabre white.

"And so we meet, Amanda, my dear."

The voice sent cold shivers through her. It came from somewhere close and yet the light made it impossible to see.

"You have been very difficult, my dear, what with your independence and your refusal to be frightened. I suppose you get that from your father."

Was he serious? She was terrified. "You're Harry Lake." The moment she said his name she recalled what Thorne had said. Harry's next move would be as Harry, not as a man in some disguise.

"Ah, and smart. But then I'm of so much importance to you that you would think of me first. As you have since our meeting on Town Beach Road."

"That was you," she whispered more in automatic response than in astonishment.

Harry chuckled. "Of course, driving skill of that caliber isn't learned from a manual."

"Where's Thorne?"

He chuckled again, as if the question was moot.

Amanda clutched the covers. "What have you done to him?"

In a neutral monotone, he replied, "Stupid bastard should have known not to tangle with me, but he's of no consequence now. My only interest is in you, my dear. Taking care of you and then delivering you to your old man so you can watch him die."

She shuddered, but her mind refused to accept that Thorne had just been brushed aside like a pesky fly. Yet she also knew that he would never have allowed Harry this close to her by choice. She did take some solace in the fact that her father was all right. At least for now.

Harry continued, as if apologizing for being late for a garden party. "A pity I had to miss poor Sally's funeral, but I did see to it that she got flowers," he said in a friendly offhand tone. "Now I know you have lots of questions, my dear, but I dislike answering questions. However, since you're being so cooperative, I will answer three."

At the moment she was more worried about Thorne than about asking questions. Amanda swallowed, her senses alert, her heart pumping painfully. She refused to believe this man could so easily get by Thorne. Lake couldn't be that clever, no matter how calm and blasé he seemed. And yet he was here and Thorne wasn't....

"I said I would answer three questions," he said with a sharp edge to his voice. Obviously he was accustomed to instant response when he said something. Or perhaps her gratitude that he was allowing her to ask any questions wasn't sufficient. Harry continued, "Momma always said, 'Boy, you ask too many damn questions.'" He sighed heavily as if bored. "No doubt you will, too, so you have three. Just three."

My God, she thought with a growing fear, he sounds like a little kid playing some game where he's made all the rules. Games, yes. One of his cat-and-mouse games. Obviously Harry viewed himself as some smug, in-control cat while all his victims were like trapped mice awaiting the tormentor. She rubbed her eyes, wanting to see where he was, but the light disoriented her so that she couldn't concentrate.

"Well?" he sneered. "I don't hear any questions."

Startled, she asked the first one that came to mind. "Why did you kill Sally?"

For a moment he was silent, then his tone became contemplative as if he were personally disconnected from her murder. "Poor Sally, I only put up with her because she knew you and she was useful for telling me when you were home and when you weren't."

"Like the night I was at the other house and you stole my dress and left the light on."

"Hmm, I used to pick locks at one time. Yours are far too simple, my dear." Then in a smooth, reflective voice, he said, "Sally insisted on carrying usefulness too far. Clinging to me and wanting my body," he said with a definite puff of pride. "She did, you know, want me desperately. My patience and kindness to the poor thing made me irresistible." Then in a curt voice, he snapped, "Second question."

She wanted to say he hadn't answered the first, just given her a view of his swelled ego, but didn't dare. Being careful not to phrase a question, she said, "The card with the flowers at the cemetery sounded as if you may have cared for Sally."

"She was useful. I don't forget those who were useful any more than I forget those who have hurt me. Momma, Delaski..." His voice trailed off with all the warmth of tumbling ice cubes.

Amanda guessed that Harry's reference to his mother as Momma, plus the childish whine in his voice, indicated some major problems with their relationship. In some ways he was a prototype of a few of the girls at the house. Terrible homes, abusive parents, a crying need for love and yet being scorned at every turn. These were the elements of a tragic childhood, and one Harry had obviously experienced. It was probably too late for Harry, which despite the danger she was in, made her feel deep sorrow for him. He had to be a brilliant man to have overcome so much and been taken into the CIA, but he had never completely put his horrible past behind him. That hair-trigger temper resulting in a death that sent him to prison, the years of plotting revenge against her father, had all culminated here with her. No wonder he was smug: he had just what he wanted.

"Second question!"

Amanda jumped. "Why are you stalking me?"

"Stalking? A pedestrian term. I do not stalk, my dear. I watch and wait and plan and then act. It is all very precise and brilliantly done. Did you enjoy the roses?"

"Which ones?" The moment the words escaped her mouth she realized it was the third question.

Harry guffawed, then in a swarmy voice to himself, he muttered, "'Which ones,' she asks, 'which ones.'" Shifting quickly to a cold dead tone, he replied, "The ones in the coffin, the ones around your body, my dear. The dead ones. How did you like all those lovely dead roses?"

Amanda knew from his voice that he was somewhere to her right, but with the light on her it was impossible to move without him seeing her. She also guessed that he was insane. Years of anger and hate had built inside him like a pressure cooker. Even wanting to hurt her, in his mind, must seem totally rational. What better way to exact the perfect revenge against Walker than to go after his daughter?

"Answer me," he roared.

She froze. "I hated them! They were horrible, ugly, just like what you did to Sally. Just like what you've done to me and my father."

"Just like what your father did to me. Locking me up in that godforsaken place. Just like what Momma did to me. Shutting me off in that locked room, closing off the light so that all I could smell was her damn roses. That's all she cared about, not me, just her damn roses." His voice rose to a falsetto. "Don't walk in the garden, boy. Don't pick my roses, boy. Don't ever get your dirty hands even near my roses, boy." He cursed, calling his mother a foul name. "You know what I did when she died? I killed all those roses and took them to the cemetery and dumped them on her grave. A rotting, stinking, maggot-crawling blanket for her to wear in hell."

Despite the horror, the fury and hatred in his voice, Amanda found herself understanding his twisted logic. And because of that twisted logic, the hairs on the back of her neck stood up in new terror.

Then he moved, not a lumbering motion but a precise and steady one. Suddenly the blinding white light was gone. Amanda blinked and blinked again, trying to soak in the darkness. Her pupils ached and burned. She couldn't see Lake in the light and now she couldn't see him in the dark. And Thorne, where was he? She knew he hadn't just left and yet could she have slept through a struggle between the two men? Not likely. But Lake was too calm, too sure of himself.

Maybe she could bluff. "Look, Thorne's going to be here any minute—"

He laughed.

"Damn you, what have you done to Thorne?" Now her terror made her body shake. Something *had* happened to Thorne. Oh, dear God, no...

"No more questions!" He was so close she could smell him, a cologne, oddly familiar. Then she knew. It was the same as what the delivery person had worn when he'd delivered that mock casket. Thorne was right. Harry was the delivery person. My God, he'd been in her house, that close.

Just as he was close now. She scrambled back. "What are you going to do?"

Instantly in her face, he roared, "No more questions!" His hand snagged a handful of her hair and yanked. She cried out at the sharp pain. Then, while holding her head, he poured something on her. It wasn't wet or dry, but sticky clumps of something. One sniff and she knew. Roses. *Dead roses.*

Amanda tried to jerk away, shuddering, but he held her, piling on the rotten flowers. Nausea pushed through her and she tried to hold her breath while struggling to get loose. Her head pounded with pain. She felt the flowers smeared on her neck, her shoulders and she clawed at them. Harry laughed, holding her by the head while she squirmed and fought.

"Let her go, Lake, or your hands are going to be holding on to your spilling guts."

Amanda's heart leapt in relief, but it was short-lived. Instead of submitting to the gun she knew Thorne must have jammed into his side, Lake screamed. A wild war whoop, his body exploding with energy as he shoved Amanda back and went after Thorne. The two men hit the floor and the next thing she heard was the explosion of gunfire.

For too many pulse-pounding seconds Amanda didn't breathe. Thorne getting shot was too awful to consider. Then, within seconds, the struggle between the two men resumed.

She pushed away the clumps of rotten roses, so disoriented by the smell, the after effects of the light and then the total darkness, she almost knocked over the bedside light. Finally she got it on to find Thorne in a life-and-death struggle to get Lake subdued.

Then to Amanda's horror, Lake got the gun. His eyes were crazed, his body wired and shaking as he tried to back up and away from where Thorne was crouched.

"I knocked you out," Harry muttered in a low croak.

"Yeah, but I have a hard head. Let me have the gun, Harry," Thorne said in an even tone.

"Answer my question. I had it all figured out. Kill you, get the girl and deliver her to Delaski. The best revenge was going to be seeing Delaski's face when he saw her body."

"My God," Amanda cried, pressing her hand over her mouth. He really had planned to kill her.

Thorne moved just slightly, a motion Amanda guessed was to put himself in a better position. All the while he kept talking. "Harry wanted to kill you first so that Walker would know that Harry had exacted the best kind of revenge. Kill someone the enemy loves and cares about. Always more damaging and satisfying to the killer than a direct hit."

Harry stared at Thorne for a long time, then aimed the gun. "I'm brilliant, you hear me! Brilliant!"

"So brilliant you forgot to be clever and smart," Thorne muttered. "Killing Sally was a stupid move, Lake."

"I had to! She wanted too much from me. She made me angry with her demands."

Thorne eased his way from his crouched position to his feet.

"Like the feelings you had for your mother, weren't they?"

"I didn't kill Momma!" he shouted, sounding tragically like a small trapped child.

"I know you didn't. She fell down some steps and broke her neck, but you were glad weren't you? All those men she brought home wouldn't come anymore. You wouldn't have to listen to your friends call her a whore. You wouldn't have to spend the night in a locked room and listen to the sounds of sex."

"I loved her! All I wanted was for her to love me! Just to love me!"

Amanda tried to swallow the sharp tightness in her throat. Despite all he'd done, she felt a deep sorrow for the circumstances of his past. As a child he'd gotten the ultimate rejection—a mother turning away from her child. Amanda couldn't help but correlate that to her own rejection by Thorne. Not the same, not even close, but each carried the same seeds of hate and revenge. God, hadn't she told Thorne she hated and despised him when in effect she loved him? What she hated was the sense of rejection and yet Thorne wasn't even remotely like Harry's mother. Thorne hadn't tormented her, dismantled her feelings one by one, and he hadn't taunted her in any way. He'd simply said no and walked away.

"Harry, let me have the gun," Thorne urged with a surprising soothing edge to his tone. Amanda wanted to scream at Thorne not to get any closer, but knew that if she made a sound it would destroy the ploy Thorne was trying to make work. Talk Harry into willingly giving up the gun.

"Stay back," Harry warned, moving his feet wider apart. Then as if a ballet had been choreographed, his foot slipped on a pile of scattered dead and slimy roses. His arms flailed and Thorne dived for his middle, taking Harry down in a single move. The weapon fired again. This time Thorne pinned Harry, turning him on his belly and pulling his arms around behind him.

Amanda scrambled off the bed and quickly retrieved Thorne's weapon. She handed him a scarf to tie Harry's hands behind him. Restrained now, the defeat showed on Harry's face. He reminded Amanda of a small child who wasn't sorry for what he'd done, but was terrified that he'd been caught.

Thorne made sure Harry was secure and then went to the window and whistled. In a few minutes the police were swarming into her house.

Amanda frowned in confusion at their quick arrival. After Harry was taken away, a few of the officers stopped and complimented her.

"Great job, Ms. Delaski."

"Outstanding. A woman cool under those circumstances is a rarity."

"Thanks, Ms. Delaski, we may not have gotten the evidence we needed without you."

Then the officer she'd talked to the night after the incident on Town Beach Road, said, "My guess is that Harry and his van are what went after you that night. Given his penchant for bright lights it would seem to fit."

"Yes, it would," Amanda said, distracted by watching Thorne.

As soon as the last of the cops had left, Thorne walked over to her and pulled her into his arms. "God, I need two things. A stiff drink and to hold you." He stared down at her face, his eyes weary and tense with concern. "Never have I been so scared or so frantic."

She gripped him feeling as if she were holding life itself. "Where were you?"

He grimaced. "Not where in hell I should have been. Protecting you." He cursed with self-directed bluntness, then lowered his mouth and kissed her. Kissed her deep and long as if he couldn't get enough. Then in a tight voice, he explained. "I heard a noise outside, but couldn't see anything. I went out to the porch and thought I saw a movement in the bushes where we saw the figure that first night. But before I could do anything, I was blinded by light and then total darkness. When I woke up, Harry was in your bedroom. Because of the light I couldn't get a clear shot at him." She saw a deadly fury in his eyes. "I wanted to kill him. I wanted to walk in there and kill the son of a bitch."

"Oh, Thorne." She hugged him, never wanting to let him go.

"I knew I had to get myself under control so I called the cops and then waited until he made a move." He kissed her, holding her against him. "Babe, I'm sorry I couldn't get to him before he dumped those dead flowers on you."

She held him with a fierce possessiveness. "Thank God you're all right." Then in a confused tone she said, "But the police talked as if I knew all along what was going on."

"Yeah, thanks to your cool professionalism, your actions spared me from looking like an incompetent jerk."

"You're not incompetent."

"Babe, the bodyguard is supposed to be in charge, not sprawled on the porch floor with a lump on his head from a high-powered flashlight. You shouldn't have had to face Lake at all. I'm just glad you were so savvy as to keep him talking."

She buried her face in his chest. "I think I could use one of those stiff drinks, too."

"I'm not sleeping in that room," Amanda said an hour later after she'd showered and put on a clean nightie. She stood in the doorway to Thorne's room. Just the bedside light was on and he was sprawled on the bed, his second glass of straight Scotch balanced on his flat belly. She'd had a glass of wine earlier, but despite the drink and the hot shower she was wide-awake. Thorne had called Walker and told him the developments and assured him that Amanda would call in the morning.

Thorne watched her, eyes hooded, his body still. The nightie covered too much of her and yet he wished it covered none of her. He was tense, wired and hot. Maybe it was the events, the sudden erasing of any reason for him to be here now, or maybe it was just that he hadn't had enough of her. Hell, hadn't he decided on that first day when he saw her for the first time in ten years that he could handle being with her? And yet, right at this moment, he knew he couldn't handle watching her in her prim nightie with its lace and silk ribbons. And here she was, an invitation too volatile to consider and too tempting to refuse.

He sighed, drained the glass and then heaved himself from the bed. "Fine, then I will. You can sleep in here."

"No."

"Amanda, the other choice—"

"Is that you will have to break down and sleep with me."

"We won't sleep and you know it."

"That's fine with me. I thought making love would be a fitting way to say goodbye." At her words, his body responded like a man dying of thirst who had been presented with gallons of clear, cool water. She added, "You *are* leaving now, aren't you, now that Harry is caught and on his way back to prison?"

"That was the plan."

"And making love would mess up those plans."

Just say yes to her and walk away, Law. But he couldn't. Hell, he didn't want to. For the first time in a very long time, he wanted something more than the next job, the next woman, the next kick of excitement. In a low voice he said, "No, making love would mess me up."

She took a step forward. "I don't understand."

He swung on her, his eyes dark, his ability to resist this time slowly draining out of him. "Don't you? Don't you know how I feel about you? How I've felt about you for ten years?"

She stared and he knew he'd done a masterful job. He'd convinced her he didn't want her. Now all he had to do was convince her it was all a lie.

Chapter 14

"Thorne?"

Suddenly he looked as if he regretted his question, as if having held back for so many years, he feared he might have stepped into forbidden territory. His eyes not quite meeting hers, he said, "You're right. Why don't we make love? We both want it and—"

But she backed away when he closed his hand on her shoulder and worked the nightie strap down.

"I want to know what and how you felt about me for those ten years."

He sighed, a mixture of defeat and resigned relief. "I thought about you. I followed your career. When I talked to Walker I asked how you were and he often told me some of his concerns." His eyes hooded to a dark intensity. "One particular concern was when you got serious with that guy a few years back."

Amanda's heart soared. Thorne had to have been more than marginally curious if he'd asked her father about her

And she didn't miss the clipped tone in Thorne's voice. "You mean Don Nicholson?"

"Yeah, from the way your father described him, he sounded as if he sold bargain-basement rugs for a living."

She grinned at his scowl. "Not quite. Actually he was president of a furniture company, but by your expression you obviously shared Dad's sentiments. He never came right out and said so, but he was distant and cool about Don. Dad made very unsubtle comments like 'aren't you rushing into this?' and 'I never did trust men who smile constantly.' He didn't realize that Don was so intimidated by him . . . Never mind. It doesn't matter now. What does is that he discussed Don with you. Dad never said a word to me about that."

"You know your father. Never one to pass on information unless he's specifically told to. Besides, not once did I ever say, give Amanda my best or say hello to her for me. Starting some sort of long-distance relationship or friendship with you would have meant eventually having to see you." Thorne wondered why they were talking about the past, since now it was so irrelevant. Then again maybe it wasn't, for at the time he'd been frustrated and terrified that Amanda would marry. He took a deep breath. "I always felt as if I was on the shadowed side of you. The bodyguard, lurking, expressionless, assuming whatever place or position was needed to keep you safe. I never felt I had the right to cross a line into wanting more with you."

Wanting more from her? she thought with a sense of new wonder. As in love? But she didn't ask. She didn't yet trust the answer.

After a pause, he gave Amanda a direct look. "You know what I dreaded?"

She shook her head, having a hard time imagining Thorne capable of dreading anything.

"Being invited to your wedding. When you were dating Don and it was looking serious I was sure you'd decide to exercise your independence and marry him despite Walker's reservations.''

"I had some of my own," she said softly. "One was that I wasn't in love with him."

"Thank God, because I have to tell you, the news that you broke off with him was the best I had that year."

Amanda didn't really want to discuss her old and forgotten boyfriend, but she couldn't help but wonder if Thorne was using Don to tell her in a less direct way of his own feelings. And those feelings about her were what interested her. She wasn't sure why, for she had no guarantee they meant any more today than they ever had, but still she needed to know.

She drew him to the couch in the living room. He sprawled in one corner while she curled up beside him.

She decided to try a different tact. "Thorne, you mentioned being glad I broke off with Don. What would you have done if I'd married?"

He shoved a hand through his hair and turned away from her. "I don't want to think about it."

"Tell me."

His eyes gleamed unmercifully with the truth. "I might have kidnapped you before the wedding ceremony."

Her eyes widened and a smile curved her lips. "Really?"

"Don't look so smug."

"I love it," she said, lacing her fingers together and closing her eyes as if daydreaming. "I can just see it. You all dark and fierce, catching me up and carrying me away to some secret place where we remained, together forever."

"Amanda, that sort of fantasy approach is what you wanted from me that night in the garden. I couldn't give you that. And coming here this time...I still can't. I have a dirty job that oftentimes has me doing things that aren't discussed in polite company. It's not as simple as not being good enough for you or us being so different. It's how I am, who I am, deep inside. I'm not idealistic and hopeful.

don't see good in people or even the potential for it. Mostly I see the dark side. Looking at you that night in the garden told me that if I touched you I would change you. I would make you see life and the world as I do. A place to kill, to watch your back, a place where terror can come from something as innocent as roses."

Amanda slipped her arms around him. She was filled with a sudden realization that protection by Thorne was much more complex than just being her bodyguard. In a soft voice, she said, "You don't even know what's happened to you since you became my problem-solver for the project, do you?"

"What happened to me? How about what happened to you? Having to give up what was so important to you because of Lake killing Sally is pretty earth-shattering."

Amanda's face saddened. "But the girls were spared dealing with Harry Lake. Leaving the counseling position was the safest thing I could do for them physically, but it also spared them emotionally. The project was designed to show them positive images and cultivate self-esteem. Instead they had a rerun of what they'd left. Murder and deceit and chaos."

"My specialties," he muttered in self-disgust. And yet there was no question that the idea he'd subconsciously been considering since Amanda's last confrontation with Olivia had grown in significance to the point where he'd made some major decisions. Decisions he planned to carry out no matter what happened with his relationship with Amanda. Yet without Amanda...

"There's much more to you than that," she said with the kind of confidence that made him even more aware of how much he needed and wanted her.

"Ever the idealist, aren't you?"

"In this case, I'm being totally realistic. I've seen many sides to you since your arrival here. Your time with Julie has changed her and given her a new outlook on life. The way all the girls responded to you, in fact, is a sign of how wonderful you are. They told me they wished they had fathers and brothers and boyfriends just like you. You listened and you cared, and you shared your past with them. You didn't try to prove you were tough or wise or better than they were. You gave them what they needed. A strong role model."

"I enjoyed all of them," he admitted, finding that Amanda's words and pride in him gave him a wellspring of good feeling. "They're bright and gutsy and savvy. Just like another young woman I knew about ten years ago. Except for one difference. The woman of ten years ago changed my life, but it took me that long to figure out how and why."

"How?" she asked simply.

He laid his hand on her bare thigh where her nightie had ridden up. In a husky voice he said, "You messed me up big time, babe. You were some innocent child that I kissed to prove I was all wrong for you only to find out that I couldn't forget you and I couldn't forget your words. You told me you loved me."

"But you rejected that. You told me I didn't have a clue what love was and that I should go back to boys my own age."

"Of course I told you that. If I hadn't, I would have wanted you for myself. But your words stayed with me. I thought about them when I was lonely. I thought about them when I was in bed with other women. I thought about them when I was seriously considering marrying Jill."

Tears glazed her eyes. "Oh, Thorne..."

He kissed her softly before continuing. "In fact, looking back, I think your words were what kept me single. I felt as if I was snagged by them. As if they had invisible wires that connected me to you. Of course, I dismissed it all as emotional rubbish. I told myself that having the hots for you was all I felt. That love was for romantics and children and that those who loved me only got hurt."

Then he sagged back and squeezed his eyes closed. She saw the pain and anger on his face, the rigid line of his jaw, a muscle ticking near his cheekbone. "Yeah, those who loved me got hurt," he said almost to himself. "For years I've tried to avoid the simplicity of that answer. It seemed whiny and immature, but it made me wary of relationships and my job just increased that wariness. But I can't deny the facts. My mother worked crazy hours because she wanted to make extra money to make a better life for me. And what did she get for being caring and concerned? A bullet in the gut and her extra money used to bury her."

He was quiet for many moments and Amanda slipped her arm around him and rested her head on his chest. She said nothing because no words were adequate.

Then on a sigh, he added, "Jill was further proof or maybe I should say she confirmed what I knew. Women who cared for me died. Oddly, after her death, I kept thinking of you. In fact that's when I started asking about you. I think I wanted to reassure myself you were all right."

"I used to ask about you, too. About your work...in fact I went to the library and read all the articles I could find about you and your agency."

He looked genuinely shocked. "Are you serious?"

She nodded, then allowed a slow grin. "And not once did I wish you a life in hell for a zillion years."

He smiled at the comment. "But you weren't happy when I walked into your house."

"Neither were you," she said. "You looked none too pleased to see me."

"Only because I wanted to kiss you and knew I couldn't. When your father called and said he wanted you protected, I kept thinking that this was no different than the time before. The biggest difficulty would be facing you after the way I'd treated you. What I didn't expect were those old feelings to come roaring back so that all I wanted was to be with you."

Amanda didn't try to stop the joy that settled on her face.

"The time with you, the project, the lovemaking—I kept finding excuses to see it as just sex. Or an old attraction revisited, but most of all I didn't want to get involved because I knew how badly I hurt you before and I didn't want to do that again."

"And then there was me telling you more times than I care to remember that I hated you...."

He hugged her. "It's okay, babe. I hated myself, too. When I came to after Harry knocked me out, I knew that I'd messed up at the exact moment when I shouldn't have. For all my promises of protecting you, of not leaving you, of refusing to even go get a haircut without you, when you needed me the most I wasn't there. Like with my mother and, yes, even like with Jill."

"You can't blame yourself for your mom or for Jill or for getting knocked out."

"Did you blame yourself for Sally getting involved with Lake?"

"It's not the same."

"Maybe, maybe not, but when people you care about die, human nature needs something to blame especially if the loss is unexpected and could have been prevented." He studied her for a moment. "When I realized Lake had you I had to mentally close down all my emotions or I would have gone in there and killed him."

Amanda stared, recalling that he'd told her that right after the police had left. "You really would have killed him?"

"Yeah." He let out a long breath. "I made myself call the police because it gave me a few extra seconds to get myself together so I could get you out alive instead of having to call Walker and say I'd allowed his daughter to die."

No longer could Amanda hold back her feelings or her words. "I love you," she said, and then as if those words needed to be reinforced, she whispered, "That's why I couldn't marry Don, why making love never satisfied me. I wasn't making love with you."

He tunneled his fingers into her hair. "Do you know I've never told a woman I loved her? Now I know why. You were the one I loved and I couldn't tell you."

"Maybe back then I was too young and you—as you so bluntly reminded me—were much too jaded and cynical for a wide-eyed virgin living in some romantic fantasy. Plus you had a career to pursue and so did I. Maybe we needed those years apart, as painful as they were, to see who we really were. Now..." She licked her lips and Thorne finished her thought.

"Now we can marry, have kids and live happily ever after?"

Amanda's heart went into double time. It was what she wanted, wanted more than anything, and yet her old fear of rejection loomed up like a monster from hell. He had admitted he loved her and she didn't disbelieve him, but her reflexes about Thorne were so automatic that even hearing those wonderful words didn't suffuse her with confidence.

He cupped her chin and kissed her. Not deeply and not passionately, but with an enduring sweetness. In a low voice, he said, "You think I'm saying the words—I love you—but you don't believe I'm going to back them up, do you?"

She wanted to say she believed him, that *I love you* was enough. But she couldn't.

He pressed his thumb against her lips. "You gave me your heart and soul and trust once, and I threw it back at you. You would be a fool to just blindly trust me." He let go of her and stood. "Stay there, I want to show you something."

She did as he asked while he went into the bedroom and returned with an envelope. "Read this."

She opened the envelope and read the short letter, then glanced up at him. "You're selling half of your consulting agency and getting out of the antiterrorist business? But why?"

"To be with you. If we're going to marry, have kids and live happily ever after, I want to be with you, not halfway around the world."

"But you love your work."

He shrugged. "At one time I did. But being with you is more important. There's a saying that when a man is on his death bed his one regret is never that he should have spent more time working, but that he didn't spend enough time with those he loved. Those days after Sally's murder, I realized in a very stark way that life can become death in an instant. No warning. I saw it with my mother, with Jill, and in those moments when Lake had you..." He lowered his head. "Suddenly you were more important than anything else I've done or ever planned to do." Then in the softest of voices, he added, "I love you and I want to be with you. I've made enough money, I've traveled and worked and seen more than my share of excitement and fast on-the-edge living. And you know what?"

Amanda was so choked up she could barely speak. "What?"

"It's a lousy substitute for spending ten minutes with you, babe."

"Oh, Thorne..."

He took her into his arms and kissed her, skimming his hands along her body.

Quickly he loosened his own clothes and pushed her nightgown aside. Her breasts, the sweet shape of her waist, the long slenderness of her thighs gathered and welcomed him in a provocative hold. Thorne slid deep inside her, his eyes shuttered, his mouth as greedy for the taste of her as she was for him.

They moved slowly, then faster, then slower again. Each time drawing deeper, taking more, glorying in their newly confessed love.

Finally as they lay spent, their bodies warm and flushed from pleasure, Amanda kissed his ear and whispered, "I love you. I love you so much. And I want to spend a zillion years telling you so."

He grinned and dropped a kiss on each of her breasts. "Now *that* I won't argue with. How about we start with you celebrating your birthday with me?"

She drew his head to the pillow of her breast. "Oh, that's right. It's next week. With all the stuff going on I forgot."

"Hmm, well, since I made such a disaster of your twenty-first, I thought I'd make up for it on your thirty-second."

"We're going to spend the day in bed?" she asked hopefully.

"The day? Hell, I planned to spend every day until then in bed."

She hugged him, loving him, wanting him and deciding that she'd never, ever been quite this happy. "Okay."

He grinned and kissed her again. "That's what I like, a cooperative woman. And while we're enjoying the honeymoon, it might be a good idea to set a wedding date."

"I agree," she said, her eyes gleaming with contentment. "When?"

"Tomorrow?"

She laughed. "Would you think it was silly and too much of a fantasy if I said I wanted a wedding in the Sutton Shores Chapel and Dad giving me away?"

"I think that whatever you want, Amanda Delaski, you should have. Just don't forget that I'm counting on being the groom."

"And the man I love."

His eyes embraced her with a new rush of feelings.

Her eyes glistened with tears of joy.

Thorne said, "And let's buy a bed. Between dead roses in yours and mine being that narrow rollaway..."

"Tomorrow we buy a bed, but tonight..."

"Tonight, babe, you can practice those fantasies you've been saving for the right man."

"Hmm," she said teasingly. "And who might that be?"

"Me, babe, just me."

Epilogue

"Surprise! Happy birthday!"

Amanda's mouth dropped open, her eyes widened and then just as quickly her hands flew to her face at the scene before her.

It had been a week since Harry's arrest and with a wedding date set for mid-July, Amanda had been so busy with details that her birthday had been pushed to the back of her mind. She'd thought she and Thorne would have a nice dinner alone to celebrate, but a surprise party...

Just this morning, Thorne had told her Olivia had called and wanted to meet her at the other house. He hadn't said what about and Amanda had assumed the older woman wanted to let her know how the project had finished up. Amanda was interested in how Julie and the other girls were progressing, but with the wedding plans and indulging herself with Thorne, she'd procrastinated calling Ginny or Olivia.

Now she didn't have to ask anyone because her answers were all beaming at her and she didn't know who she wanted to hug first.

Ginny stood in the doorway to the kitchen beside a two-tiered, pink-and-white decorated birthday cake with thirty-two candles. When Ginny told her that she and the girls had made it and decorated it, Amanda felt a new rush of tears. Olivia and the committee smiled and greeted her warmly. There was Julie, her hair beginning to grow in, her clothes fresh and stylish, but most of all she and Lisa were giggling and chatting away, like the best friends they'd become.

Walker Delaski, tall and trim with gray hair and the infectious smile of a doting father, walked up to her and kissed her. "Happy birthday, honey."

She grinned and hugged him. "Did you do all this?"

"Just helped Monk and Ginny blow up balloons. Thorne did all the arranging."

She glanced around. "Where is Thorne?"

Monk, taciturn as ever, gave her a bear hug and managed the vaguest of smiles. "You were surprised, huh?" he asked in a deep voice, then without waiting for an answer, he added. "You're not gonna have balloons at the wedding are you? My lungs couldn't take it."

She gave Monk a quick kiss on the cheek. "No balloons. I promise."

Platters of food filled a long table compliments of Bing. Bottles of champagne and cans of soda sat in buckets of ice. Music played as all the guests came up and wished her a happy birthday. She accepted the congratulations and good wishes, but her eyes searched the room for Thorne.

Then she saw him in the shadowed hallway where he'd kissed her that first day for luck. She quickly excused herself and crossed the room. Stepping into the darkness, she curled her arms around his neck.

"You did this, didn't you?"

"Just made some phone calls. Everyone was excited, especially the girls. Ginny and the girls worked liked beavers. Are you enjoying seeing everyone again?"

"It's wonderful. You're wonderful and I love you," she said, her heart overflowing with happiness.

"I knew there was a reason I wanted you all to myself. Do I get to kiss the birthday girl?"

"You make me feel like sixteen."

"But you make love like a pro."

"Which now that I think about it," she added with a provocative smile. "If you hadn't accosted me in the shower I would have been here earlier."

"And spoiled the surprise." He leaned down and sniffed. "How do you always manage to smell so good?"

"Good loving."

He drew her into his arms, covering her mouth in a deep kiss. She wiggled closer and he pressed his thigh between hers.

"You want me," she murmured, brushing her hand down his slacks.

"When don't I?" he asked, cupping her breast and stroking her gently. "Think anyone would notice if we left?"

"Probably."

"Yeah, I was afraid of that."

He gave her another kiss, dropped an arm around her and led her back to the living room. Congratulations were given to Thorne on getting such a wonderful woman and to Amanda for the success of the project. The food was consumed with relish, "Happy Birthday" was sung and finally the cake was cut.

"Amanda," Olivia said in a loud voice, getting everyone's attention.

Amanda put down her piece of cake and Thorne slipped an arm around her. Olivia walked forward with a gaily wrapped flat box. She looked as pleased as if she were presenting one of her checks to a worthy cause.

Amanda took the package, which was quite heavy. "You didn't have to buy me a gift. All of you here was gift enough."

"This is from all of us, Amanda," Olivia said, a mischievous glimmer in her eyes.

Thorne stood close and the rest of the room grew silent. Amanda carefully opened the wrapping and then removed the tissue paper.

She stared at the object, her eyes filling with tears, her lips trembling. There, on finished wood that had been cut in the shape of a house, were the words: Amanda Delaski's House For Young Women.

Olivia said, "The project was such a success thanks to you that the committee decided to fund a series of projects throughout New England and call them the Amanda Delaski House projects. Thorne has begun a scholarship fund for the girls who complete the sessions and want to further their education."

Amanda was so overwhelmed, she turned and buried her face in Thorne's shirt.

"I think she likes the idea," he said as he hugged her close.

She took a deep breath and turned around. "I don't know what to say. To have a project named for me and then to see it expanded and with scholarships." She gulped down the solid lump of joy in her throat. "It's just a fabulous birthday gift."

Everyone clapped while Amanda stared at the sign, still filled with awe and disbelief.

Later back at her house as she and Thorne cleaned up after having Monk and her father for dinner, Amanda said, "I certainly have to say that was the best birthday ever."

He lifted her up and swung her around, kissing her and letting her slide down his body. "Hmm, now it's time for our party. Just you and me."

She grinned. "I thought we'd never get to just you and me."

He led her into the bedroom. "I was saving the best for last. Here's to a zillion more years to enjoy and make love with each other."

Amanda sighed with contentment as he lowered her onto their new bed. "A zillion or two..."

* * * * *

MILLION DOLLAR SWEEPSTAKES (III)

No purchase necessary. To enter, follow the directions published. Method of entry may vary. For eligibility, entries must be received no later than March 31, 1996. No liability is assumed for printing errors, lost, late or misdirected entries. Odds of winning are determined by the number of eligible entries distributed and received. Prizewinners will be determined no later than June 30, 1996.

Sweepstakes open to residents of the U.S. (except Puerto Rico), Canada, Europe and Taiwan who are 18 years of age or older. All applicable laws and regulations apply. Sweepstakes offer void wherever prohibited by law. Values of all prizes are in U.S. currency. This sweepstakes is presented by Torstar Corp., its subsidiaries and affiliates, in conjunction with book, merchandise and/or product offerings. For a copy of the Official Rules send a self-addressed, stamped envelope (WA residents need not affix return postage) to: MILLION DOLLAR SWEEPSTAKES (III) Rules, P.O. Box 4573, Blair, NE 68009, USA.

EXTRA BONUS PRIZE DRAWING

No purchase necessary. The Extra Bonus Prize will be awarded in a random drawing to be conducted no later than 5/30/96 from among all entries received. To qualify, entries must be received by 3/31/96 and comply with published directions. Drawing open to residents of the U.S. (except Puerto Rico), Canada, Europe and Taiwan who are 18 years of age or older. All applicable laws and regulations apply; offer void wherever prohibited by law. Odds of winning are dependent upon number of eligible entries received. Prize is valued in U.S. currency. The offer is presented by Torstar Corp., its subsidiaries and affiliates in conjunction with book, merchandise and/or product offering. For a copy of the Official Rules governing this sweepstakes, send a self-addressed, stamped envelope (WA residents need not affix return postage) to: Extra Bonus Prize Drawing Rules, P.O. Box 4590, Blair, NE 68009, USA.

SWP-S994

Dark secrets, dangerous desire...

Lovers DARK AND DANGEROUS

Three spine-tingling tales from the dark side of love.

This October, enter the world of shadowy romance as Silhouette presents the third in their annual tradition of thrilling love stories and chilling story lines. Written by three of Silhouette's top names:

LINDSAY McKENNA
LEE KARR
RACHEL LEE

Haunting a store near you this October.

Only from

...where passion lives.

INTIMATE MOMENTS®
Silhouette®

You've met Gable, Cooper and Flynn Rawlings.
Now meet their spirited sister, Kat Rawlings, in
her own installment of

THE WILD WEST

by Linda Turner

Kat admitted it—she was once a spoiled brat.
But these days she focused all her attention
on making her ranch successful. Until
Lucas Valentine signed on as her ranchhand.
Sexy as hell, the bitter cast to his smile pointed to
a past that intrigued her. The only problem was
that Lucas seemed bent on ignoring the sparks
between them. Yet Kat *always* got what she
wanted—and she was readying her lasso,
because her heart was set on Lucas!

Don't miss KAT (IM #590), the exciting
conclusion to Linda Turner's Wild West saga.
Available in September, only from
Silhouette Intimate Moments!

▼ INTIMATE MOMENTS

™ Silhouette®

NIGHT SHIFT, NIGHT SHADOW, NIGHTSHADE...
Now Nora Roberts brings you the latest
in her *Night Tales* series

NIGHT SMOKE
Intimate Moments #595

The fire was under control when American Hero
Ryan Piasecki got there. But he was an arson
inspector, so the end of the fire was the
beginning of his job. He scanned the crowd,
looking for that one face that might give him a
clue, a lead. Then he saw her.

She was beautiful, elegant, cool—an exotic
flower amid the ashes. She was an unlikely
candidate as an arsonist, but as a woman...

As a woman she probably wouldn't even give
him the time of day.

**Look for Ryan Piasecki and Natalie Fletcher's
story in NIGHT SMOKE, coming in October to
your favorite retail outlet. It's hot!**

SILHOUETTE... Where Passion Lives

Don't miss these Silhouette favorites by some of our most
distinguished authors! And now you can receive a discount by
ordering two or more titles!

SD#05750	BLUE SKY GUY by Carole Buck	$2.89	☐
SD#05820	KEEGAN'S HUNT by Dixie Browning	$2.99	☐
SD#05833	PRIVATE REASONS by Justine Davis	$2.99	☐
IM#07536	BEYOND ALL REASON by Judith Duncan	$3.50	☐
IM#07544	MIDNIGHT MAN by Barbara Faith	$3.50	☐
IM#07547	A WANTED MAN by Kathleen Creighton	$3.50	☐
SSE#09761	THE OLDER MAN by Laurey Bright	$3.39	☐
SSE#09809	MAN OF THE FAMILY by Andrea Edwards	$3.39	☐
SSE#09867	WHEN STARS COLLIDE by Patricia Coughlin	$3.50	☐
SR#08849	EVERY NIGHT AT EIGHT		
	by Marion Smith Collins	$2.59	☐
SR#08897	WAKE UP LITTLE SUSIE by Pepper Adams	$2.69	☐
SR#08941	SOMETHING OLD by Toni Collins	$2.75	☐
	(limited quantities available on certain titles)		

TOTAL AMOUNT	$_____
DEDUCT: 10% DISCOUNT FOR 2+ BOOKS	$_____
POSTAGE & HANDLING	$_____
($1.00 for one book, 50¢ for each additional)	
APPLICABLE TAXES*	$_____
TOTAL PAYABLE	$_____
(check or money order—please do not send cash)	

To order, complete this form and send it, along with a check or money order
for the total above, payable to Silhouette Books, to: **In the U.S.:** 3010 Walden
Avenue, P.O. Box 9077, Buffalo, NY 14269-9077; **In Canada:** P.O. Box 636,
Fort Erie, Ontario, L2A 5X3.

Name:_____

Address:_____ City:_____

State/Prov.:_____ Zip/Postal Code:_____

*New York residents remit applicable sales taxes.
Canadian residents remit applicable GST and provincial taxes.

SBACK-SN